T0265905

REEFS, ROYALS, RECKONINGS

Also by John Keyse-Walker

The Teddy Creque mysteries

SUN, SAND, MURDER
BEACH, BREEZE, BLOODSHED
PALMS, PARADISE, POISON *

A Cuban Noir Novel series

HAVANA HIGHWIRE *

The Bert and Mamie 1930s mysteries

BERT AND MAMIE TAKE A CRUISE *

* *available from Severn House*

REEFS, ROYALS, RECKONINGS

John Keyse-Walker

SEVERN HOUSE

First world edition published in Great Britain and USA 2023
by Severn House, an imprint of Canongate Books Ltd,
14 High Street, Edinburgh EH1 1TE.

severnhouse.com

British Library Cataloguing-in-Publication Data
A CIP catalogue record for this title is available from the British Library.

ISBN-13: 978-1-4483-1124-8 (cased)
ISBN-13: 978-1-4483-1125-5 (e-book)

All Severn House titles are printed on acid-free paper.

Typeset by Palimpsest Book Production Ltd.,
Falkirk, Stirlingshire, Scotland.
Printed and bound in Great Britain by
TJ Books, Padstow, Cornwall.

Praise for the Teddy Creque mysteries

"A tropical treat like no other"
Kirkus Reviews Starred Review of *Palms, Paradise, Poison*

"Keyse-Walker smoothly integrates Caribbean lore and
culture into the narrative, which is peopled with distinctive,
well-wrought characters . . . Readers will look forward to
Teddy's further adventures"
Publishers Weekly on *Palms, Paradise, Poison*

"Plenty of action, entertaining and appealing characters,
and colorful depictions of island life . . . A solid read-alike of
Agatha Christie's *A Caribbean Mystery* and Bob Morris's
'Zack Chasteen' series"
Library Journal Starred Review of *Beach, Breeze, Bloodshed*

"An intriguing look at island life with a likable hero whom
readers will want to get to know better"
Booklist on *Beach, Breeze, Bloodshed*

"Spectacular as a Caribbean sunset, Keyse-Walker's debut is
a well-paced puzzler no one should miss"
Kirkus Review Starred Review of *Sun, Sand, Murder*

"A strong debut that vividly evokes its Caribbean locale"
Booklist on *Sun, Sand, Murder*

"Features a beautiful Caribbean setting, vibrant characters,
lively plotting and pacing, and a memorable villain who
will surprise you"
Library Journal on *Sun, Sand, Murder*

About the author

John Keyse-Walker practiced law for thirty years, representing business and individual clients, educational institutions and government entities. He is an avid salt- and freshwater angler, a tennis player, kayaker and an accomplished cook. He lives in Florida with his wife.

Sun, Sand, Murder, the first book in the Teddy Creque mystery series, won the Minotaur Books/Mystery Writers of America First Crime Novel Award. As well as the Teddy Creque series, John is also the author of the Cuban noir novel *Havana Highwire* and historical mystery *Bert and Mamie Take a Cruise.*

johnkeyse-walker.com

To my kid sister, Mary Jane

ONE

'You're a handsome man in a tuxedo, Teddy Creque,' Jeanne Trengrouse said, her deep blue eyes sparkling with mischief. 'But you need to work on the charm, especially with the Royals in town. Standing there with your mouth agape is not very James Bond.'

I tried to speak. I couldn't form an adequate thought to describe the dazzling woman before me, let alone spit out a word. Something akin to a cough or a squeak finally came out, drawing a merry laugh from Jeanne, making her all the more alluring. Finally, my panic dredged up a favorite phrase of my Dada's.

'You are a Coca-Cola bottle woman.'

'Oh, Teddy, you are so suave,' Jeanne fake-gushed. 'You might want to save some of that for Princess Portia this evening.' I felt the heat of embarrassment rise to my ears. I was saved when Lord Anthony Wedderburn, Viscount of Thetford, known on Anegada as De White Rasta, popped out of the door behind me.

'My God, Jeanne Trengrouse, you are the most glorious example of feminine magnificence I have ever set eyes upon,' De White Rasta blurted. The aristocracy get all the best invitations, such as that night's reception, in part because they know all the best words to say.

'Now that, Teddy, is how you compliment a lady,' Jeanne said. 'Especially a lady who has had to do her hair, make-up and dress in the locker room of a police station after a ten-mile open-water crossing of the Sir Francis Drake Channel in a boat with no cabin.'

Jeanne bowed to De Rasta and executed a little twirl to show off her sapphire-blue gown. 'Now you, Anthony,' she giggled. Anthony, just changed into a kilt, fur-trimmed sporran and short jacket, the formal attire of his ancestors on his mother's side, started a matching twirl. I caught him by the shoulders, halting his pirouette just as the kilt began to rise above his knees. I'd dressed with Anthony in the gents' locker room; his ancestors apparently felt no need for underwear beneath the family tartan. Anthony was following the family tradition this evening.

'No need to spin, Anthony,' I said. 'I think Jeanne can fully appreciate your outfit without any additional gyrations.'

'Spoilsport,' Jeanne teased.

'No knickers,' I explained.

'Oh,' Jeanne said. I thought I detected a flush of color on her tawny cheeks.

'Oh, my. I completely forgot.' Now it was Anthony's turn to color up.

'Well, don't cross your legs and keep your knees together when you sit, Lord Wedderburn,' I said. 'You don't want your – what do you lads from the mother country say? – twigs and berries waving in the wind in front of the Royals.'

'Boys, boys,' Jeanne interjected. 'Don't you know that when you come out of the locker room you leave these kinds of conversations behind? A little decorum, please. Think of the grand occasion we are about to attend.'

'Duly admonished, ma'am.' A grin cut across Anthony's look of contrition. 'But I will be the most comfortable man in Government House tonight, I can assure you.'

'If you two didn't look so manly, I'd think my escorts for the evening were two thirteen-year-old boys,' Jeanne said. 'Now, don't we all look fine?'

'We all do,' I said. 'A credit to Anegada.'

'Then shall we conduct ourselves to the event as lady and gentlemen?' Jeanne said. 'The Royals await.'

'Yes, ma'am,' De Rasta and I chorused. We stepped out the door of the Royal Virgin Islands Police Force Marine Base and walked along Waterfront Drive toward Government House, an elegant woman in an evening gown, a man in a tuxedo, and a nobleman, a lord, in a kilt, sporran and red sash. Along the way we drew stares from the Road Town belongers, clothed in their customary tattered T-shirts and shorts, and the cruise ship tourists, in their pristine, purchased-just-for-the-trip fanny packs and comfortable walking shoes. They would have stared even more if they had known that the man sporting the black satin bowtie was carrying an ancient Webley top-break revolver in a shoulder holster concealed by his tuxedo jacket.

Ten days before Jeanne, Anthony and I strutted along Waterfront Drive in our finery, I had received a call from Consuela Lettsome, the longtime assistant to my boss, Royal Virgin Islands Police Force Deputy Commissioner, Howard T. Lane.

'Please hold the line for Deputy Commissioner Lane, Constable Creque.'

A moment later, the DC's voice traveled from RVIPF headquarters in Road Town, on the BVI's main island of Tortola, along the cable beneath the waters of the Sir Francis Drake Channel, to the administration building and police station on Anegada, the most remote of the sister islands of the BVI, to erupt in all its stentorian glory in my always unprepared ear.

'Constable Creque, I take it that you have the RVIPF in good order and discipline on Anegada this morning?' the DC boomed.

'Yes, sir.' I guessed I could vouch for the RVIPF's good order and discipline on Anegada since I was the only member of the force stationed on the island and I was upright and functioning at the time. 'To what do I owe the pleasure of your call, Deputy Commissioner?'

'The Royals are coming, Constable Creque. Well, not all of them. Princess Portia, seventh in line to the British throne, and her husband, the Viscount of Newent, are due to arrive in three days. They had planned the trip as a vacation, the usual fly-in to Lettsome International Airport, and then straight to Necker Island, but the Governor has just informed me that they will be spending two days as his guests at Government House in Road Town. Horrible security mess. They want a parade along Waterfront Drive when they arrive and then a formal reception and ball at Government House the following day. I suspect it's all the doing of the Viscount of Newent. Damn Americans don't know how to behave.'

Jeremy Sutherland, the Viscount of Newent, the New York real-estate mogul and playboy, had caused an earthquake at Buckingham Palace when he swept Princess Portia, a rare Royal spinster, off her feet a couple of years ago. The Princess, easily old enough to be Sutherland's mother, had ignored an admonition against the marriage delivered in a private tête-à-tête with our late HRH Queen Elizabeth. The Princess had publicly proclaimed the marriage to be a match founded on true love which could not be denied. The skeptical believed it had more to do with the Princess's inherited millions from her family's Midlands coal mining operations. The rumor was that Jeremy Sutherland had been swimming in debt from overextended, poorly managed condo developments and that his creditors were questionable banks with ties to the Russian mob. Following the whirlwind romance and marriage of the playboy and the spinster, the debt was satisfied. The Queen reluctantly followed tradition and bestowed a minor title on the pushy new American relative, naming him Viscount of Newent, an ancient and inconsequential market town near the Welsh border. Sutherland flaunted his new title and finances. The tabloids, usually uninterested in the lives of Royals so far down the line of succession, made an exception for the dowdy princess and her flashy new husband, whose lack of tact and crude manners earned him the label of 'the Wanker.'

'The Princess and the Viscount have chosen not to travel with their usual Royalty and Specialist Protection officers on the trip,' growled the DC. 'Apparently, the Viscount finds them intrusive. So the RVIPF will be providing security. Every uniformed officer from every shift will be along the parade route and form a perimeter contingent for the reception and ball at Government House. Except you, Constable Creque.'

'Except me, sir?' I tried to fathom what offense I had given to warrant exclusion from this important duty. I could think of none. Or, I should say for the sake of honesty, no recent examples.

'Yes, Constable,' the DC said. 'You have a knack for getting your nose in places where it shouldn't be and conducting yourself in . . . unorthodox ways.'

'I see, sir.' I was crestfallen.

'So you have been assigned to special duty as a plainclothes officer at the reception and ball. You will be one of the two armed RVIPF officers inside at the event, me being the other. You will dress as a guest and mingle with the attendees, keeping an eye out for trouble. You will bring a companion . . .'

'A companion?' I asked.

'A date, Constable.'

I could feel the DC roll his eyes all the way from Road Town. 'I am bringing Mrs Lane. Are you not acquainted with a suitable young lady on Anegada you can bring?'

I was taken aback. Not by the need to arrive with a companion; of course, Jeanne Trengrouse would be the belle of the ball. No, the shock came from learning I would meet Mrs Lane. My image of the Deputy Commissioner had always been spit-and-polish, always by the book, always on duty and in command. The thought of meeting the woman who saw him at his pipe-and-slippers ease at home, a woman who did not snap to attention and salute when he entered the room, shook my world. Momentarily at least. 'Yes, sir. I can bring Ms Jeanne Trengrouse, my . . . domestic partner.'

'Very well, Constable. Please remember the occasion calls for your very best formalwear.' The line went dead.

Formalwear?

Luckily, a hole-in-the-wall shop on the high street in Road Town had a small collection of rental tuxedos with a jacket in my size. The trousers, though quickly altered, were slightly tight and bunched a bit in an uncomfortable location. Climbing the white steps to the polished mahogany door of Government House, I should have been impressed. Instead, each step reinforced my discomfort and my envy of De White Rasta's free and easy formalwear.

On the top step, our progress ground to a halt as event-goers bunched at the entrance. The rise of voices and the clink and tinkle of glassware beyond confirmed that the cocktail reception was in full swing. I took a nervous step to the side and waved Anthony ahead. He must have attended something like this in his distant past. Jeanne and I would follow his example.

'Lord Anthony Wedderburn, Viscount of Thetford,' a familiar voice proclaimed as De White Rasta stepped through the door. Only then did I see Inspector Rollie Stoutt of the RVIPF Scenes of Crime Unit beside the door, announcing each guest as they entered. Attired in the dress white uniform of the RVIPF, Rollie called to mind a rotund snowman displaced to the tropics. The image wasn't helped by the ridiculous headgear he wore, a white pith helmet with an ostrich plume, which replaced the regulation checked-band uniform hat.

Rollie gave me a wink and called out, 'Mr Teddy Creque and Miss Jeanne Trengrouse.' I guess my undercover status meant no mention of my police rank, but I was not so undercover that my name couldn't be bellowed into the reception hall at full voice. Fortunately, no one paid Jeanne and me one whit of attention. De White Rasta, the only resident nobility in the BVI, had already stolen the show, at least until the Royals arrived. Always popular with the ladies, he was in his element, surrounded by a gaggle of femininity ranging from turkey-necked dowagers to taut-abbed teens.

'Anthony certainly seems to be enjoying himself,' Jeanne said. 'It's difficult to believe he once led the life of a hermit on Anegada.'

'Perhaps his time in the wilderness accounts for the attraction of the ladies to him. His glow of enlightenment, you know,' I said.

'With this crowd, Teddy?' Jeanne asked. 'I'm guessing his magnetism has more to do with his family coat of arms than his zen outlook on life.'

I glanced around at our fellow roisterers. There were silver-haired men in tuxedos, encrusted with every sash, medal or other form of official decoration they could muster to prove their traditionalist chops to the guests of honor. On the distaff side, perfectly coiffed women sported cascades of diamonds and hawsers of pearls, with the youngest also displaying tasteful amounts of thigh flesh and décolletage outside the boundaries of their dresses and the more mature wearing gowns which extended those boundaries to cover any imperfections.

'I guess you are right, Jeanne,' I said. 'Not the usual crowd found dancing on the sand at the Cow Wreck Beach Bar & Grill.'

A short-coated waiter offered us drinks from a tray. 'Oh, champagne, lovely!' Jeanne said. 'This doesn't usually appear at Cow Wreck either.'

'For you, sir?' the waiter asked, offering the tray.

'No champagne for me, thank you,' I said, remembering my on-duty status. 'Is anything softer available?'

'At the bar, sir,' the waiter said, nodding to the far corner of the long room.

'Do you mind?' I asked Jeanne.

'Of course not, Teddy. I will wait right here for you.'

I struck off for the bar, turning back toward Jeanne at the halfway point. An antediluvian duffer wearing a CBE neck decoration was engaged in rapt conversation with her. An attractive woman is never alone at a party for long.

For such a civilized occasion, the throng at the bar was behaving miserably. The crowd of serious drinkers there, unsatisfied with the lightweight champagne offered by the circulating waiters, pushed forward in a scrum, shouting orders for gin and tonics and desert-dry martinis at the harried barmen. I fell in at the back of the fray. It's easy to be patient when the reward at the end of the line is a Schweppes on ice with a twist.

I felt a light hand on the forearm of my jacket and turned in its direction. I found myself staring into a pair of eyes the deep green color of a cool mountain lake.

'Hello, Teddy,' the owner of the eyes said. 'It's been a while.'

TWO

There are, in life, many forms of the unexpected which produce the emotional reaction called surprise, agitation or disquiet – the sudden death of a friend, the end of what society considers to be an institution, a blindside break-up with a lover. Intellectually, we know such events occur in every life, so we should prepare for them, but somehow when they come we are caught off guard and unready, gut-punched and reeling, unable to gather ourselves and react appropriately. Or even to react at all.

That was the situation I found myself in after the woman so reminiscent of Nefertiti touched my arm and spoke to me in a tone of voice that at one time sent chills down my spine and lightning heat into my loins. I started to speak but no words came. I choked. My mind flashed back to events seven years in the past – a stolen afternoon making love on a quiet beach; the clap of a gunshot and its punch into my chest; this very woman working frantically to save my ebbing life, and then abandoning me in a moonlit clearing in favor of a shagreen bag of emeralds and a life on the run.

I stammered.

She laughed, the laugh I remembered from our first meeting, no girlish giggle, a woman's laugh, warm and full. A laugh unchanged despite her incarceration for the past seven years in His Majesty's Prison.

I finally managed to get a single word out. 'How?'

A wry smile crossed her lips. 'How what, Teddy? How did I get out of His Majesty's most proper hellhole of a prison? How did I end up here tonight? Or how did I find you?'

'All of that, I guess.'

'That's just like you, Teddy, wanting it all, or at least thinking you deserve it all. The easy question first – how did I find you? Well, the Stay Puft Marshmallow Man with the feathers on his head by the front door just roared your name out for everyone to hear. I don't mind telling you, I was quite surprised to learn that you were here. This doesn't seem like your kind of crowd, but maybe things have changed for you in the last seven years. I saw the arm candy you brought in and she sure didn't strike me as an Anegada sistren.'

I started to speak. She touched a long finger with a flame-red nail to my lips. 'No need to explain, Teddy. By the look of her I'd say that you are doing very well for yourself. Now, what were the other questions? Oh, yes, how can I be out of His Majesty's Prison and invited to this uptown bashment, as the Rasta daughters in the cell block would call it? Simple, Teddy. I behaved. For seven years I made sure I said "yes, ma'am" and "no, ma'am" when spoken to. I didn't talk back to the matrons. I followed every rule. I went to church services on Sunday and sang in the choir. I tutored some of the other inmates for their classes. When I worked in the laundry, I made sure every shirt was ironed just so. When I worked in the kitchen I made sure every pot was scoured until it shined. When I finally worked my way up to being a trusted inmate assistant to the Superintendent of Prison, I made sure he had a smile and a nice word from me every time he passed by, but never anything more, just enough so he took a liking to me but not enough so he wanted to keep me around forever. The first time I came up for parole release, everybody agreed I was rehabilitated. And I was.'

'And . . .?' I said.

'How am I here tonight? I still fly, Teddy. VI Birds wouldn't take me back, but Edmund Steinmetz was more than happy to hire a good pilot who knows the area. That's right, *the* Edmund Steinmetz – entrepreneur, billionaire, philanthropist. I've been flying for him for the past six months, mostly taking him from his place in the U.S. Virgin Islands to San Juan and Road Town. Fortunately or unfortunately, never to Anegada. He's not much of a beach guy and we all know there's not much to Anegada beyond the beaches. And, yes, he knows, Teddy – the prison sentence, the emeralds, the killing, everything. And he's been very understanding.' She smiled and touched her necklace of emeralds anchored by one the size of a pigeon pea. 'I'm here as his plus-one tonight. He and the Viscount of Newent go way back. They've partnered on a couple of real-estate deals in New York

City. Edmund stood as best man at his and Princess Portia's wedding. So, of course, Edmund received an invitation to this evening's reception. Now, Constable Creque, why don't you tell me about your life these last seven years, as long as we are catching up. Is the young lady you're escorting this evening something more than a date or are you now among the ranks of the eligible?'

'I . . . er,' is what came out as I stumbled over my tongue. Again.

'Well, Teddy, I thought I had lost you,' said an icy voice behind my shoulder. 'Why don't you introduce me to your friend?'

I turned to face Jeanne. She didn't appear to see me. She was locked in on her perceived rival, and vice versa, cool green eye to appraising blue eye, the air between them crackling with electric animosity. I worried for a moment that they might come to blows.

Jeanne extended a hand. 'Jeanne Trengrouse.'

The hand was accepted. 'Mary Catherine Wells. My friends call me Cat.' The skirmish moved to a new front as the two gripped hands like a pair of testosterone-fueled arm wrestlers.

'Cat Wells,' Jeanne said. 'Teddy has told me a great deal about you.'

'Oh, my. I hope at least some of it was favorable.'

'Some. He said you were lovers.'

'I prefer to think of us as friends. Very good friends. And you?'

Jeanne's eyes flared. I knew if I didn't step in now there would be a scene that might get out of hand. At least, I hoped that I was enough of a – what? A catch? – to have a scene over. 'Jeanne is my . . .' And I was again at a loss for words. How could I describe her?

'Partner,' Jeanne said. 'Domestic partner.'

'Teddy always was the domestic type,' Cat said. 'Congratulations.'

'Thank you. So, how are you occupying your time these days? Wrecking homes? Stealing?'

'I've reformed. I've given up those pastimes.'

I looked around the room for rescue and spotted Deputy Commissioner Lane and an elegant woman in a pale green gown alone in a corner. They stood silently, looking away from each other.

'Nice to see you, Cat. I've got to check in with my superior. Come with me, Jeanne.' I took Jeanne's hand and started away.

'My regards to the Deputy Commissioner, Teddy. He was very kind to me the last time we spoke,' Cat called after us. I assumed the last time they spoke was when the DC had interrogated her after she was caught trying to leave the country the day after I was shot.

Jeanne pulled her hand away from mine and hissed, 'You didn't tell me that woman was going to be here.'

'I didn't know, Jeanne. I thought she was still in prison. And even if she was out, the last place I expected to see her was here. I guess her nickname is right. A cat always lands on her feet.'

'Cat is the right name for her, in more ways than one,' Jeanne huffed. 'That woman is bad news, Teddy.'

'No one knows that better than me, Jeanne.'

'Just make sure you remember it.'

We had made our way across the reception hall as I was receiving my admonition from Jeanne, and for the first time in memory I was relieved to see the slightly scowling face of the Deputy Commissioner. The graceful middle-aged woman with him seemed upset, her arms crossed and her face a mask of concern. It was probably a bad time to speak with the DC but he had told me to report to him as soon as I saw him at the reception.

'Good evening, Deputy Commissioner.' I did not salute. I had been ordered not to. I was, after all, undercover.

The Deputy Commissioner was wearing his formal uniform – a white tunic with a respectable but not excessive number of medals over his left breast, black cloth web belt pinching the tunic at the waist, and black trousers with a single gray stripe along the outer seam. A bulge beneath his left arm told me that he, too, was carrying a weapon.

'Good evening, Mr Creque. May I present my wife, Letitia. And I don't believe I have had the pleasure of meeting this young lady.' The Deputy Commissioner's words were cordial but their tone was strained. His face betrayed an odd mix of pique and something I'd never associated with the man: upset.

'My domestic partner, Jeanne Trengrouse.' I nodded to Letitia Lane. 'How do you do, Mrs Lane?'

'Better some days than others, Const . . . er, Mr Creque.' She smiled at me, a beneficent smile meant to put me at ease. She turned to Jeanne. 'How are you enjoying the evening, dear?'

Jeanne managed to smile in return. 'Well enough, though some of the guests are not quite the type I expected.'

'I know what you mean, Jeanne – may I call you Jeanne?'

'Of course.'

'Sometimes I think these glamorous affairs bring out the worst in people.' Letitia Lane's smile disappeared and she shot a sidelong frown at the Deputy Commissioner, then turned back to Jeanne. 'I'm going to the ladies' to powder my nose.'

'I'll go with you,' Jeanne said.

The DC slowly shook his head as they departed. 'Why must females travel to the loo in pairs and packs?'

'I don't know, sir,' I said. 'I am finding there are many things I don't know about females.'

'It seems to be a difficult evening all around,' the DC admitted.

'My evening was fine until I ran into Cat Wells,' I said. 'I had no idea she was even out of prison.'

'I must confess,' DC Lane said. 'I knew she was out. I thought she would return to the United States, so I didn't inform you when she was released. I thought I would spare you the news. Then I heard she got a job with that Steinmetz fellow, but I certainly didn't expect to see her here as his companion tonight.'

'She has a way of getting what she wants.'

'So does Steinmetz. A powerful chap. Close friend of the premier, the Governor, and he was the best man of Lord Sutherland at his wedding to Princess Portia last year. In any event, I had no idea Ms Wells would be here tonight or I would have told you in advance. Or maybe assigned another officer. I'm sorry.'

'That part of my life – and Cat Wells – is all behind me now.' Now all I have to do is convince Jeanne of that, I thought.

'Very well then.' The DC moved with alacrity from the discomfort of apology to his personal respite of command. 'I will work close security for the Royal couple, staying in proximity to them. You should circulate, primarily away from the Royals, keeping an eye out for suspicious persons or activity.'

'Yes, sir.'

'Ah, here come the ladies. To work.'

Just as Jeanne and Mrs Lane reached us, the room fell hushed and all eyes turned toward the entrance. Inspector Stoutt stiffened his jelly-roll body to ramrod attention and bawled out: 'Her Royal Highness Princess Portia and Lord Jeremy Sutherland, Viscount of Newent.'

The Princess entered with a practiced bearing that seemed a bit ridiculous, given her squat, wide body. She wore a gown that matched the ivory white of the sand at Loblolly Bay. The dress and her carriage were of no real help for her appearance. She looked like a regal bowling ball. The Viscount of Newent, formerly of Brooklyn, New York, was a contrast in all ways to his wife. Tall and trim, with what some would call classic good looks, he slouched and shambled his way into the room. In a hall full of men in dress uniforms, tuxedos and even formal swallowtail coats, the Viscount wore black trousers and a white dinner jacket with a tiger print bowtie. The couple stopped for a moment inside the door, the unlovely Princess nodding solemnly left and right, while Lord Sutherland clapped his hands together, shouted 'Let's get this party started' and snagged a glass of champagne – for himself, none for the Princess – from a passing waiter.

'Well, wasn't that special?' Letitia Lane remarked. 'Perhaps next the Viscount will lead us all in a round of line dancing. Or maybe the Macarena.'

'Letitia, please,' the Deputy Commissioner whispered.

'What, Howard?' she shot back. 'Surely you don't think the man would be offended. My God, look at him. How could he be offended by anything?'

A sound somewhere between a rumble and a growl emerged from deep within the DC. He steered Mrs Lane in the direction of the Royals to begin his close protection mission.

'Trouble in paradise?' I asked Jeanne when the Lanes were out of earshot.

'No more than for you,' she said. I guess the dog house was large enough for occupancy by both the Deputy Commissioner and me.

'Please, Jeanne. I didn't know she would be here.'

Jeanne sighed. 'I know, Teddy. Even though she's in your past, the sight of her fired up a little jealousy in me, I guess. I'm sorry. I know I can trust you. But from what you've told me, I also know Cat can't be trusted.'

'Point taken,' I said. 'But you don't need to worry. Someone as wonderful as you should never worry.'

Jeanne flashed a warm smile. 'You are one smooth talker, Teddy Creque.'

THREE

When we received our respective invitations to the Royal reception, De White Rasta had warned me: 'If the memories of my youth serve me right, these affairs begin with a great deal of fanfare and then quickly settle in someplace between dull and downright dreary.'

He was right. The pomp and ceremony of the Royals' introduction, the women and men in their best dress, the string quartet in the corner, the gleaming crystal chandeliers and polished mahogany wainscoting of Government House, and the waiters catering to every whim, failed to forestall the drift of the evening into a stodgy tedium that even liberal applications of booze could not enliven.

Jeanne and I circulated among the lesser lights, which were somehow quickly culled from the herd of the more monied, titled, and famous. We had just concluded a scintillating conversation about asset protection with the private banking manager of the Road Town branch of Barclays and his twittering wife when De Rasta sidled up.

'Are things a touch more lively in the hoi polloi half of the room?' he asked, glancing over his shoulder as if pursued.

'Only if you're interested in bond prices and the benefits of tax havens,' I said. 'Is someone after you?'

'I think I've made my escape, but one can't be too sure,' Anthony said.

Jeanne gave an inquiring look, seeking further explanation. Anthony, following the same mode of nonverbal communication, directed his eyes, and ours, to a bejeweled dowager across the room, chatting with a heavily tanned man a third her age.

'That is Lady Paulette Sakach, the third wife and widow of Sir Dennis Sakach of British Petroleum fame,' De Rasta said. 'Sir Dennis and Lady Paulette were friends of my mother and father. The younger gentleman is Lady Paulette's personal secretary, Javier. I suspect Javier's secretarial skills are rather limited.

Lady Paulette was always a bit of an adventuress, if you catch my meaning. Even tried her Mrs Robinson efforts on me when I was a lad of seventeen.' Anthony Wedderburn blushed for the first time I ever remembered.

'So, Anthony, was she pleased to renew her old acquaintance with you?' Jeanne teased.

'Quite.' De Rasta's coloring deepened. 'Uncomfortably so. She kept lowering her eyes to my . . . kilt. Even felt the cloth at the top of my thigh. "Oh, such a fine worsted wool. It must be uncomfortably warm here in the tropics, though, Anthony. Might be a relief to get shed of it." And while she's saying that, young Javier there thinks I am out to nick his hustle. Whenever she'd let her eyes stray low on my kilt, he'd mouth "sod off" at me.'

Jeanne began laughing. Her merriment was infectious and soon Anthony and I had to do everything we could to keep from making a spectacle of ourselves.

Suddenly Anthony stopped tittering. 'Oh, I say, isn't that . . .?' he blurted, and then realized.

'Yes, Anthony, that is Cat Wells,' I said. Cat and her benefactor-escort, the patrician Edmund Steinmetz, were in animated conversation with Princess Portia and Lord Sutherland. The 'Wanker' appellation that the tabloids had given him seemed particularly appropriate now. He had installed himself as the center of attention in a circle that included Steinmetz, Cat, the Governor and the premier arrayed around him. Princess Portia, looking pained and uncomfortable, had been pushed off to one side. While it was impossible to hear what was being said in the din of raised voices and colliding crystal, the Wanker could be seen periodically guffawing at his own jokes, slapping shoulders and, most embarrassing for Her Royal Highness, ranging his eyes and hands freely over Cat's arms, shoulders, the small of her back, and at one point, *below* the small of her back.

Deputy Commissioner and Mrs Lane hovered nearby. When the Princess finally couldn't take it any more, she broke for the ladies' room, quickly trailed by Cat, who was probably relieved to have an excuse to put distance between herself and the handsy Wanker. After a short conference between the DC and Mrs Lane, the latter followed Cat and the Princess. The Wanker, looking now like he was relaying confidences to the Governor and the premier, spoke for a few minutes more, and then made for a side door which opened into the acre of gardens at the rear of Government House.

The DC, torn, looked toward the ladies' room and then to the garden door, his Royal charges now split. After a second's hesitation, he followed Lord Sutherland, apparently feeling Princess Portia had at least some protection in the company of his Letitia. Who knows, maybe he had commissioned Letitia as a special constable before the reception.

The separation of the Princess and the Viscount was problematic from a security standpoint. Because the DC had followed Lord Sutherland into the gardens, I assumed he expected me to cover the interior, including the Princess when she emerged from the ladies'. 'Excuse me, Jeanne,' I said. 'Duty calls.'

I thought for a moment and said, 'Do you mind if I take Anthony? It should only be for a short time.'

'Of course, Teddy.' Jeanne shot me a sly smile. 'Who knows, with all these distinguished codgers around, maybe I'll locate an Edmund Steinmetz of my own.'

'Don't try too hard. Come on, Anthony.'

We edged through the crowd that seemed to have grown with a number of late arrivals – island time, I guess – and took up station twenty feet from the door. No sooner had we done so than Cat emerged, followed by Letitia Lane, and Princess Portia. The Princess had bloodshot eyes and a red nose. She appeared to have been crying. She immediately made for the garden door through which the Wanker had disappeared. Letitia Lane scurried ahead and exited before the Princess.

'Quickly, Anthony, introduce yourself to the Princess,' I said, recognizing that a delay of a minute or two was needed to set up at least a shred of security outdoors before the Princess exited into the darkened garden.

'Of course,' Anthony said, moving to intercept Her Royal Highness just as she was about to exit the room. He tried to do as requested, approaching the Princess and bowing deeply. Princess Portia, however, was on a mission. She skirted Anthony like a rugby half-fly on the way to a try, and dashed out the door. Anthony, surprised by her speed and agility, took a moment to recover and then, as ungraceful as I have ever seen him, tripped and took a full fall in the doorway. The doorway jammed up with people trying to help Anthony up and me trying to follow the Princess. The end result was that my exit and De Rasta's return to standing on two feet both took much longer than they should have. Finally, after our Marx Brothers moment, or maybe minute, we shed those trying to assist and dashed out into the night.

Anthony and I both halted when we emerged from the door.

The Princess was nowhere to be seen. Indeed, it was impossible for a long minute to see anything, stepping from the bright lighting of the reception hall into the velvet darkness of the gardens lit only by the smallest crescent of the moon and the smattered stars of the Milky Way overhead.

The only nearby sound was a chorus of coqui frogs and insects. Farther afield the sounds of reggae and fungi music echoed off the hills.

It was then that the snap of a pistol shot could be heard coming from the depths of the garden.

FOUR

As I fumbled my Webley out of its shoulder holster, trying not to panic, I could hear the sound of running footsteps, their direction and destination not discernible in the blackness.

'You go that way, Anthony,' I said, pointing to the right. I took the left, not knowing what I was looking for or would find, other than trouble. There were more running footsteps, someone breathing heavily and, in the direction I was traveling, a scream. A Royal scream, I recognized. The Princess was in danger but she was also a sound beacon, as her scream went on and on.

I could smell night-blooming cereus, its perfume almost sickly sweet in the heavy air, as I ran in the direction of the Princess's wailing. I was soon drenched with sweat, crashing through the garden, not following the footpath, taking the most direct route to the sound. I wondered where the Viscount of Newent was, wondered what had resulted in the shot I'd heard and what was causing the shrieking of the Princess, which now had become a constant, a background soundtrack of terror to the otherwise soft tropical evening and the elegant party taking place in Government House.

And then I was upon her. She was kneeling on a patch of manicured grass, a rare thing in the British Virgin Islands, in the midst of a riotous growth of croton bushes. Her dress was soiled where she had knelt in the dampness. Her eyes, barely visible, spoke of terror, but not injury. She had fallen silent when I approached.

'Your Royal Highness, are you injured?' I asked.

She said nothing, now seeming unable to make a sound after making so much noise, and lifted her arms to me. I knelt beside her and held her as she trembled, trying to discern if she had suffered any harm other than fright.

'Please, Your Royal Highness, if you are able, let's stand and get you to somewhere you will be safe,' I said.

She made a mewing noise then, like a kitten, and pointed into the nearby gloom. She was pointing at two figures, one supine and one standing over the first, looking down at the figure on the ground. The prone figure seem to be clothed all in white, illuminated by the pewter slice of moon overhead. The standing figure wore white too, a white jacket or coat which, over dark trousers, made it seem like a detached torso floating over the person on the ground.

My first concern was the safety of Princess Portia. I placed my body between her and the two figures, shielding her from any danger they might pose. I would have to deal with them later, whatever their circumstances. With a boost up, the Princess stood, compliant and not so terrified now but still unable to speak. She began sobbing, quiet tears running on to my neck as she clung to me.

'Come, Your Royal Highness,' I said, steering her away from the two dim figures, away from the shadows in the garden, toward the lights of Government House. Men in dress uniforms and formalwear were already spilling out the garden door, some with drinks still in hand, drawn out by the sound of the shot like fire ants fanning out from underground to protect their nest from an intruder.

'Deputy Commissioner! Anthony!' I shouted as we approached the expanding crowd. Cat Wells came out the garden door and moved quickly to the Princess's side. Then Anthony and several uniformed RVIPF officers, who had been on perimeter security on the road and at the edge of the grounds, materialized and took up positions nearby. I began to feel that the Princess was in a safer situation but was still discomforted by the absence of Lord Sutherland and the officer in charge, the Deputy Commissioner. Were they safe? Was the gunshot I'd heard to do with either of them?

'Anthony, have you seen Deputy Commissioner Lane?' I asked.

'No,' he said.

'You men,' I said to the uniformed officers. 'Have you seen the Deputy Commissioner?' Heads shook in the negative all around.

Cat had Princess Portia wrapped in a protective embrace. 'Let's move the Princess inside,' I said to her, and we headed toward the door, the Princess shivering despite the warmth of the evening. Suddenly, though, a thought seemed to register in the Royal mind. The Princess halted, wild-eyed, and screamed, 'Jeremy!'

The eyes of the crowd cast about for the lanky presence of the Wanker but he was nowhere to be seen. Hysteria gripped the Princess. She struggled against the efforts of Cat and several uniformed officers to move her inside, shouting for the errant Viscount over and over again.

'Please, Your Royal Highness, go inside where it is safe,' I said, to no effect.

The Princess relented only when Cat stated in a calm voice, 'Come inside, Your Royal Highness. These men must stay here to protect you as long as you're outside. There is an anteroom off the reception hall inside. We can wait there and it will free up some of the men to look for Jeremy.'

Inspector Stoutt, in his silly Gilbert and Sullivan pith helmet and plume, chose this moment to arrive. As the ranking member of the RVIPF on scene, he was expected to take charge but he dithered until I suggested he take several uniformed officers inside with him to protect the frantic Princess.

'Yes, I'm doing that,' he said. 'Constable Creque, take the remaining men and find the Viscount.'

As Rollie and the uniformed officers were unarmed, I offered him my Webley, holding it out to him butt first. You would've thought I was handing him the tail of a cobra but he took it, realizing that the House of Windsor might be under attack, and that part of what remained of the empire was under his care. To replace the Webley, I borrowed a torch from one of the uniforms.

I took De Rasta and two uniformed officers back out into the darkness, sending the group of us to the four corners of the compass in hope of locating the Viscount, the Deputy Commissioner and the source of the gunshot.

My course took me west, back toward the clearing where I had found the Princess only a few minutes before. Besides locating the Viscount, I wanted to see who the shadowy figures were who had been in the clearing and if they were injured or worse. I moved quickly, not on a run but stepping fast, and nearly collided with a man in a waiter's uniform, looking back over his shoulder.

'Boxcova!' The man said as I gripped his shoulders to prevent a full-on collision. 'You scare de wit out mi. I tink you was a duppie.' At these close quarters, the man smelled strongly of ganja and champagne. Apparently, the Royal reception had spawned some lower level partying among the Government House staff.

Realizing that he was in the grip of a man wearing a tuxedo and that was one of the persons who he should be serving, the waiter said, 'Sir, you gave me a fright. My apologies for not paying attention to where I was going.'

I decided a quick conversation in patois would get me information more quickly. 'Wha yuh name, mon?'

'Jubbie.'

'Yah true name?'

'Glenroy Watson.'

'Yuh hear de shot?'

'Ya, mon.'

'Wah yuh see of it?'

'No ting.' Jubbie's face showed concern. Why was he being interrogated by this tuxedoed stranger about shots fired? 'Surely no ting, sah.'

'Yuh ugh bak by de 'ouse, stay der, sight?'

'Yah mon.' Jubbie double timed it toward the lights of Government House, trailing the burned herb scent of ganja behind him.

Another fifty feet in the dark had me away from the noise and confusion of Government House and back at the clearing where I had found Princess Portia. It had been only minutes before but it seemed an eon had passed until I saw that the same two figures were still in the same positions at the edge of my vision. I approached them quietly, flipped on the borrowed torch, and called: 'Police!'

The beam of the torch reflected from the lifeless eyes of the figure on the ground. It was Letitia Lane. The figure standing over Mrs Lane turned toward the light so slowly it seemed as if he was underwater.

It was Deputy Commissioner Lane.

He had a gun in his hand.

FIVE

R are is the individual who can go for long periods in life without receiving a shock that disrupts their otherwise even keel of existence. A decade, a year, or even a few uneventful months is an unusual stretch for some, or even most, of us. I had been in the unwonted position of no shocks, pleasant or unpleasant, for most of the forty years before what seemed a lifetime's worth of bolts from the blue came piling in during the space of a week. Those bolts, culminating in my shooting, the death of my wife, Icilda, and the solution of the crime of the century in the BVI, were seven years in the past now. Other, lesser, shocks since then – finding love for the first time in my life, a good shock; solving a murder; surviving a dangerous hurricane and an even more deadly encounter with the super-natural – had convinced me that my ingenuous life through middle age had been tempered in the fires of my most recent years, and that, as a consequence, I could handle almost anything.

Nothing, however, could have prepared me for the shock of seeing Deputy Commissioner Lane, my commander, my mentor, my most unflinching critic and most stalwart supporter, a man who was the epitome of moral rectitude, standing over the still-warm corpse of his wife with what could very well be the murder weapon in his hand. I panned the torch light across the tragic tableau. Had the Deputy Commissioner really shot and killed his wife of many years? Why had he chosen to do it here and now, at the very seat of the Virgin Islands Government and on a night when an heir, albeit a distant heir, to the throne was being feted?

I said nothing. Nor could DC Lane, it appeared, say the words necessary to provide a reasonable explanation for the situation in which he found himself. He stared at me and my torch, a look of confusion or bafflement or incomprehension on his face, and said nothing. Indeed, he made no movement, simply stood there, his service revolver pointed at the ground, his dead wife at his feet, his entire being conveying nothing so much as a complete lack of understanding of what had taken place in the dark garden of Government House.

I fell back on the police officer's standard operating procedure. I acted. Shining the torch in the DC's eyes, I stepped quickly to his side and took the gun from his hand. He allowed the heavy Smith & Wesson Military and Police .38 to be drawn from his fingers with no resistance whatsoever.

'My God, what the hell is this?' called a loud American voice from my right. I swung the torch in that direction, full in the face of Jeremy Sutherland, Viscount of Newent. 'Get that damned light out of my face, you,' he said.

'Please step back. This is a crime scene.' I searched for the right honorific since the Queen had not seen fit to bestow a royal highness designation on the Wanker, and settled on 'sir'.

The man's sense of entitlement wouldn't allow him to be shooed away so easily. 'Don't order me what to do, you officious copper. Do you know who I am?'

'Yes, sir, I do, and this is still a crime scene and you are still to step back. There may be danger to you here. Please, return to Government House directly and tell the first police officer you see that an officer needs assistance here.'

'You don't tell me what the hell to do,' Lord Sutherland said and, much to my surprise, took a step in my direction. I was pondering how to deal with this when the Deputy Commissioner let out a low moan and dropped to all fours beside his dead Letitia.

Lord Sutherland was distracted from his belligerence by the Deputy Commissioner's actions. 'Did that cop shoot that poor woman?'

'I do not know.' I grasped the horrid realization. 'It would appear that he may have done so.'

'What kind of a place is this, with cops shooting women right here next to a civilized party? I have a mind to tell the Governor,' Sutherland ranted.

'Then do that, sir,' I said. 'Do it now. Please just go do it now.'

Lord Sutherland, probably used to his threats to take matters to a higher authority resulting in an obsequious response from underlings like me, was taken aback. Luckily, Anthony Wedderburn and two uniformed officers chose that moment to ride in to the rescue, drawn by the sound of our voices.

De Rasta, sensing the tension, deployed his winning smile and innate charm. 'Lord Sutherland, are you safe? Her Royal Highness and the other guests are very concerned about you. It is good to find you unharmed.'

In the face of Anthony's unabashed fawning, the Wanker puffed up. 'I heard the shot while I was out taking the air. I thought someone might need help, but when I came upon this –' he gestured vaguely in the direction of me, the Deputy Commissioner, and Letitia Lane's body – 'I was met with insolence. Me, simply trying to be a good Samaritan.'

'The police can be uncouth at times.' Anthony cast a reproving eye in my direction. 'I am sure you will wish to speak to the Governor about your poor treatment after you reassure Princess Portia that you have come to no harm. These two officers will escort you back to Government House.'

Satisfied that his affront was appropriately recognized and about to be rectified by punishment of the offender – yours truly – Lord Sutherland allowed himself to be escorted away. The two uniformed officers parted with an assurance to me that they would send more help.

'The damn Royals are more trouble than they are worth,' I muttered after the Wanker and his police escort was out of earshot.

'There are some in Mother England who have been saying that since 1639,' Anthony said. Catching sight of the Deputy Commissioner beside Letitia Lane's body, Anthony exclaimed: 'My God, what has happened?'

'I'm not sure, Anthony, but I don't like the look of it,' I said. 'I've got to secure things here.'

With the distraction of the Wanker gone, I turned quickly to the work before me. I unloaded the pistol that I had taken from the Deputy Commissioner. There were four unfired bullets and one spent shell in the gun's fifth chamber. I placed the bullets and the fired shell in the silk-lined pocket of my trousers.

I bent to touch Letitia Lane's carotid artery for a pulse, a gesture I knew was futile from the fixed stare of her open eyes and the expanding pool of blood now soaking my shoes. The blood reached to where the Deputy Commissioner crouched on all fours at his dead wife's hip, painting his pant legs and palms in a gory profusion.

I stood, grasped my superior and mentor by his upper arm, and lifted him to his feet. He was docile, his body cooperating in levering him up from his knees. But the man who belonged to the body seemed not to be there. I shined the torch to provide indirect light to his face. His eyes were dull, unfocused, uninterested, his jaw slack. He worked his mouth in an effort to speak, but the only sound to emerge was a nonsensical garble of grunts and gurgles, accompanied by drool. I took a handkerchief from my pocket and wiped the Deputy Commissioner's face, then moved to clean the gore from his hands until I thought better of it. The state of his hands was evidence, not to be altered for purposes of propriety, personal dignity, or simple human kindness until it could be photographed to preserve his condition for the coming investigation.

The copper-sweet perfume of Letitia Lane's blood mingled in the still night air with the cloying scent of the ceres and the pungent animal smell of sweat from me. Then I detected another odor. I swung the torch to a spreading stain on the uniform trousers of the DC where he had voided. This embarrassment, like all other aspects of his condition and the horrific circumstance in which we all found ourselves, produced no effect on the Deputy Commissioner. None.

'Step over here, Deputy Commissioner.' I steered him a few steps away from the corpse, an action which he neither resisted nor assisted, moving with automatous disinterest.

'Deputy Commissioner, what happened here?' I did not think to give the DC the caution, equivalent to the American Miranda warning, that we in the RVIPF give to inform criminal suspects about their right to silence and that their words might be used against them. I could not fathom, despite the damning evidence before my eyes, that the DC was responsible for his wife's death.

There was no response, no acknowledgment of my question, or even any acknowledgment of my presence.

'Deputy Commissioner, tell me, please,' I begged the big bear of a man standing before me like a confused child. I shook the arm I held, hoping to gain his attention. Only then did he, mouth open and slack, lift his lightless eyes to mine.

A single tear trailed down Deputy Commissioner Lane's cheek and dropped noiselessly on to the medals above his heart.

SIX

Inspector Rollie Stoutt arrived at a sprint, or at least at what he would describe as one, though in truth it was more like the casual lope my nonagenarian Dada, Sidney Creque, would employ kicking around a soccer ball with his great-grandchildren. The two officers I had sent to get help trailed him closely, barely winded but loath to embarrass their superior by dashing past and away from him on the way to the crime scene.

Rollie carried a camera which must have been borrowed from one of the photographers recording the reception for posterity. He also had a sheaf of resealable plastic baggies, probably grabbed from the kitchen at Government House, in his hands. He stopped short and, eyes wide, said, 'Jeezum, what happened?'

'Mrs Lane has been shot,' I said.

'Jeezum!' Rollie gathered himself. 'Do we need the rescue service?'

He probably already knew the answer. The two uniforms had told him enough to cause him to bring the basic crime scene tools of camera and evidence bags. He knew when he ran down the path that he might be working a death scene.

'No,' I said. 'She is dead. We will need the morgue van eventually.'

Rollie turned to Deputy Commissioner Lane. 'I am so sorry, sir.'

The Deputy Commissioner did not even acknowledge Rollie's presence, let alone his offer of condolences. Rollie's eyes, in the half-light of the torch, asked an unspoken question of me.

The best I could do was to shrug in response. Rollie, clearly needing more, took charge. 'Sergeant, please stay close to Mrs Lane's remains and make certain nothing is disturbed. Corporal, please stay with the Deputy Commissioner. Constable Creque, can you step over here with me for a moment?' He moved out of earshot of the scene, under the canopy of a white cedar tree and its showy spring finery of pink flowers. As we stood there, a confetti of tiny rosy petals sprinkled down, the cascade of beauty juxtaposed against the carnage a few yards away.

I spoke first. 'My assignment and the Deputy Commissioner's assignment tonight was security for Her Royal Highness and the Viscount. That must still be my primary concern. Are they both safe?'

'They are. The reception has been canceled. The guests have been sent home. The Princess and Viscount are secure inside Government House. We have cordoned Government House with every on-duty officer on Tortola. In addition, all the off-duty officers have been called in, as well as all officers from Virgin Gorda. The Commissioner has taken command at Government House. Now, what happened?'

I related what I had seen and heard in the last half-hour, including my interactions with Princess Portia and Lord Sutherland, trying to be as factual as possible. At the end of my report, Inspector Stoutt pursed his lips and looked me directly in the eye.

'Can you handle it, Teddy?' he asked.

'Handle . . . what, sir?'

'This investigation. The homicide investigation into the death of Letitia Lane.'

'But, Inspector Stoutt, I'm not even a sergeant, let alone an inspector. I don't have the rank or training for a homicide investigation.'

'True, you don't have the insignia on your uniform or the formal education and training that several in the RVIPF do. I suppose I could ask Derek Fahey to do it. He's an inspector and he has a good case clearance rate, but those cases are mostly low-level felonies – theft, fraud, domestic abuse. He's dogged but he's not the best in the RVIPF. Trust me, I know. Scenes of Crime gets to see everyone's investigations. I know who gets the job done, Teddy. You do. And this is important. This is one of our own. This has to be done right.'

It was true that, by sheer luck or by simply inserting myself where I wasn't supposed to be, I had investigated and solved as many homicides as any police officer in our relatively homicide-free islands. Those circumstances didn't make me feel that I was a seasoned homicide investigator, though. If anything, they served to convince me of my imposter status. I was sure I was a policeman who would be found out at any time and demoted in rank back to special constable, that kind of half-policeman endemic to the British Virgin Islands. And after that, when further truths about me were revealed, I would be out of the Royal Virgin Islands Police Force altogether, shunted back to Anegada to pull lobster traps, dive for conch and guide sunburned Yankees out to the East End flat in search of cruising bonefish.

'Are you sure Inspector Fahey wouldn't be better for this case?'

'This case is for you, Teddy. It's important for the RVIPF. It's important that it's done thoroughly, for the sake of the Deputy Commissioner and the sake of Mrs Lane. I have confidence in you that I can't say I have in anyone else on the force. Now, will you take it on?'

I thought about my times standing before the spit-and-polish Deputy Commissioner, and his dogged efforts to do what was best for the Virgin Islands and the RVIPF. His efforts, despite the growling reprimands and tough discipline, to shape me into a real police officer.

I snapped to attention, as I had learned at the Regional Police Training Centre in Barbados, and as I had done so many times in the presence of Deputy Commissioner Lane. 'Yes, sir,' I said.

'Good.' Rollie Stoutt, uncomfortable with a command role, was ready to get back to what he knew best. 'I will get to work on the crime scene. The investigation is yours, Constable Creque.'

'There is one thing, Inspector, that I would like if possible.'

The wary 'yes' from Rollie was prolonged and pregnant with dread.

'I'm hoping you can see your way to assign an RVIPF civilian administrative assistant to the investigation,' I said. 'To aid with the paperwork and such.'

'Anthony Wedderburn, I suppose.' No flies on Inspector Stoutt. 'Yes, sir.'

By way of answer, Rollie heaved a heavy sigh which he intended, and I took, as approval of my request.

We walked a short distance back to where Letitia Lane's earthly remains lay on the manicured turf of the Government House garden. I borrowed a set of handcuffs from the corporal there and snapped them on the wrists of her husband and my superior officer and mentor.

SEVEN

When I was a child I knew exactly who the important people in my life were and how they became so. There was Madda, who fed, clothed, nurtured and comforted me. There was Dada, who taught me how to run a boat, how to fish, and how to become a man. There were my many siblings, who supplied lessons on how to get along and not get along with others, how to stand up for each other, and how to have fun. How did they all become important to me? They were there, just there, and they have always been and will always be there.

When I became an adult, I got to choose who was important in my life. There was Icilda, my wife, the woman who I selected to be my partner in life, who was that for many years and then ceased to be so, and who was now gone. There were our children, Kevin and Tamia, who we chose to bring into this world and who no one can match in importance for me as a parent.

And then there are the people who become important in an unexpected way, almost as a surprise. Lord Anthony Wedderburn, known to all on my home island as De White Rasta, who stumbled into my life from the deck of a fuel barge, bleary-eyed, smelling of ganja, goat and diesel fuel, and who became my closest friend and the savior of my life on at least two occasions. Jeanne Trengrouse, a lovely woman on a bicycle with a scarlet macaw on the handlebars, who became the love of my life. Her special boy, Jemmy, now a second son to me, brought into my life through a murder investigation in which the killer's weapon was, of all things, a shark. And Deputy Commissioner Howard T. Lane, at one time a distant, detached authority figure on a far-away island, a man who gave me a job, that became a career, that became a calling. A man who shielded me in that process from the harm brought on by my own failings or the actions of others, and shepherded me through to the place where I am in the RVIPF, and in life, today.

Now I gently led the Deputy Commissioner through the silent garden toward the bright lights and the hubbub of the disrupted reception at Government House. I wondered what had actually transpired that led to his Letitia's death. I wondered how I would determine the degree of the Deputy Commissioner's involvement, if any, in that killing. I say 'if any' despite the overwhelming circumstantial evidence and Deputy Commissioner Lane's unwillingness, or at least inability, to speak about what had occurred. I say 'if any', hoping against hope that there was more, that this was all some terrible mistake, and that the man I so admire – no, revere – who is already suffering from the death of his wife, will not be made to suffer further by being blamed for her demise.

The Deputy Commissioner did not speak a word during our walk to Government House, stumbling silently at my side like a zombie. When we arrived we were met outside the garden door by the Commissioner of the Royal Virgin Islands Police Force, Sir Fleming Miles. Sir Fleming was new to his post and new to the Virgin Islands, the latest in a long line of RVIPF Commissioners sent out from the home country to command the local island force. Some of Sir Fleming's predecessors had arrived in near disgrace, not guilty of any crime or malfeasance, but rather of having risen to the pinnacle of their capabilities, only to find that pinnacle to be of a middling level. The home country's police administration found the almost crime-free Virgin Islands a convenient place to cast away such mediocrities. Others had come seeking retirement-in-place, a cushy assignment in a balmy climate, a prelude and a practice run at their golden years of shed responsibility and indolence. Sir Fleming, I had heard through my tenuous connections to the RVIPF grapevine, did not fall neatly into either of the two categories of his antecedents. The rumor mill had not stuck a label on him yet, an uncomfortable situation for those under his direct command but not a concern to line officers in the sister islands, such as me. Until now.

Sir Fleming met me outside the garden door, flanked by two uniformed officers. Casting a wary eye on the Deputy Commissioner, he demanded: 'What the bloody hell has happened here, Constable?'

'There has been a homicide, Commissioner.' I temporized by

ending my explanation there, trying to think of an explanation as to why I had the Deputy Commissioner in manacles while avoiding naming him as the prime suspect in his wife's death.

'Who has been killed?' The Commissioner did not appear rattled at the prospect of a homicide during the reception for Princess Portia and Lord Sutherland. Perhaps it was acceptable to him, as long as it was not one of them.

'A woman. One of the guests at the reception.' I was dubious as to how much longer I could avoid implicating the Deputy Commissioner.

The Commissioner turned his focus to the DC, hoping to get more information than he was receiving from the somewhat dim constable standing before him. 'Deputy Commissioner Lane, what is going on? Explain yourself, man.'

The DC didn't even lift his eyes to his superior, and made no attempt to answer his question. At that point, the Commissioner spied the handcuffs on the DC's wrist.

'Constable . . . what was your name?'

'Creque, sir.'

'Creque. Oh, that one.' Sir Fleming gave me a knowing, and unsettling to me, look. 'Constable Creque, why is the Deputy Commissioner in handcuffs?'

'For his own . . . safety, sir.'

'Ridiculous, man. A ranking officer in the Royal Virgin Islands Police Force restrained like a criminal? Remove those handcuffs at once, Constable.'

'I will follow your orders, sir, but doing so will be contrary to the RVIPF manual and force policy, sir.'

'What? Don't quote manual and policy to me, man. What policy could possibly require the Deputy Commissioner to be restrained?' Sir Fleming allowed his irk to show in the form of a twitch at the corners of his mouth.

'The policy that requires persons suspected of a violent felony to be handcuffed when they are detained and to remain handcuffed until they are transported to a secure facility, sir.'

'Deputy Commissioner Lane suspected of a violent felony? Don't be ridiculous.' The Commissioner's irk became anger, his face, still without a Caribbean tan, turning red. 'What is the felony? Stop beating about the bush, Constable.'

'Yes, sir. It is my sad duty to report that the homicide victim is Letitia Lane, Deputy Commissioner Lane's wife. She was shot. I found the Deputy Commissioner standing over her body, his service revolver in his hand. The weapon had been fired. When I arrived on scene, Princess Portia was present, and may have been a witness to events leading up to the shooting, as well as the actual shooting itself. Deputy Commissioner Lane has provided no explanation for the circumstances. In light of the evidence at this stage, I felt I had to place the Deputy Commissioner in custody.'

'The Princess, a witness to a murder? Good Lord.' The Commissioner's concern for the DC seemed to drain away in light of the involvement of the Princess, his face slowly turning from crimson to pale white.

'I cannot say with certainty to what the Princess is a witness until she is fully interviewed, of course,' I said. 'But it is likely that she is a material witness.'

To punctuate my statement, several bright flashes occurred in the direction from which I had come. Inspector Stoutt had begun to photograph the crime scene. It was as if lightning and storm had come to the peaceful quietude of the BVI evening.

'Is the Deputy Commissioner's weapon secure?' The Commissioner, like all our RVIPF officers, was acutely aware of the Virgin Islands laws against the possession and use of firearms. We all, from the Commissioner down to the lowliest special constable, work hard to keep guns off the street and away from our island home.

'Yes, sir. I turned it, and four undischarged bullets found in the weapon, together with one spent shell, over to Scenes of Crime.' Meaning I turned them over to Inspector Stoutt, the only RVIPF Scenes of Crime officer. As if Rollie sought to remind us of his important work, more camera flashes lit the far end of the garden. The guests who remained began murmuring, questions on their lips as to the meaning of the periodic flares.

'I see. Very good, Constable.' The Commissioner paused for a moment and thought. 'I suppose Deputy Commissioner Lane should be placed in His Majesty's Prison, and interrogated at the earliest by the investigating officer. Normally, the Deputy Commissioner would have assigned the investigating officer for a homicide but he obviously cannot do that here. The task falls to the next ranking officer of the criminal division, who I believe in this case is Inspector Stoutt. I assume he will conduct the investigation and the interrogation of the Deputy Commissioner, himself.'

'I think not, Commissioner. Inspector Stoutt has already assigned another officer.'

'Who?'

'Me, sir.'

'You? A mere constable?' The Commissioner felt no need to conceal his disdain for Inspector Stoutt's choice. 'There must be more qualified investigators available.'

Maybe it was the condescending tone the Commissioner took. Maybe it was my need to see that my mentor and respected superior received the best possible investigation of this tragedy. Maybe it was – though I like to think not – my pride. 'I remind the Commissioner that I have been involved in the investigation of several homicides and other major cases, with what I believe can be categorized as satisfactory results.'

'Yes. By the skin of your teeth in each instance, as I recall. Oh, very well, it is Inspector Stoutt's selection under the chain of command. I hope he doesn't regret it but I shan't interfere with it. Off to His Majesty's Prison with Deputy Commissioner Lane. Segregated custody for him, of course. We wouldn't want him mixing with the general prison population.' Sir Fleming turned to re-enter Government House.

'Beg pardon, sir, but I believe Deputy Commissioner Lane has suffered some kind of . . . injury. Or illness. I would like to take him to Peebles Hospital instead.'

The Commissioner opened his mouth, I thought, for a moment, to disagree. After a bit of hesitation, he said, 'As you wish, Constable,' before walking from the dim garden to the luminescent glamour of the reception hall.

EIGHT

The patrol officer I found to transport us dropped Deputy Commissioner Lane and me at the door of the preternaturally quiet emergency department of Peebles Hospital. When we entered, the lighting was subdued almost to the point of being suitable for a seduction. Or a nap, which is precisely what the mousy receptionist, clad in a wool cardigan against the air-conditioned frigidity of the reception area, was doing when we stepped in. There was no nurse or doctor in view.

'Miss, this gentleman needs assistance,' I said as she roused herself from the surface of her desk.

She cast an appraising eye over the Deputy Commissioner. He was obviously under his own power, upright, and with no broken bones or other visible injuries. 'There no doctor here now, only one on call. What is wrong wit de ole man?'

I glanced at the DC and realized that he had ceased to be the imposing, spit-and-polish policeman I knew and had indeed become an old man during the short span of the evening. The word 'doddering' came to mind. 'Is there a nurse, then?' I asked. I was not about to be satisfied with the drowsy receptionist's triage.

'Not in de department,' she said, with indifference.

'*Anywhere* in the hospital? This *is* a hospital, isn't it?' My exasperation showed through the polite veneer of my questions.

Affronted, the receptionist played what she thought was her trump card, sure to send us packing after a quick and skeptical exam. 'Dey a nurse here, in de ICU. I call her down.' A mumbled conversation on the phone, and the receptionist said, 'She be right down,' leaving unspoken the 'And she will fix you, policeman' that could be read in her eyes.

After a silent three minutes standing in the darkened reception area, the double doors to the emergency department bay burst open in a flood of fluorescent light. A stocky woman in full 1960s nursing regalia – a white dress with starched collar, sensible white shoes with crepe soles, white hose, and a white winged nurse's cap – was framed in the sickly light, her lips twisted into a grimace of displeasure. Ignoring both the DC and myself, she immediately turned her attention to the drowsy receptionist who had summoned her.

'What is it you need so urgently, Alondra, that you pull me off the floor in the middle of my rounds?' If looks could kill, Alondra would have been headed to the coroner's office for the slab next to Letitia Lane. 'I heard no ambulance arrive.'

'Des mens . . .' Alondra began, nervously fluttering a hand in the direction of the DC and me. The laser look from the nurse's eyes shifted away from sleepy Alondra to me. The grimace of displeasure brightened into a broad smile.

'Constable Teddy Creque, as I live and breathe,' Nurse Rowell exclaimed. 'And Deputy Commissioner Lane. I have not seen you two gents in donkey's years.' The smile left her lips when she looked more closely at the DC. She moved to take him by the arm to bring him into the emergency department proper. When she did so, the chain of the handcuffs clinked. Nurse Rowell cast a questioning look in my direction.

'The Deputy Commissioner needs . . . medical assistance.' I stumbled over the words, unsure of what the DC's mysterious condition required.

Nurse Rowell steered the DC toward a bed. He complied as a child would, dropping to sit on the bedside after Nurse Rowell turned him and gently pushed down on his shoulders.

'There, dear man, just relax,' she murmured to the DC. To me, she said, 'Take these handcuffs off. I cannot help him with them on. And this is a hospital, not a prison.'

I found the key in my pocket and removed the cuffs. Usually when that is done, the prisoner will massage his wrists and flex his fingers to restore circulation. Deputy Commissioner Lane didn't even seem to notice that the restraints had been removed.

'Now, Deputy Commissioner, let's have a look at you,' Nurse Rowell said. She began by tilting his head to shine a penlight in his eyes, all the while talking to me. 'Why have you brought him in, Constable?'

'He was involved in a very traumatic event.' I skirted around using the words 'homicide' or 'crime.' 'He has been like this since I came upon him after the incident.'

'How long ago was that?'

I glanced at my watch. 'Two hours ago.'

'He has blood on his trousers and on his hands.' Nurse Rowell picked up one of his hands and prepared to wipe off the now-dried blood with a towel.

'Don't wipe off the blood yet,' I said. 'Not until it has been photographed.'

Nurse Rowell harrumphed. 'I need to see if his hands are injured beneath the blood.'

'They are not,' I said. 'The blood is not his.'

Nurse Rowell's eyes widened but she made no comment. She placed a stethoscope on the Deputy Commissioner's chest and listened. Then she said, 'Deputy Commissioner Lane, where are you injured?'

There was no response.

'Deputy Commissioner, can you hear me?'

The DC's head sagged against his chest with not a flicker of recognition that he was even being spoken to.

Nurse Rowell lifted the DC's chin in her hand and said, 'Open wide and say ah.' The DC stared blankly into the distance.

'Has he received a blow to the head?' Nurse Rowell ran her hands over the Deputy Commissioner's close-cropped skull as she asked.

'Not that I know of,' I said.

Nurse Rowell continued to run her hands over the DC, checking his arms and legs and then pulling off his tunic, shoulder holster and singlet. 'There doesn't appear to be any physical trauma,' she said. She struck each of his knees with a reflex hammer, causing his legs to kick in a normal response.

'Deputy Commissioner, have you taken any medicines? Any pills? Any drugs of any kind?' The only response from the Deputy Commissioner was a continued blankness. 'Do you know if he has taken any drugs, Constable Creque?'

'I'm not aware that he has, but I wasn't with him for much of the evening. We were working security at Government House during the reception for Princess Portia and the Viscount of Newent.'

'Whose blood is on his hands and trousers?'

'His wife's.' A severe glance from Nurse Rowell to me. 'She was shot and killed this evening.'

'Dear God. The poor man.'

'He is our prime suspect in the murder.'

'Oh. Oh.' Nurse Rowell refused to be surprised, I suspect a product of her standard medical demeanor, but her attitude toward the Deputy Commissioner seem to change. She took an iPhone from her dress pocket and photographed his hands and trousers. She then took a device that looked like a spatula from a cabinet, scraped dried blood flakes from each of the Deputy Commissioner's hands into plastic baggies and handed them to me. I scribbled the information concerning the date and contents on to a piece of medical tape, taped each bag shut, and pocketed them.

'I'm going to draw some blood for the lab,' Nurse Rowell said, to me as much as to Deputy Commissioner Lane. He didn't flinch as the needle went in and blood flowed into the glass sample vial.

'The lab will be open on Monday and we should have the results then. I will do what I can to expedite them.'

I looked at my watch. It was just after midnight on Sunday.

'Is he in danger?' I asked.

'He doesn't appear to be. His vital signs are certainly not normal but nothing seems alarming enough to bring in the on-call doctor, who is an orthopedist and probably would defer to me in any event.' Nurse Rowell said this last part as a matter of fact, not as a boast. She was undoubtedly right. 'I am going to keep him for observation until he comes out of whatever the state is that he's in. If this continues long enough, we may need a psychiatric consult.'

'I was taking him to His Majesty's Prison.' I wasn't sure if what I said was an explanation or a plea to let me carry on with my duty. Or a request to find some way to prevent me from carrying on with my duty.

'He could take a turn, Constable. Do you want that on your head?'

'No, of course not, Nurse Rowell.'

'Then he stays. We don't have a prison ward, as you know,

but one section of the intensive care unit can be locked and the windows there are impact glass for hurricanes. He will be secure. I will keep an eye on him.'

'I will send over a constable.' I had no doubt that Nurse Rowell was more than capable of keeping the Deputy Commissioner where he was supposed to stay, but regulations required an officer on guard.

'As long as he stays out of my way. Help me get these bloody clothes off the Deputy Commissioner so we can get him into a gown.'

It was one in the morning by the time the constable I summoned to act as guard arrived. As I walked out of the ICU with the Deputy Commissioner's once meticulous, now bloodied, uniform in a plastic bag in my hands, I turned back. Deputy Commissioner Lane, his eyes confused, his large frame hunched, shuffled toward his ICU room. His backside was almost exposed by the too-small hospital gown. He was a man who, in a single evening, had lost his wife and his dignity, very likely his career, and most probably his freedom. And I was the man tasked with carrying out the latter two deprivations.

NINE

The grand reception hall at Government House was anything but grand at half past one in the morning. The place had an air of being dismantled. Waiters hustled away silver centerpieces from tables. Busboys clattered china and glassware into plastic tubs to be carted into the kitchen and washed. Flowers were being removed, chairs folded and stored. The high and mighty dignitaries had long ago taken their leaves. A phalanx of police officers remained, stationed about the interior and exterior of the Virgin Islands seat of government, commanded by the RVIPF Commissioner, who had the place on a war footing.

Of the guests from earlier, only Anthony Wedderburn and my Jeanne Trengrouse, still lovely in her evening gown, remained. They were seated in two folding chairs along the wall, out of the way, and out of the concern of all around them. They rose as one when they saw me, and Jeanne rushed to my arms.

'Anthony told me, Teddy,' Jeanne said. 'It's horrible, so horrible.'

It was only then that the horror of the evening struck home for me, too. Up to that point, I had been occupied, first dealing with the possible threat to Princess Portia and Lord Sutherland, then securing the crime scene, and finally seeing to the Deputy Commissioner. Now the shock came in a rush. Gunfire near an heir to the throne on my watch, the murder of a dignified and warm-hearted woman with whom I had been chatting moments before, my superior and mentor the prime suspect in the homicide, and that same man, who I respected and admired, reduced to a doddering shell in the hospital. It all seemed too much for a moment. And then it did not. It was all part of my duty, the imagined stentorian voice of the Deputy Commissioner said in my ear. Or was it in my mind? It was all part of being a policeman, to be unruffled when others are shaken; to continue on when others would require rest, or comfort, or recovery; to be strong when the situation should have sapped all your strength. I had once been unsure that I had what it took to be a policeman. It had taken exposure to danger, to heartache, to death to convince me, not that I had what it took to be a policeman, but to know that the only way any policeman survived was to endure, to proceed, to carry on, when the world seemed to be crashing down around you.

'You are safe, Jeanne.' I held her close. 'I am safe. The Princess is safe.'

'But poor Letitia. Dead by her own husband's hand.' Jeanne burrowed more deeply into my neck, seeking shelter from the thought.

'We cannot assume that to be the case.'

'What?' Jeanne drew back and looked into my eyes. 'Anthony said you saw him with a gun in his hand, standing over the poor woman's corpse.'

''Tis true, Teddy,' De Rasta said. 'I know you consider the man to be something akin to a father figure, but the evidence at this point is exceptionally damaging, you must admit.'

'I will admit that is how it appears, but I know the Deputy Commissioner and I know he would never do anything like that, no matter what the situation was between him and his wife.'

'The situation?' Anthony asked.

'Deputy Commissioner Lane and Mrs Lane appear to have been . . . to have had a falling out over something before the reception began,' Jeanne said. Then, looking over my left shoulder, she stiffened and her nostrils flared.

I turned and there was Cat Wells, still in her evening finery.

'You haven't seen my clutch, have you? I'm afraid I lost track of it in all the confusion,' she said.

'I thought you had gone home.' This from Jeanne, with a sharp edge to her voice.

'No, Edmund and I are staying here tonight at the request of Lord Sutherland. The Princess was very upset by what she saw. A doctor has been in and given her a sedative. Jeremy thought that having someone other than a nurse present when she awakens would be helpful. Or, as he put it, "I cannot abide any more of this weak-ass crying jag alone." He and Edmund are off in the Governor's library, soothing their nerves in a more manly way, with double brandies, one after another.'

'I had intended to interview both the Princess and the Viscount about what they witnessed yet this morning,' I said.

'I can tell you, Teddy, that whatever the doctor gave the Princess put her out like a light. He said that she would sleep for at least twelve hours.' Cat made a disapproving face. 'And as for Jeremy Sutherland, let's just say that both he and my dear Edmund are feeling no pain. I'm guessing that, while Jeremy may not be asleep for a full twelve hours, he won't be in any condition to answer your questions for at least that long.'

'Here it is.' Jeanne had broken away while I was speaking with Cat. Now she waved Cat's missing clutch like a prize as she returned to us from across the room.

'Thank you,' Cat said, taking the handbag. 'Where did you find it?'

'Where I expected. On the corner of the bar. At least now you can get back to the Princess.' Jeanne sent out a vibe that I hadn't seen a woman send out since I watched one of those American television shows – the real housewives of someplace or the other – with Tamia on one of our father-and-daughter nights.

Cat arched a catty brow to Jeanne and almost hissed. 'I guess I can. Thank you.' To me and to Anthony, she smiled her best seductress smile, said, 'Gentlemen,' and swept from the room.

'I don't like that woman,' Jeanne said when Cat was out of earshot.

'You don't say.' De White Rasta drew a dagger eye from Jeanne for this remark. Undaunted, he went on. 'Well, Teddy, it looks like you have no witnesses to interview, your suspect is uncommunicative and locked away in the hospital, and the ballistics report and forensics from Scenes of Crime are certain not to arrive tonight. I am at your disposal, though, for whatever we can get done in the four hours before dawn and during the sleepy Tortola Sunday morning that follows. What now, Kemosabe?'

I thought about what Anthony had said. Thought first that his Eton-Oxford diction and vocabulary was being supplemented with faux Native American words and phrases learned by watching reruns of the Lone Ranger on satellite television with Jemmy every afternoon at five o'clock, and wondered if it could be considered detrimental or an improvement. It certainly had made De Rasta's vocabulary more colorful – now a mélange of

Rastafarian patois, American TV slang, and extremely proper English. Once beyond the 1950s Cowboys and Indians jargon, I thought secondly about what really would be accomplished in the next few hours, given the state of all involved. And remembered, thirdly, the teachings of Captain Grimsby of the Montserrat Police Force, my course instructor in Felony Investigations at the Regional Police Training Centre in Barbados. He had emphasized, or maybe a better description is *harped upon*, the fact that the first forty-eight hours of an investigation are the most important, and that it was crucial that the time be used to the best advantage by the investigator.

Considering that last thought, I had a course of action. 'Come, Jeanne, Anthony. It is time to go home to Anegada and get some rest.'

TEN

Sometimes it doesn't seem right that each and every day should dawn bright and blue and immaculately perfect. But that is the way every day dawns on Anegada, other than the tropical storm or hurricane days that darken our skies once or twice a summer. If it is a day for a wedding – flawless. If it is a day for a funeral – the same perfection. The blackest of moods, the lightest of hearts, the grimmest of life's challenges, the most glorious of its celebrations, all have the same impeccable backdrop of gentle breezes, lambent sun and balmy temperatures. It should make the difficult days easier, the good days even better, the best days an ecstasy.

But not even the relentlessly perfect sameness of the Sunday morning following our late-night return to Anegada could lighten the dark mood at the breakfast table at the Creque-Trengrouse household.

I should say the dark mood of the adults because the children, unaware of events, bubbled with questions, especially after having seen Jeanne and me in a try-out of our finery a few days before. Then, Tamia had oohed and cooed at Jeanne's outfit. Even Kevin and Jemmy had shown a young male disinterested-interest in my rented tuxedo and its accessories.

'Did all the women look as beautiful as you, Madda?' Tamia had taken to calling Jeanne 'Madda' in the last few weeks, a change that had gladdened Jeanne's heart and strengthened the bond between them.

Before Jeanne could respond, the lads chimed in.

'Did the Princess wear a crown?' Jemmy asked.

'Who cares about a crown? Did anybody have swords?' my budding teen, Kevin, asked. Then, as the oldest and most sensitive to adult moods, he said, 'Something is wrong, isn't it?'

Balancing breakfast plates of eggs, johnnycake and fried snapper on her way from stove to table, Jeanne said, 'Someone was killed at the reception.'

'It wasn't the Princess, was it?' Tamia's earlier enthusiasm fell into solemnity.

'No,' I said. 'It was Mrs Lane, Deputy Commissioner Lane's wife.'

One might expect childlike questions or a sense of detachment from the news. After all, none of the children had known Letitia Lane and barely knew of the Deputy Commissioner, having only heard tales of him around the dinner table. But, despite their tender years, they all knew unexpected death. My two had lost their mother, and almost their father, to violence. Jemmy had witnessed three deaths and seen his mother wounded by a gunman.

As it was, they showed they were all children of a policeman.

'Are there any suspects?' Kevin said.

'Yes.' All three youngsters knew from experience not to ask who the suspects were.

'Are you on the investigation?' Jemmy's small voice usually betrayed no emotion. Today, though, it held a hint of apprehension. For me. I thought about how unfair it was to Jemmy, to them all, to be the child of a policeman, even in a place as sedate as Anegada. They hadn't signed on for the worry, the concern, they had to carry in the back of their mind on even the most ordinary day, and the actual fear that had to be just below the surface when they knew their dada was chasing a murderer.

'I am in charge of the investigation,' I said. Faces fell around the table. 'It will be all right. It will be over soon. But I am going to be spending some time on Tortola until it is over.'

'When?' said Tamia. Dada's girl.

'Starting today. I'm going when you all go to church.'

The rest of the meal was eaten in silence and then we all piled into my beat up RVIPF Land Rover to pick up my parents, Sidney and Lily, and go on to worship at the little Methodist church in The Settlement.

When we stopped to pick up Madda and Dada, my Dada noticed I had on my uniform. 'Police business that won't wait for church?' he asked.

'I'm afraid so, Dada.'

'Is it that terrible business at the Princess's reception at Government House? We heard about it on the radio news.'

'Yes.' More silence now, from all of us in the Land Rover until I let them out at the door of the church. Dada leaned in the passenger-side window. 'Watch your hide, son.' He then took Madda's hand and shepherded everyone in the family but Jeanne through the mahogany front door.

Jeanne forced a smile, tears welling at the edge of her azure eyes. 'You watch that hide like your Dada said, Teddy. It belongs to me now, and I expect to get it back in one piece.'

'Not a problem, my love. I'll be gone a couple days at most and will return, hide intact.'

Little did I know how many people would be after my hide, and how powerful they were.

ELEVEN

A police officer investigating the crime of murder is one of the most unconstrained employees on the face of this green and blue earth. True, there are ultimately reports to superiors to file, but when a case is turned over to the lead investigating officer no one directs to whom he is to speak, where he is to go, and how he should conduct his inquiry. I suspect this is because society recognizes unrestrained inquiry is a necessity in this most important of not just police but societal functions. Bringing a murderer to justice overrides the niceties of protocol and convention. At least I thought so.

'You want to do what?' De White Rasta shouted above the noise of the outboard engine of my skiff, the *Lily B*.

'Well, Anthony, I really don't want to, but I may need to.' The wind tore away my words as I navigated the boat across the pale green waters leeward of the Horseshoe Reef, headed south to Road Harbor, and the RVIPF Marine Base there.

'But, Teddy, old man, you are not just talking about an ordinary . . .' De White Rasta struggled for the word. 'Citizen. These people are different. They're not even people in the true sense of the word.'

'Oh, really? What are they?'

'They are . . . Royals. This may be the Virgin Islands, Teddy, but it is really England and in England you don't mess about with the Royals. You don't even joke about it.'

'I'm not joking, Anthony.'

'That, old friend, is exactly what I feared. But is holding Princess Portia and Lord Sutherland in the Virgin Islands as material witnesses the only way to skin this obstreperous cat? Surely there is a way to investigate and convict without keeping the Princess and, worse, her consort, the Wanker, here until the case is concluded.'

'If there is a trial, we will need her testimony. Even short of a trial, I will need to interview her as a part of the investigation. Unless . . .'

'Unless what, Teddy?'

'Unless a confession is secured from the suspect.'

'That seems the clear answer to this knotty problem, doesn't it, Constable Creque.' Now De Rasta was going all formal title on me.

'I would prefer not to subject Deputy Commissioner Lane to an interrogation of the type designed to procure a confession. Facts need to be developed, and the man was in no condition for questioning the last time I saw him, anyway.'

'Not to offend your delicate sensibilities respecting your mentor, but didn't you see him just last night standing over the body of his wife, soaked in her blood, with his service revolver in his hands? Just how much deference does that circumstance deserve?'

The *Lily B* carved an arc across the entrance to Road Harbor. I thought about another day, another circumstance, where a police officer was found in proximity to that officer's deceased spouse, his service revolver at the murder scene, and the deference the investigating officer had displayed toward his fellow. On that other day, the investigating officer was Deputy Commissioner Lane and the officer in suspicious circumstances was me. But what was it that I owed to Deputy Commissioner Lane? I found the answer in the way I remembered he had treated me then. He had questioned me. Fairly, with sensitivity. I owed him the same.

'OK, Anthony, I take your point. We will begin with the Deputy Commissioner.'

'Good man,' Anthony said, stepping on to the marine base dock with the bow line as I cut the *Lily B*'s engine.

'He had a rough night, Constable.' Nurse Rowell's no-nonsense eyes peered up at me from the charting she was doing at the ICU nurses' station. 'Not so much physically as emotionally. He sat up crying most of the night. Not loudly, just staring, tears running down his cheeks. We haven't done much for him, just IV fluid replacement for some slight dehydration. He's responding to simple commands but still not speaking. I finally got him down in bed at dawn.'

'I need to speak to him,' I said. 'About some very serious matters.'

'He is not really in shape to speak, Constable.' Nurse Rowell spared me her usual gruff nobody-upsets-my-patients attitude; her tone was gentle. 'I have asked Dr Ramoutar to see him today.'

'Dr Ramoutar?'

'He is a psychiatrist.'

'I see. Still, I need to see the Deputy Commissioner.'

Nurse Rowell's entire being clouded when I insisted, but apparently there was no good reason to restrict me from seeing my superior officer/suspect. 'Do not expect much of a response.' She cast a wary eye at Anthony. 'Only one visitor at a time.'

'Of course,' I said. Best to be satisfied with small victories when confronting a force like Nurse Rowell.

We walked to the single ICU room dedicated to containing infectious diseases, which, with its lockable door, doubled as the only holding room in the hospital. Nurse Rowell produced a key and swung the door open. 'Five minutes, Constable. No more.'

The Deputy Commissioner was sitting on his bed, his eyes downcast, staring at the gray linoleum floor.

'Good morning, Deputy Commissioner.'

He lifted his eyes to mine. I thought I saw a spark of recognition but he said nothing before dropping his gaze to the ground again.

'I'm sorry, sir. I know this is a difficult time for you.' I considered whether to give him the warning concerning his rights and decided that I must. The words had no effect on the man.

'Sir, please tell me what happened last night.'

No response.

'Sir, I wish to help you but I cannot without your assistance. Can you tell me what happened at the reception for Princess Portia? Any information you can give will aid me in finding the person –' I struggled for the right words – 'responsible for your wife's death.'

The wall of the ICU seemed as likely to provide answers as the big man sitting on the edge of his bed in a hospital gown. I begged, cajoled, implored Deputy Commissioner Lane for any information for the full five minutes of my time with him. The primary suspect in Letitia Lane's murder wouldn't say a word.

Not a word to help me find his wife's killer nor a word to confess that he was the man who had killed her. At the end of my allotted time, Nurse Rowell stepped inside the room and beckoned me to leave. I rose and was almost into the hallway when the Deputy Commissioner finally spoke.

'Who killed Letitia?' The question was uttered in the smallest of voices by the hulking figure on the bed. I stopped and turned to meet his eyes.

'Who?' he said and began to cry.

Nurse Rowell took my arm and moved me into the hallway. 'Enough. The man is in bad shape. No more interviews until Dr Ramoutar sees him.'

Anthony, waiting down the hall, turned to me expectantly. 'What news?'

'I have been given an assignment, Anthony. Deputy Commissioner Lane has asked me to find the person who killed his wife.'

TWELVE

'I am sorry, Constable, but Princess Portia is indisposed.' Anthony Wedderburn and I had been admitted into Government House and shunted to the library, where Sir Roger Chamberlain met us and immediately uttered those words. As special assistant to the Royal family, Sir Roger was known in the home islands as 'Sir No'. He coupled his words with a smile formed just with his eyes, making you think that he was doing you a favor by putting you off and keeping you away from any contact with the Royals. Indeed, that had been his job since he was brought in by the Crown four years ago, for the stated purpose of 'fostering improved relations between the Royal family and their most worthy subjects.' In fact, he had been selected for his position for his unique ability to say 'no' in the nicest way possible. He was good at his job, took pride in it, and was one of the most oily characters I had ever encountered in my days as a police officer. I was able to make this determination after only a couple of minutes in his presence.

'When will she be available, Sir Roger? It is urgent that I speak with her concerning the death that occurred at the reception last evening. She may have seen things which prove valuable in locating and convicting the killer,' I said.

'The Princess was sedated due to that unfortunate incident.' Sir Roger unleashed a full visual charm offensive, a knowing, just-between-us-men-of-the-world smile. 'I am afraid it is not possible to say when her physician will feel she is sufficiently recovered to answer questions concerning the matter. I am certain you understand the delicate circumstances we are dealing with here.'

'Well, then, I shall have to make do with an interview with the Viscount of Newent for the time being,' I said. 'Is there a quiet room available where we may speak?'

'Lord Sutherland is nursing a hangover as big as the humpback whales I used to see when I was flying along the north shore of

Anegada.' The voice saying those words over my left shoulder was familiar. It used to whisper sweet nothings and lewd suggestions into my ear back in the day.

'Good morning, Ms Wells,' I said, turning from Sir Roger's Cheshire cat visage to the more enticing feline countenance of Cat Wells.

'Good morning, Teddy.' Cat turned to Anthony. 'Good morning, Rasta. You two are out and about bright and early today, at least compared to the men folk here at Government House, Sir Roger excepted.'

Anthony made a show of glancing at his wristwatch. 'Bright and early at the crack of eleven o'clock in the morning. It reminds me of those halcyon days before I put myself to rights. Top of the day to you, Ms Wells.'

Sir Roger took his cue. 'I'm sorry, gentlemen, but it seems the Viscount is also indisposed.'

'Indisposed. Such a useful word,' Anthony said. 'It saves the recipient from the indignity of an unadorned "no."'

Sir Roger, cognizant of his place in the noble hierarchy, gave De White Rasta, a.k.a. Lord Wedderburn, a deferential simper but no verbal response. Why say no when you have already said it?

'Trust me, Teddy,' Cat said. 'Neither Princess Portia nor Lord Sutherland are in any condition to see you.'

Cat's request for me to give her my trust seemed a bit of cheek, since at the last time I had seen her before yesterday's reception at Government House, she'd had the choice of getting a shot and bleeding Teddy Creque to a hospital or walking away with a fortune in emeralds, and she had chosen the latter. Still, with two gatekeepers shutting us out, discretion required a deferral of these two crucial interviews. That did not mean, however, that the two interviews would never take place. I had to make certain of that.

'Very well, Sir Roger, we shall return tomorrow to make inquiry of both the Princess and the Viscount. I trust they will have sufficiently recovered by then.'

Sir Roger gave a noncommittal nod and said nothing. Cat shot him a look that I couldn't quite fathom, but then I had been failing to fathom looks cast by females for most of my life. Anthony and I made our exit.

When we emerged into the bright sunshine made brighter by the white-painted steps and walls of Government House, Anthony said, 'Did you pick up the message, Teddy?'

'What message?'

'The message that Ms Wells' lovely face conveyed.'

'I saw something but I couldn't read it.'

'The message that I read was that when Sir Roger nodded, he was holding something back,' Anthony said.

'Like what, Anthony? Something about the Royal couple?'

'I don't know, old chum. But Ms Wells certainly does.'

'Bah, Anthony, Sir Roger wouldn't hold anything back about the Princess and Viscount that would affect our murder investigation. It's just that the Princess is shocked and Lord Sutherland is hungover. That is thoroughly understandable on her part. It is not very commendable on his part, but he didn't earn his nickname by leading a commendable life. We will talk to them tomorrow. They will both be better able to respond to our questions when they have had time to recover from the insults to their respective systems.'

'You know best, Teddy. You are the trained investigator. Where to next? And to speak to whom?'

'I think we need to pay a visit to the below-stairs portion of Government House. I have a feeling that the staff here are of stern enough stuff that some questions about last night won't offend their delicate sensibilities.'

THIRTEEN

'I don' care if you de police or de President of de Unite' States, you wan' to talk to one of de kitchen staff here, you tells me why an' you gets me permission. I start here back in seventy-four sweeping de floor for ole Governor Cudmore. I dust his damn seashell collection and housekeep till Governor Davidson's kitchen lady quit and I can finally show dem I can cook. Now I am de master of this kitchen. And no one, not even de Governor, do nothing here without through me.' Myrthlyn Nibbs planted her hands on her ample hips, effectively blocking entry to her domain at the first floor, rear, of Government House, although I supposed I could almost vault over her since her height was slightly less than her width. I couldn't decide if I was amused or terrified of the kitchen manager.

De White Rasta, undaunted by any female he had ever encountered, proceeded to ladle out copious portions of charm. 'So you are the one responsible for the delightful food served at last night's reception? I must say, I have lived on Anegada for years, and never had such a delectable fish and fungi. And the conch stew – magnificent!'

'Dem Anegada girls not know how to make fungi likes de Tortola girls. You livin' a deprive' life out at dat backwater island, Mr . . .?' Myrthlyn melted like a schoolgirl in the glow of De Rasta's smile.

'Wedderburn, ma'am. Anthony Wedderburn. I am so pleased to make your acquaintance.' What's next, I wondered. Would he kiss her hand?

'An' I am pleased to make your acquaintance, Mr Wedderburn.' She cast a chary eye toward me, and focused solely on Anthony. 'Now, what can I do for *you*, Mr Wedderburn?'

'I, er, we, that is Constable Creque and I, would like to speak to one of your kitchen chaps about the killing last night.'

'Dat a tragedy, dat lady bein' shot right here in de garden.

Who you want to talk to, Anthony?' First names already, Myrthlyn?

Relegated to the role of De White Rasta's sidekick, I waited until he gave me side-eye permission and then said, 'Glenroy Watson. He goes by the name of Jubbie.'

Myrthlyn, studiously ignoring me, Anthony's mere minion, turned to De Rasta and said, 'Can't talk to him.'

'But why ever not, dear lady?' Anthony obviously didn't believe in hard-hitting interrogation any more than I do.

'Him gone. Him was scheduled to bus lunch but call first ting dis morning and say he quit.'

'Did he say why?' I asked.

The reward for my question was a look of disdain from the pugnacious kitchen manager and a response directed to Anthony. 'Only that him's not ever coming back.'

'Where does he live, love?' Sugar wouldn't melt in De Rasta's mouth.

'Out at Long Trench.' Myrthlyn gave an address. 'Did him kill dat lady?'

'Not as we know, love. We just want to talk to him.'

'I knew him not trus'worthy,' Ms Nibbs huffed as we exited her domain.

'Where now?' Anthony asked.

'Where your girlfriend said, Anthony. Long Trench.'

Anthony was nothing if not pleased with himself as we entered the RVIPF Land Rover that we had been loaned by the Road Town station. 'You can cast all the aspersions you want, Teddy, but I guarantee you this – I'll never starve.'

FOURTEEN

L ong Trench, northeast of Road Town among the steep hills of Tortola, was a pretty upscale neighborhood for a waiter to live. At least it appeared that way to me as we traveled along the Ridge Road that runs on the spine of the island. Multi-million-dollar homes clung to the hillsides, with sapphire swimming pools cantilevered out into space beyond the homes' conspicuous bulk. Other than a few gardeners and handymen, the faces in the yards were white, another sign of wealth and an indication that Glenroy Watson was not likely to be found here.

'It doesn't look to me like many of the residents of Long Trench make their living as champagne waiters and bus boys,' I said as I juked the Rover around a gaggle of Mercedes and BMWs parked encroaching into the narrow roadway. EDM music from a pool party the cars' owners were attending could be heard from behind one mansion's concrete privacy fence.

'Lucky for us I know some of the locals,' De Rasta said. 'Turn down this side road.'

A furlong down the side path Anthony had suggested placed us in a different world. The shacks that leaned into, away from, and at right angles to the road made The Settlement in Anegada look like the upper west side of Manhattan. Not that I had ever been to the upper west side of Manhattan, but I do have television. With walls made of plywood scraps, driftwood, and stacked concrete blocks, and roofs of tarpaper, the entire neighborhood was one category-one hurricane away from being wiped off the face of the hill. Chickens roamed. Babies cried. Dogs slept in the road.

As we drove along, eyes appeared in the dark recesses of the glassless windows of some of the shacks. It went without saying the Royal Virgin Islands Police Force was not a frequent visitor to the area. It seemed that the reception might be hostile. Men began to appear in doorways and around corners, big, bared-chested men, with copious dreadlocks on their heads and machetes and cricket bats in their hands.

Anthony read my concern. 'Not to worry, old man. I have a former associate who resides just at the end of the boulevard. Down there.' De Rasta pointed to a shack indistinguishable from the others save for an extra helping of hulking toughs in its dusty yard. I drove to the end of the road and managed a three-point turn before halting. Our reception thus far gave me a desire to have the vehicle pointed in the direction of the exit.

By way of greeting, the largest of the rough boys in the yard said, 'What you want, mon?' Not the usual mannerly salutation given by citizens to RVIPF officers and delivered in a downright unmannerly tone. That most of the men took menacing steps forward, shaking their long knives and bats, reinforced the less than cordial reception.

'I have this, Teddy,' Lord Wedderburn, the Viscount of Thetford said. Then, out the window to the big man in the yard: 'I-mon here to talk to Boss Claudie. Him a fren mine, sight?'

The surprise of hearing a white man in a police car speak Jamaican patois wore off quickly. The largest of the men said, 'No mon dat name heh. G'weh, policemens.' He gave a brushing wave-off like we were two pesky flies.

The rough boys all took a collective step toward the Land Rover when we didn't immediately depart, but Anthony persisted. 'I-yah ax Claudie him not wan' see him ole cumbolo Ant-nie.'

A jolly voice boomed from the darkness inside the doorway of the shack. 'Ant-nie, yuh ragamuffin, 'ow hab yuh bin?'

The bruisers in the yard immediately relaxed their aggressive postures, lapsing back into the languor they had exhibited when we first approached.

'I am well, Claudie,' De Rasta said, emerging from the Land Rover. 'How is life treating you these days?'

'It has been fine, though I am not so sure now that my old friend arrives on my doorstep with Babylon in a police car.' The man who stepped from the dimness of the shack certainly didn't fit my expectations. He was well dressed, in dark slacks, expensive Italian loafers, and a crisp, white guayabera. And he was old, patrician old. My experience with Jamaican gangs, all gleaned by way of be-on-the-lookout dispatchers from RVIPF headquarters, was that their leaders consolidated their power in a particular gang by their mid-twenties and were usually dead by age thirty. And the men arrayed around Boss Claudie certainly looked like a Jamaican gang.

'This gent may be Babylon, Claudie, but he is a right fellow and a friend,' Anthony vouched. 'Constable Teddy Creque, meet Boss Claudie. And we are not here about your business operations, Claudie.'

Boss Claudie extended a hand. 'Any friend of Anthony's is a friend of mine. And, Anthony, I have no business operations these days. I'm retired. These boys are mostly nephews and cousins. They don't deal or enforce; they are here to protect me. This is what retirement looks like for a drug lord. Live quietly. Live modestly. And have enough muscle around to discourage the settling of old scores. I study now, getting the education I never bothered with when I was young and foolish. Philosophy, mostly. I was just wrapping up a morning of deontological moral theory. Kant, you know. But you and Constable Creque did not come all the way up here to discuss the moral rightness or wrongness of a man's actions, did you? At least not in the philosophical sense.'

'No, sir,' I said. 'We are looking for someone. A possible witness to a murder.'

'Not the one that took place at Government House last night?' Word of murder travels quickly, even to the hill country, on the tame Virgin Islands.

'The same, sir. Anthony says you or your . . . nephews may know of this witness's whereabouts. His name is Glenroy Watson. He goes by Jubbie.'

'I know him, Constable. Jubbie is a good boy. Goes to church. Isn't mixed up with any bad elements. In fact, he is a friend of my nephew, Raymond. Raymond!' Boss Claudie yelled.

Raymond emerged around the corner of the shack, munching on a chicken leg. Apparently, we had interrupted his mid-morning snack.

'Raymond, ave yuh si Jubbie todeh?' Claudie asked.

'Nuh, uncle. Him gaan.' Raymond chewed the hen leg through his answer.

'Gaan weh, Raymond?'

'I-mon don' know. Him roommate Georgie say him pack up an' cut in di miggle addi nite. Georgie tell I-mon dat Jubbie nah seh wah mek ar weh.'

'There you have it, Constable. Out in the middle of the night to who knows where. Sounds like Jubbie saw something he's none too anxious to discuss. With anyone, let alone the police. Raymond, weh Jubbie guh wen he waah bi alone?'

Raymond was now savoring the gristly joint at the top of the hen leg, but he managed a 'Mi nuh know' as he gnawed. 'Him 'ave an auntie en St Lucia. Mebbe deh.'

I didn't think Jubbie could have scraped up a ticket out of the Virgin Islands so quickly on a Sunday morning; Saturday is changeover day for most of the bareboat charters and, between that and the sabbath, there are almost no flights into or out of Lettsome Airport on Sundays. But that didn't mean he wasn't trying. 'Thank you, Raymond, and thank you, Mr . . . Claudie. Come, Anthony, we have work to do.'

'Farewell, Claudie,' Anthony said. 'Best of luck with the studies.'

'Drop by any time, Anthony. We can discuss Wittgenstein's *Tractatus Logico-Philosophicus*.' Boss Claudie shook his venerable gray locks. 'Back ten years ago, I would never have thought I would be making such an offer to you.' He smiled.

FIFTEEN

'What do you think, old friend?' Anthony Wedderburn asked.

I thought about responding to his question with a few of my own about his White Rasta days and his acquaintance with Jamaican crime kingpins who retired to the Virgin Islands. I decided to save my questions for another, less busy day. 'I think that Glenroy Watson may have witnessed something more than just a bunch of duffers and dowagers drinking champagne to excess last night. I think with what he saw we may be able to eliminate the need to do an extensive interview of Princess Portia and the Viscount of Newent about events. Nothing would make me, Sir Roger and, probably, the Governor and the Commissioner more happy than to avoid that unpleasantness. But first we have to find him and the initial step to that will be a material witness warrant to prevent him from leaving the Virgin Islands.'

'So you, a constable from the remote sister island of Anegada, are going to knock on the door of the judge of the High Court on a Sunday morning and ask him to issue a warrant for some poor soul who you have a hunch may have seen *something*, while you yourself have seen the deceased's husband standing over her body with a gun in his hand?' In my police career up to now, it had been Deputy Commissioner Lane who had asked me penetrating and often uncomfortable questions about my investigative choices. Now that the DC was out of commission, Anthony seemed to have taken over that role.

I answered De Rasta with all the certainty I usually reserved for the Deputy Commissioner. 'I guess so.'

The chirp of the radio in the Land Rover saved me. 'Unit Twelve, public service a female caller.' They gave a number I did not recognize. I took out my cell phone – a new acquisition for me, since Anegada had only recently erected a cell tower and most of the long-time residents still used the traditional method of communication on marine radio channel 16 – and rang the number.

'Hello.' A sultry voice that still sent chills down my spine answered.

'Hello, Cat. It's Teddy. I'm returning your call.'

'Hold on a minute.' There was mumbled conversation in the background and then the click of heels on a tile floor. 'Teddy, I'm so sorry,' Cat began.

'For what?' Cat certainly hadn't chosen now to apologize for leaving me bleeding on the East End of Anegada seven years ago.

'I should have told you about this the minute Sir Roger gave you the smiling omission treatment earlier. Teddy, Princess Portia and Jeremy Sutherland are leaving tomorrow morning, first thing. The arrangements are all set. Sir Roger knew and didn't say anything when you said you'd be back to interview them tomorrow. They will be long gone unless you plan to be here at the crack of dawn.'

'But don't they understand that they are witnesses – important witnesses – to a capital crime? I need to speak to them. It may be vital to the case.'

'The departure plans were made this morning before you and Anthony arrived.'

I absorbed what I was hearing and said, 'Well, OK. I can come and get their statements now, and if they saw nothing important, or if what they saw is duplicative of another witness's recollection –' what other witness I had no idea – 'they can leave as planned. We can be there within the hour.'

'Teddy, the Princess is still sedated. No, that's not really accurate. She is out like a light. She woke up, screaming, and Jeremy had the doctor give her another shot. She is so out of it that the plan for a departure ceremony has been scrapped and she is to be transported to the airport in an ambulance.'

'Well, I can at least interview Lord Sutherland.'

'He won't talk to you, Teddy.' There was a long pause. 'I lied to you. I'm sorry. Jeremy wasn't hungover. He can drink until he passes out and pop up the next morning fresh as a daisy. That's what happened last night and he is fine today. When Sir Roger reminded him that you wanted to question him today, he said, "I'll be damned before I'll talk to that piss-ant yokel." He told Sir Roger and me to put you off with the hangover story for a day and he and Princess Portia would be gone and you would still be cooling your heels. I went along for the sake of Portia. She really needs to get this whole thing behind her. But then I saw that it was wrong, Teddy, and that you needed to know about it.'

'We'll still come over, even if it is to be turned away again.'

'It won't do any good, Teddy. Sir Roger will never let you at either of them. He will obfuscate and delay until they are gone.'

Cat was right. Sir Roger was a master at his job. And he undoubtedly had the Governor's ear and possibly his unspoken approval of the plan to spirit the Royals back to England without my interviewing them. I thought about going to the Commissioner, but his actions last night and the fact that he, like the Governor, was on an overseas posting from the mother country did not give me a great deal of hope that he would side with me against . . . my God, against someone in the line of succession to the throne. I was a mere lawman. What could I do? Then I realized the answer was right there in my colloquial title. I was a *law*man. And even the Royals, all of them but King Charles himself, were not above the law.

'You're right, Cat,' I admitted. 'Persuading Sir Roger is a futile errand. But you have done the right thing by telling me about their deception and their intentions. I just need to decide how to use the information, if at all.'

'Then forgive me, Teddy,' Cat said. 'For this morning, I mean.'

'For this morning, yes,' I said. 'Goodbye.' I punched off the phone.

Anthony had heard only half of our conversation but he understood the gist. 'I take it, old friend, that we are now off to storm the gates of Government House and free the Princess, or some such thing. Capital! I have always wanted to do that.'

'Actually, no, Anthony.'

'Where are we going, then?'

'To find a typewriter, of course.'

SIXTEEN

I rapped tentatively, and then forcefully, on the polished mahogany front door of the stately plantation house that was now the home of David Shapiro MD, Coroner of the Virgin Islands. After what seemed an eternity, De Rasta and I were greeted by Mrs Shapiro, a grandmotherly type, who seemed a bit frazzled despite the Sunday morning quiet.

'He's this way, out in his *jardin sauvage*, as he calls it. Relaxing among the hibiscus and oleander after his predations of last night, the same as he does every Sunday morning.' She pointed us in the right direction at the edge of the garden and scurried away.

Dr Shapiro drained off the contents of a crystal old-fashioned glass and placed it on the stone table beside his seat as we approached. He was wearing a brown batik sarong and no shirt or shoes. He may have been drowsing in the solitude of the garden but had quickly come alert when Anthony and I approached. The good doctor, catching his wife's remark about predation with his razor-sharp-for-a-ninety-year-old hearing, grinned at us and said, 'She begs for it every Saturday night and complains about it every Sunday morning. The sacrifices I make to satisfy the carnal needs of that woman. I am, in case you haven't noticed, no longer a young man. My cardiologist, killjoy that he is, told me that I could no longer continue with the drinking, the cigars and the sex, that I had to cut back. So I gave up the cigars.' His eyes grew misty. 'I loved those cigars. Now, Constable Creque, the last time I saw you, you had two unfortunates on ice in your office on Anegada and a shortage of quality rum on the island in the aftermath of Hurricane Leatha. I hope nothing that serious brings you to me today.'

'Almost that serious, Your Worship. A matter of material witnesses in a death on your inquest docket,' I said. 'I come to apply for a warrant.'

'As I told you back on your home island, save the "Your Worship" tommyrot for the courtroom.' The old man poured

himself two fingers of rum and held the glass aloft to examine
the golden liquid in the sun. 'Next thing you know that damn
cardiologist will cut me off from this elixir and I will be down
to just the Saturday night romp with Mrs Shapiro. But you didn't
come here today to listen to my petty problems. You want a
warrant. Such matters are within my jurisdiction but most police
officers here on Tortola apply to the High Court for warrants.
The High Court has concurrent jurisdiction, and Judge Highsmith
has much more criminal procedure experience than I do.'

'I am not acquainted with Judge Highsmith, Dr Shapiro, so I
chose to come to you with the request.'

'Didn't think you could get by Highsmith with it, eh?' Dr
Shapiro looked at me with undisguised skepticism. 'All right,
Constable, I'll bite. Show me your papers.'

I drew out the warrant materials I had prepared for holding
Glenroy Watson as a material witness, including my affidavit
raising the risk of his fleeing to St Lucia to avoid testimony. Dr
Shapiro scanned the papers. 'A flight risk? All right, I will grant
your application. Do you have a proposed order?'

I handed the coroner the order and he scratched out his
signature on it. Then I said, 'I have two more applications related
to the same inquest. They are also flight risks.' I passed him the
papers.

Dr Shapiro began to read and became very focused. 'Excuse
my crude American slang, but holy shit, Constable! You want a
warrant to hold two members of the Royal family as material
witnesses? Do you know what this will bring down on your head?
On *our* heads?'

'I believe they are a flight risk. They may have crucial information about the circumstances of the death of Letitia Lane. I
intend to treat them as I would treat any other witnesses in the
same circumstances.'

'Well, Constable, I hope to hell the confidential informant you
rely on in your affidavit isn't blowing smoke up your skirt.'

'I don't believe she is, sir.' I decided to omit the fact that she
had recently been released from His Majesty's Prison.

'All right, what's sauce for the goose is sauce for the gander.
If Glenroy "Jubbie" Watson is to be prevented from travel as a
witness, the blind eyes of Lady Justice require the same treatment

for Princess Portia and the Viscount of Newent. I hope you know what you are doing, Constable.'

'So do I, Dr Shapiro. For both of our sakes.'

'I am ninety years old, Constable. What can they do? Fire me? The next morning would find me in this lovely spot, sipping this golden potion, with Mrs Shapiro, as usual, harping at me about something. In short, I am impervious, bulletproof. My life is unchangeable and would be unchanged. You, on the other hand . . .'

'I know, sir. But, the requirements of duty.' I shrugged.

'Many's the conscientious man hoisted on the problematic petard of duty. Watch your back, Constable Creque.'

'I shall, Your Worship.'

The ancient physician adjusted his sarong to avoid revealing too much leg. 'I told you, Teddy, save the "Your Worship" for the courthouse. I will see you there. Good luck.'

The coroner's warrants in my hand seemed to scream that I would need that good luck.

SEVENTEEN

J ubbie Watson was elusive, but the handling of his material witness warrant was relatively easy. I called dispatch and informed the shift supervisor of the warrant. In thirty seconds, a radio call went out telling every police and customs officer in the Virgin Islands to locate and hold the errant wine waiter.

The subjects of the other two warrants proved easier to locate and impossible to detain.

'Did you consider, Teddy, that it might be prudent to inform your immediate supervisor that you have just obtained and are on your way to serve warrants to place a member of the Royal family and her spouse in custody?' De White Rasta asked as we drove in the sunny balm of the early afternoon along the seaside road to Government House. 'Just a thought, mind you.'

Of course, it was prudent. If I'd had to face Deputy Commissioner Lane with that information, I probably would have dodged Anthony's reasonable suggestion. But my immediate supervisor now was Inspector Rollie Stoutt, he of rotund girth and faineant manner. I figured I could handle him with a quick telephone call and I was right. 'Jeezum, Teddy, I'm on my way,' was his breathless response after I gave him my best two-minute summary of the situation. 'Jeezum.'

Anthony and I were walking up the steps of Government House when the car bearing Inspector Stoutt, blues and twos activated, roared into the driveway. So much for a discreet approach. I expected Rollie to emerge from the RVIPF car in his dress whites and ostrich plume helmet and was relieved to see he was wearing a regular duty uniform. American size 48 by the look of it.

'Teddy, Teddy – I mean Constable – a word before you go inside.' This breathless sentence followed Rollie's sprint up the dozen steps to the front entrance of Government House.

'Yes, sir.' I saluted my superior officer, fingers together, palm out, as I had learned from the Deputy Commissioner when I was a green special constable. I guess Rollie expected an argument or at least some form of resistance. He was caught speechless when I stopped and waited. Flustered, he finally spat out, 'You can't do this.'

'The manual of procedure recommends obtaining warrants and detaining material witnesses who are about to flee the jurisdiction. I am following the sanctioned procedure, Inspector.'

'But. But. . . . they're Royals.'

Anthony came to my aid. 'Trousers on one leg at a time, just like the rest of us, Inspector.'

'Princess Portia doesn't wear trousers, Mr Wedderburn, and for our current purposes neither does Lord Sutherland,' Rollie sputtered.

'The Viscount of Newent might take offense to your remark about his lack of trousers,' De Rasta grinned.

'Must you find lewd humor in everything?' Rollie was truly rattled now. I saw my opening.

'Are we to treat them differently?' I asked.

'Yes.' Rollie's knee-jerk response caused him to pause, looking for the right justification. 'No. Just . . . be a tad . . . sensitive. Please.'

'Always, Inspector. Always.'

'Criminal legal process against a member of the Royal family? No, two members!' Sir Roger sputtered, flushing red and putting on a BAFTA-award-worthy performance of perfectly controlled fury. 'This is an outrage. I shall not permit it.'

After his explosion at me, he turned his practiced indignation on the closest person he thought could rein me in. 'Inspector Stoutt, is it? My God, man, you must see how inappropriate, how positively *profane* this is. Are you not his commanding officer? You must override this.'

Rollie elevated squirming to a new level but held firm. 'The warrants are proper, Sir Roger,' he peeped. 'And they are not truly criminal process. They simply require the Princess and the Viscount to remain in the Virgin Islands to aid in the murder investigation and any attendant prosecution as witnesses. Constable Creque could even speak to them now, if possible, and the warrant could then be withdrawn if their testimony is determined to be unnecessary after they have answered all of the Constable's questions.'

Sir Roger put on his best I-want-to-speak-to-the-manager face and voice. 'I had hoped to avoid further unpleasantness, but that seems to be impossible, Inspector. Please radio the Police Commissioner and tell him he is required at Government House. Now.'

Rollie blanched as much as a black man could and reached for his portable radio.

'I am sure the Commissioner will come forthwith,' said Lord Anthony Wedderburn, my assistant and Sir Roger's clear superior in the arcane pecking order that is British aristocratic society. 'And he will fully inquire into the circumstances giving rise to the warrant request, won't he, Constable Creque?'

'Yes, of course,' I agreed. Where was De Rasta going with this?

'And I suppose you will be required to reveal that your action seeking the warrants was prompted by you learning of a secret plan to remove Princess Portia and the Viscount from the Virgin Islands.'

Sir Roger's false choler was replaced by a flush of genuine perturbation. 'How dare you . . .?'

'Oh, Constable Creque dares, and dares often, I can assure you, Sir Roger.' Anthony smiled benignly, eyes aglow.

The unctuous fixer changed his tactics. 'Surely you do not seek to hold the Princess and the Viscount when their personal safety is at risk. And don't tell me His Majesty's Prison is an option. Even you must realize that cannot happen. And Government House is not secure; the bullets flying through the air last night proved that. Located in the middle of Road Town as it is, with no suitable walls or security structure in place, means that even your entire police force cannot protect the Princess. She must leave Government House tomorrow, with her husband, for both their safety. And no other place in the Virgin Islands is secure enough to house them. They must return to England.' Sir Roger, believing he had successfully played the safety card, allowed a look of triumph to pass across his countenance.

'There is one place in the Virgin Islands which can be easily made secure enough for two Royal guests,' I said. 'And there is a residence there where they will be quite comfortable. Anegada.'

'Anna what?'

'Anegada. An island to the north of Tortola,' I said.

'Ah, yes. That backwater? Where is there a residence that befits a Royal on that place?' Sir Roger said.

'There is a fine Italianate villa on an empty bay on the island's south side, off by itself. The land approach to it can be easily guarded by two officers; the sea approach is through a maze of coral reefs. The RVIPF police boat, the *St Ursula*, can be anchored just offshore to prevent anyone from approaching by sea and to provide a base of operations for the security detail. The villa's wine cellar is well stocked and I know of a local chef who can see to meals. That is, unless you are prepared to offer the Princess and the Viscount for an immediate interview and their evidence proves unimportant.'

Bluff called, Sir Roger had no choice. 'As I told you, Constable, both Her Royal Highness and Lord Sutherland remain indisposed. And how do you propose to safely transport them to this villa? I suppose you will levitate them across the water.'

'No, Sir Roger. I propose that they be transported by helicopter. I know a reliable pilot with whom they are both well acquainted. The trip will take mere minutes.'

EIGHTEEN

'You want to put Princess Portia and Lord Sutherland in the Setting Point Villa?' Lawrence Wheatley, proprietor of the Reef Hotel, had a tone of glee in his voice that marked an innkeeper about to see his humble, and humbly priced, lodging appear on the international map, with jet-set room rates to match. 'Of course, it is available.'

'And for meals, we need a dedicated chef. No restaurant food. I think you should get Belle Lloyd from Cow Wreck.'

'Consider it done, Teddy. When can I expect them?'

'They will arrive today, sometime before sunset. They will come in by helicopter. Anthony will be with them. He will need to have land transportation available at the villa for emergencies. Send someone to get my Land Rover and have it waiting for him. The keys are in it.' I know what you are thinking. Leaving the keys in a police car for anyone to walk up and drive it away? And a police officer asking someone to do just that? But – this is Anegada.

The instruction concerning the police car didn't phase Lawrence, but having Anthony in charge did. 'Teddy, are you sure De Rasta is the right person for this? I mean, with the ganja and all?'

'Of course, Lawrence. He's an aristocrat. He understands exactly what makes them tick. That's why he had to smoke all that ganja in the first place.' I clicked off my cell phone and turned to the task of enlisting the helicopter pilot, walking across the room to where Inspector Stoutt and Sir Roger were huddled.

'We are all set on the security arrangements for Anegada,' Rollie said, seeing me approach. 'The *St Ursula* embarks within the hour for the island, with her crew plus six uniformed officers to handle the landside security.'

'That's fantastic, Inspector,' I said. Turning to Sir Roger I said, 'I will need to speak to a member of the Royal entourage now.'

'But I have already told you, man, the Princess and the Viscount are unable . . .' Sir Roger began.

'Not them. I need to speak to Ms Wells,' I said. I thought I heard Anthony inhale and catch his breath. I thought I saw him give his golden Prince Valiant mane a negative shake. I chose to ignore both.

'Yes, Constable. I will have her join you in the library.' Sir Roger scuttled away.

'He will be coming with them, you know,' Anthony said when Sir Roger moved out of earshot. 'I know his type. There are dozens of them scattered among the aristocracy back home, their whole existence wrapped up in insulating the upper crust from any 'untoward events' and their consequences. They can be very dangerous to careers. Do not think that you are done with Sir Roger just because you had the element of surprise this morning.'

'That's why I want you to shepherd the Royals in Anegada, Anthony. Keep an eye on things while I work on the case here. Both you and Cat Wells.'

'Do you think involving Ms Wells is really a good idea, old man?'

'I need eyes on the inside, Anthony. I trust her.'

'I hope for your sake your trust is not misplaced.'

The library at Government House had a sad air of disuse about it. A fine veneer of dust coated the leather-bound volumes brought in by a succession of colonial governors. The books had never been touched once they had arrived in the Caribbean, their owners instead preferring the attractions of indolence, rum and other native pursuits to the habit of reading they had cultivated during the dreary winters in England. I waited there among the decaying volumes, as instructed.

'Ms Wells,' Sir Roger announced like some over-paid butler, stepping aside to allow Cat Wells to enter and then closing the door.

'I hope you haven't called me in to scold me, Teddy.' She wore an emerald-green sheath dress, simple and clearly obscenely expensive, that brought out the similar hue of her contrite eyes. I tried to decide if the contrition was genuine and finally gave up.

'I'm not here to scold you, Cat.' She had, after all, done the right thing after a wrong step or two along the way. That seemed to be a pattern with her. It seemed to be a pattern with me. It seemed to be a pattern with most of humanity, I decided. 'I came to ask for your help. I need a helicopter pilot.'

'My chartering days with VI Birds are over, Teddy. They have a company policy of not placing convicted felons on the payroll.'

'I am not looking for a charter, Cat. This is a special mission. I want you to fly Princess Portia and Lord Sutherland to Anegada. We're taking them there for security reasons. They will be staying in the Setting Point Villa.'

'Putting them in a gilded cage until they deign to speak with you?'

'Possibly.' I had not given it much thought, but that was exactly what I was doing. I had been spending so much distracted time getting the Royal run-around that I was letting the investigation of Letitia Lane's murder slide. I needed the Royals away, safe and isolated, so that I could do my job until they would speak to me. I already had a watchdog for them in Anthony. But I needed someone on the inside, someone closer to them, to let me know of any further Royal machinations.

'Well, I can fly them there on Edmund's Bell Jet Ranger. I assume you want Anthony along, too. And then there is Sir Roger.'

'I had not planned for him to make the trip,' I said.

'Oh, he'll be on board, Teddy. He has turned into Lord Sutherland's right-hand man on this trip. You had best plan on him being there. Anyway, I can pop them over to Anegada within the hour and be back to take Edmund to the USVI in time for our daily sundowner. So, yes, I'll do it. I owe you that much.'

'The thing is, Cat, I was hoping you could make more than just a quick hop to Anegada. I was hoping you could stay.'

A barely detectable flash of surprise passed across Cat Wells' lovely green eyes, followed by an even briefer look of desire that I recognized from the times years ago when such looks would linger between us for hours on end. As quickly as they arrived, the expressions of surprise and passion were replaced by curiosity. 'For what purpose, Teddy?'

'To keep an eye on the Princess and let me know the truth about her condition. I need someone who will tell me the un-varnished truth, as you did earlier today. I don't believe it will be for more than a day or two. Will you do it, Cat?'

'It won't be more than a day or two if they stop giving her the sedatives they've been feeding her like candy. But, yes, Teddy, I'll do it. I guess I owe you that much. Will you be there, on Anegada?'

'I'll be staying on Tortola for the time being,' I said. I had a murder to investigate. And it was past time to talk again to the prime suspect.

NINETEEN

'You do not have to say anything, but it may harm your defense if you do not mention when questioned something which you later rely on in court. Anything you do say may be given in evidence.' I paused, took a deep breath, and went on. 'My condolences on your loss, sir.'

I had never expected to greet Deputy Commissioner Howard T. Lane with anything other than a snap to rigid attention and a crisp salute, much less a reading of the right to silence given to criminal suspects before interview throughout the United Kingdom. But then again, the dejected man in a too-short hospital gown seated on the side of his bed in the Peebles Hospital ICU bore almost no resemblance to the spit-and-polish superior officer I had answered to for my entire two and a half decades in the Royal Virgin Islands Police Force.

'Thank you, Constable Creque. For the condolences and for the warning.' The DC sagged into himself, shrinking his six-foot-six-inch frame into that of wizened old man before my very eyes, like some pathetic magic trick. 'I cannot believe Letitia is gone that way.' He hesitated, lost, and then said, 'I have a splitting headache.' As a way of explaining, I supposed.

'It is important that we speak. The first forty-eight hours, you know, sir, is the crucial time frame for gathering evidence in a case of . . .' I was loathe to say the word but could not think of a suitable euphemism. 'Homicide. But I can return in a couple of hours if you consider yourself in an unfit condition for an interview. Or . . .' More loath to say this. 'If you wish to avail yourself of the protections of the Right to Silence.'

'I will not exercise my right to silence. And I will speak with you now, for Letitia's sake as well as my own.' The DC tried to gather himself, to rally for the daunting difficulty of explaining why he had not killed his wife, but faltered and fell back in upon himself again, awaiting my first question with hopeless eyes.

'Tell me what happened last night, Deputy Commissioner.' If

he would talk, I would allow him an open-ended ramble to start, to see if . . . damn, to see if he would confess. Or explain, if there could ever be a suitable explanation for standing over the body of your wife with a smoking gun in your hand.

'We fought. Fought while we were dressing for the evening. Fought while we were putting on our finery and getting ready to attend an event most of the people in the United Kingdom would have given their eye teeth to attend, with all the pomp and the proximity to Royalty and the fine wines and the food and the sheer pageantry of it all.' DC Lane stopped, eyes brimming.

'Letitia didn't want to go?' I prompted.

The barest start of a smile appeared at the corner of the DC's lips and then vanished. 'Oh, she wanted to go. She could carry it off. So dignified, so articulate, so . . . noble. She fit in with that crowd. She had the cultured bearing. She could converse with them. Charm them. She knew it and she loved the rare chance she had at it. Imagine that, a simple little churchgoing girl grown up in Free Bottom, rubbing elbows with those people. It was not that we were going that was the problem. It was how we were going, Constable, that caused the difficulty between us.'

I filled the pause in the Deputy Commissioner's monologue with silence and it worked. He continued.

'She didn't want us to go "that way" as she said. Carrying a gun. On duty. "Leave that work to the younger men, Howard." She wanted me to retire, if you can imagine. We had sparred about it for many months off and on. You know how it is, making major decisions in a marriage, Constable. But it all seemed to come to a head yesterday. She said she was going to the reception but that she had had enough, she was going to pack a bag and spend the night at a friend's house and retrieve the rest of her things in the morning – this morning. Only this morning, she is dead.'

'What happened at the reception, sir?'

'We reached a truce on the drive to the reception. We agreed that we would get through the evening and would not carry on our dispute in public. No scenes. We would just carry out our respective duties – as a Deputy Commissioner's wife, Letitia had duties, too, uncompensated and not formally stated but duties nonetheless – and then home to . . .' The DC stopped here, searching for the right word and appalled at the one he found. 'Separate.'

'You saw how it was between us during the evening, Constable. Cold. Distant. Silent. It was almost a relief when duty called and I had to follow Lord Sutherland out into the garden.'

I waited for Deputy Commissioner Lane to continue but he did not. Instead, his brows furrowed, eyes searching not for something outside the man but for something within. Either the DC was the consummate actor or he was confused and at a loss. And I did not believe that I was in Peebles Hospital with the Virgin Islands' version of Sir Laurence Olivier.

'I cannot remember anything from the moment I exited the door of Government House into the garden until I awoke in this bed this morning.'

'How did you know about Letitia?'

'Her death? Nurse Rowell told me when I asked why I was here. She explained that Letitia had been shot and killed. That I was a suspect. The only suspect. But I remember nothing of it. Did I do it, Constable?' The big man asked the question in the bewildered voice of a small child.

'I don't know,' I said, more hopeful that my response was true than certain of it. All the evidence pointed to the DC as his wife's killer, and now he had supplied me with what might pass muster as a motive. I knew if there was to be any chance for him, either a chance for a determination of innocence or a chance for some slight mercy in sentencing, it would probably hinge on any information that could be extracted from him. So I tried, mightily, for the next half hour, using all of the tricks and techniques I had learned to jog the memory of a witness at the Regional Police Training Centre in Barbados. And the DC was cooperative; I could sense he was trying his best to recall what had occurred in the ill-lighted garden of Government House the night before.

But it was all to no avail. Whatever the DC had seen, heard, or otherwise sensed in those few minutes between when he entered the garden and when I found him standing over his wife's body remained locked away in his mind, unable to be retrieved through his best efforts and mine. At the end of half an hour, he was more tired and dejected than he had been at the start, and I was no more enlightened.

'I believe that is all I have for now, Deputy Commissioner,' I said, rising from the single chair in the room to leave. 'I will be in touch with any further questions.'

'Constable, you must find the truth. Even if the truth is ugly, unsettling, and harmful.' The DC, avoiding my eyes, gazed out the window into the blue-green waters of Road Harbor, where a sailboat cut a smart tack in the freshening breeze. 'I have an ugly truth to tell you, one of which I am ashamed. A truth I am certain is relevant to your investigation.' The DC stopped for a moment. It seemed he would not go on but then his spine stiffened. 'I have been involved in an affair for the past two decades.'

I fell back into the seat from which I had just risen, not because this new development would require more questioning but because this shocking information took me down at the knees. Deputy Commissioner Lane having an affair? Her Royal Highness Queen Elizabeth, in her nineties, having an affair seemed more likely than my staid, upright, rule-following mentor. I opened my mouth to speak but no words came out. Thankfully, the DC continued unprompted.

'Letitia knew. She found out about it ten years ago. She told me it didn't matter, that she was keeping me despite it. And, fool that I was, I kept on with both women. And they each kept on with me, both knowing that the other knew, both never mentioning the other. I'm no prize; I don't know what they were thinking. But you need to know for your investigation. And you need to know that I would not kill Letitia because of what was going on, or for any other reason. I would never harm her.'

An interviewer of a criminal suspect is schooled to not be judgmental. Disapprobation conveyed to the suspect, even by an officer not known to the accused, can shut down an interview. But I couldn't begin to conceive of being judgmental. I remembered when I was in the same situation, Icilda dead, the stain of an affair on my reputation. The DC had been asking the questions then and had treated me with sensitivity. Was it because he was involved outside his marriage at that time, too? Of course, I still had to do my job. 'Who is the lady, Deputy Commissioner?'

'Consuela Lettsome. Spare her as much as possible. She has

had a long career with the RVIPF and I would hate to see it damaged unnecessarily. This will be bad enough for her as it is.'

'I shall spare her as much as possible.' This revelation explained much about Ms Lettsome's fierce loyalty to her boss, as well as her intimate knowledge of his working activities. 'Thank you for your candor, Deputy Commissioner. I will take my leave now. I hope you will make yourself available for further questions as necessary.'

'Of course.' The DC settled back, a weight removed from his shoulders. 'And, Constable Creque, please find the truth. For Letitia's sake. For my sake. No matter how awful it is. No matter who is damaged by it. She at least deserves that.'

'Yes, sir.' I saluted. Force of habit, I guess. As I turned to leave, there was a commotion in the hallway outside the door. I recognized Inspector Fahey of the RVIPF, engaged in a heated conversation with Nurse Rowell. An officer from His Majesty's Prison stood off to one side, doubtless hoping to avoid the fray.

'I do not care who you are, officer, nor who sent you here. This patient is to have only one visitor at a time.' Nurse Rowell planted hands on hips and placed her formidable bulk between Inspector Fahey and the door to the DC's room.

'I am on orders from the Commissioner. I shall see him now.' Inspector Fahey moved to step around the redoubtable nurse. 'I have papers to deliver to the prisoner, and this officer is to take him to His Majesty's Prison now that he is medically discharged.'

'I don't care if you have the Ten Commandments on stone tablets to deliver. One visitor at a time. And I have no written order from a doctor discharging this patient. Until I do, he stays in this hospital.' Nurse Rowell set her jaw. Nobody pulled rank on her in her own domain. At least nobody who wanted to survive.

I stepped from the ICU room, as much to end the confrontation as to depart.

'You may step in now, Inspector,' Nurse Rowell growled. When the prison officer attempted to follow, she planted a hand on his chest. 'Not you.'

With the inspector already in the ICU room, the prison officer backed away. After a couple of minutes, Inspector Fahey emerged and beckoned the officer. 'Let's get this inmate ready to transport.'

'Inspector, you don't need to take Deputy Commissioner Lane to His Majesty's Prison, do you? He's in no condition,' I said.

'He's not Deputy Commissioner any more. He is suspended pending resolution of the charges against him. *Your* charges, Constable Creque. The Commissioner had me deliver the notice of suspension to him personally. I am to escort him to prison with this officer. He's been discharged from the hospital.'

'By whom?' Nurse Rowell bristled.

'By the hospitalist, Dr Patel. I spoke to him by telephone just a few minutes before I left to come here,' Inspector Fahey said.

'I thought I heard Dr Patel tell you to keep him hospitalized for further observation,' I said, directing my comment to Nurse Rowell. My grasp at this straw was exceedingly transparent but more than enough for an angry Nurse Rowell.

'He did mention further observation,' she said. 'And I have no order for his discharge in my chart.'

'I told you what Dr Patel told me,' an exasperated Fahey said.

'Well, Inspector, let me tell you about our discharge rule. It requires a written order from the patient's treating physician, in this case the hospitalist. I have no such order. Deputy Commissioner Lane stays right where he is until I have one.' Nurse Rowell gave a sharp stamp of her foot for emphasis, which was lost in her crepe-soled nurse's shoe's collision with the linoleum floor. 'And if you wish to remove him in violation of that rule, you will be assuming liability for any medical difficulties he experiences. And you will have to go through me to do it.'

Inspector Fahey wasn't used to having his authority challenged. He noisily took in a lungful of air. I thought him about to explode in anger. But somewhere in his past, he had encountered a woman like Nurse Rowell. Maybe his mother, or his auntie, or a teacher in school. He had learned a lesson in that long-ago encounter, a lesson we have all learned at one time or another when dealing with such redoubtable members of the female sex. 'I'll be back to pick him up later today. When his discharge order is signed,' he grunted.

Nurse Rowell watched him depart over the top of her reading glasses. Her lesson to Inspector Fahey on intimidation was matched or exceeded by her subsequent tutorial in the delivery of the stink eye.

TWENTY

I was probably standing with my mouth agape and an expression of slight amusement on my face when Nurse Rowell turned her attention to me. 'There is no way that poor man in there –' pointing to the DC's room – 'should be subjected to a prison cell in his condition.'

I certainly agreed with her sentiments but even if I did not, I would've been hard pressed to challenge her. 'My view exactly, Nurse Rowell. But the written discharge order will surely arrive soon. Dr Patel did tell Inspector Fahey that the DC would be discharged.'

'I think it may be delayed.' Nurse Rowell was coy.

'I – and I am sure the DC – appreciate what you are considering doing, but you don't want to get in trouble by ignoring the written discharge order when it finally arrives.'

'I suspect young Dr Patel won't be writing a discharge order today or any time soon. I'm guessing he will agree with my suggestion that we keep the Deputy Commissioner here for further observation. Indefinitely. Observation, Constable, is a powerful thing. Just like my observation two days ago of the extended time Dr Patel spent in the ICU supply room. He said he was checking inventory. But he had help, a new and very voluptuous nurse's aide who emerged from the supply room three minutes after the doctor. Adjusting her clothes. I think I am in a position to ask the doctor, quite pointedly, if he agrees that there should be further observation of Deputy Commissioner Lane after I remind him of those facts. Will a few extra days give you enough time to complete your investigation?'

'I honestly don't know. There is much to do. There seem to be difficulties at every turn.'

'Well, I can supply some information that may be of help. I called in a favor with the lab tech. Had her come in this morning to run tests on the DC's blood sample we took immediately after you brought him in last night. His blood had flunitrazepam in it. Judging by the way it metabolizes, quite a large dose.'

'Flunitrazepam? What is that?'

'You may have heard of it by the more common name, Rohypnol. The street name is "roofies" or "roach". I'm sure you know it is illegal in the United States and a prescription-only medication in the United Kingdom.'

'Yes, Rohypnol. I didn't recognize the longer generic name. It's the date-rape drug, isn't it?'

'Exactly, Constable. It is misused for that purpose and similar purposes because of its strength and its effects. It is seven to ten times as strong as Valium. Its effects can be almost paralyzing; one who ingests it will be compliant or unable to act although completely able to observe events. It also often causes retrograde amnesia. One is unable to remember what happened while under the influence of the drug. That is why it is used so often for date rape. The victim is essentially helpless while the rape occurs and remembers none of the assault afterward. And it is easy to administer covertly, because it dissolves quickly in liquids.'

'So would Deputy Commissioner Lane have been able to pursue his wife, and aim and fire a gun in his drugged condition?'

'The amount of the drug in his blood, even hours after the incident, was substantial. The Deputy Commissioner is a big man but the dose he received would have been enough to bring down a horse. Well, maybe not a horse but it would drop a pony to its knees. Your DC would have had to muster every ounce of his strength just to remain standing. And, since it is like a deeply drunken state, his ability to carry out the somewhat complex task of aiming and firing a handgun would have been severely impaired. Even if he could lift the gun and pull the trigger, he likely couldn't have hit the proverbial broadside of a barn.'

'And if he witnessed someone else killing his wife, he wouldn't remember it because of the drug?'

'That is more difficult, Constable. I would say yes and no. If he witnessed his wife's death, the drug would put a kind of haze over the event. His mind would register the circumstances and her death on some level but the drug would prevent him from knowing it in a conscious manner and being able to remember it. He would experience the horror of seeing the murder and the grief of losing his wife but he would not really know what happened or how to describe it. He would experience it on an emotional level, like the victim of a date rape. His mind would understand that something tragic had happened. He would experience the emotions associated with the tragedy. He would be depressed. He would cry. Just like a date rape victim cries and feels violated. But like the rape victim, he cannot remember why he feels the way he does, what occurred, or how it occurred.'

'How do you know so much about this?'

'I have seen what the drug does. It was about a year ago. A nice young woman, Dutch, was here on a sailing vacation. She spent a last night in Road Town for dancing and a drink at one of the clubs. The last person who saw her in the club, one of the sailboat crew, thought she was drunk, by the way she staggered out the door. But she had been fed a roofie. Whoever did it must have followed her out but no one really paid attention. She was raped in a vacant lot nearby and left there. A police patrol found her and brought her in early the next morning in a condition very similar to the condition of the Deputy Commissioner last night except she was found with her skirt and panties torn. We did a sexual assault forensic examination and found that she had been raped. A drug screen revealed that she had been given Rohypnol. She could not remember anything that happened. The police never found who did it.'

TWENTY-ONE

There is nothing quite like being on the Caribbean Sea on a moonless night. The wind usually dies down, and if you shut off your boat engine, the whisper of the water against the hull is the only sound accompanying the dazzling spectacle above, the dome of the Milky Way spread horizon to horizon, God's handiwork on display for the lucky few who venture on to the dark waters. It was a sight that I had seen many times pulling lobster traps or long-line fishing for wahoo in the deep waters of the Anegada Passage, not a care in my head other than arriving home in time for my scheduled shift at the power plant or the morning start time for the day's bonefishing charter.

Now, the sky was the same unchanging sky but the cares were larger and more numerous. How to learn exactly what happened in the garden at Government House? How to properly do my duty, even if it meant sending my mentor away in disgrace and to prison for the rest of his life? How to safeguard a member of the Royal family on Anegada, and while safeguarding her, convince her that I had no bad motive in literally arresting her and her spouse, and that she should recount to me an evening of horror that she likely preferred to forget? How to locate Jubbie Watson, an absolutely vital, or absolutely useless, witness who had fled into the impenetrable hinterland of the small islands of the Windward and Leeward chain? These questions all remained unsolved and seemingly insoluble after I completed my crossing from Tortola to Anegada, tied the *Lily B* up to the fishermen's dock a stone's throw from The Settlement, and walked its silent and unlighted streets to their end and the only house with the lights still on, my home. I turned out the lamp left on in the living room, slipped into the bedroom and managed to worm into bed beside a sprawled Jeanne Trengrouse, drawing a mumbled welcome from her before she eased back into slumber's gentle grasp. I rolled on to my back and pondered all the questions before me, finally falling asleep an hour or two before dawn.

'Your Madda said that she saw Minnie George and Ruth Lloyd at Dotsie's Bakery yesterday, and they said that Princess Portia and the Viscount of Newent are at the Setting Point Villa,' Jeanne said, after awakening me with a perfunctory kiss as dawn flooded our bedroom. Dotsie usually closed the front room bake shop at her house at five o'clock to prepare the evening meal for her husband, Enos. Using this information, I calculated that the Royal couple had been on the island for an hour and a half, at most, when my mother received this intelligence. Such was the Anegada version of the famed coconut telegraph, frequently inaccurate but always blindingly rapid.

I opened one eye, gave a groggy grunt, and pulled the sheet over my head.

'And that you had them arrested for murder and ordered them imprisoned there until their trial,' Jeanne continued.

That sat me bolt upright.

'You know that is not true,' I said. 'They are here because they are material witnesses and they need a safe place to stay. And they certainly are not charged with murder or any other crime. You see Minnie and Ruth, you tell them that. Or anyone else who spreads that rumor.'

'Then they are not being held at the villa?' Why is it that the members of your own family always have a knack for asking the penetrating questions that even the most astute news reporter would shy away from?

'I suppose technically they're being held, but really, Jeanne, don't spread the rumor.' More awake now, I was feeling less like the man who had brought a knife to a gun fight than I had moments before.

'There's a helicopter there.'

'Yes. And Anthony Wedderburn is there to help take care of them, in addition to the police officers in the security detail. And Sir Roger Chamberlain is there as well. Is there anything else you care to know?'

'Who flew the helicopter in?' Jeanne asked in the quiet tone that usually tells me that I am in trouble.

'Cat Wells.'

There was a little explosion inside the pupil of each of Jeanne's lovely blue eyes. Little because, of course, the pupils of one's eyes are little. Otherwise, the little explosion would have reminded me of the eruption of Krakatoa. I waited for the rest of the cataclysm. Jeanne instead managed a suppressed, 'Is she staying on the island?'

'Someone needed to stay with the Princess. So, yes, she is staying on the island. Cat is a friend.'

'A friend of the Princess? Or a friend of yours? Did you ask her to come to Anegada or did the Princess ask?'

Honesty was not just the best but the only policy if I was to emerge from this interrogation unscathed. Or less scathed than I already was. 'I asked Ms Wells to come to Anegada because she is a friend of Princess Portia and because I needed someone I trust to keep an eye on things at the villa until I am able to interview the Royal couple.'

'Oh, you trust *her*?' Jeanne gave the 'her' a sing-songy inflection to emphasize the word.

'I do.' Because I am a fool, you are about to tell me.

'I don't,' Jeanne said. 'I don't trust her because of what she did to you and to your family. I don't like her because of what she did to you and your family.'

'I understand, Jeanne, but . . .' I got that far before the eruption gained momentum.

'No, you don't understand, Teddy. You don't understand that that woman is a manipulator and that you are putty in her hands. You don't understand the hold she had on you once and how susceptible you are to being in her hold again. You don't understand what a danger she is to *our* relationship and happiness. I don't understand how you are so blind to her ways and to your vulnerabilities when it comes to her. Her presence here is bad for you, bad for *us*.'

'I think you are exaggerating . . .' was all I was able to say before the detonation and the full blast swept over me.

'I am *not* exaggerating, Teddy Braithwaite Creque. I am trying to save you. Trying to save us.' I saw a softening in Jeanne's eyes, and then steely resolve. 'I want that woman out of our home. I want her gone from this island.'

'She will only be on the island for a day or two. Just until Princess Portia leaves. I really need her to stay until then,' I tried to explain.

'Fine, Teddy. I will leave your breakfast on the table. Eat it and then do what you need to do. But don't expect a warm and happy welcome from me each day when you come home from work as long as she is here. Because I am not happy. And you better think, Teddy, think long and hard, about your own happiness. Are you happy? If you are, do you want to upset that happiness?' Jeanne crossed her arms, her body language for 'discussion's over.' 'I will leave you to your thinking.'

After a lonely breakfast, I headed for the police station. I carried a toothbrush in my shirt pocket and a change of clothes in a duffle bag, as a precaution.

TWENTY-TWO

Early arrivals are not a specialty of Pamela Pickering, Anegada's administrator and one of the three public servants on the island, together with me and our shared administrative assistant, Anthony Wedderburn. I expected Pamela's cubbyhole office across from mine to be vacant when I arrived at eight o'clock. This is because Pamela usually doesn't start her five-day work week, which she artfully manages to cut to three and a half days through a combination of well-crafted excuses and blatant tardiness, until slightly after noon on most Mondays.

On this day, however, the smell of freshly brewed Jamaican Peaberry coffee emanated from the office across the hall from mine. I dropped my duffel inside the holding cell located behind my desk and followed the scent.

'Top of the morning, Teddy,' Pamela greeted. 'Come on in and have some coffee. It just finished brewing two minutes ago.'

Made wary by Pamela's uncharacteristic morning cheer, I poured some coffee and wondered what was elevating her spirits. I didn't have long to wait.

'Everybody's saying that Princess Portia and Lord Sutherland are staying at the Setting Point Villa for a few days.' Ah, that was it. Pamela has a love of gossip and what better fodder for gossip than having an heir to the throne pop into the neighborhood for a few days?

'Their presence here is supposed to be secret, for their privacy and security,' I said.

'But everybody knows. You know there ain't no secrets on this island. Now, Teddy, as Administrator, the highest government official on Anegada, I think it is not only appropriate but necessary that I go to the villa to welcome the Royal couple, and to see if all their needs are being met. That sort of thing.'

Only then did I notice that Pamela was decked out in her Sunday finery, sans a particularly tacky hat with a plastic bird nesting in a clutch of artificial flowers. Then I noticed the hat hanging on the clothes hook on the wall.

'I'm afraid that won't be possible, Pamela. No visitors are permitted for security reasons,' I said. 'Even high public officials such as yourself.'

Disappointment clouded Pamela's brow. 'Well, you enjoy that cup of Peaberry, Teddy. Seems there ain't enough in the pot for you to have no more. Now, if you'll excuse me, I have some important work to do,' she said, turning to her antiquated Acer PC. People Magazine Online filled the screen.

Cast out by two of the very few women in my life within a half-hour, I retreated to my office and resolved to avoid further disappointment by not visiting my madda today. I decided to gather my thoughts and list all the potential witnesses to Saturday night's murder with whom I had not yet spoken. The list turned out to be ridiculously short, if eclectic:

Princess Portia
Lord Sutherland
Glenroy Watson

A more knotty issue was whether one or more of the listed individuals was something more than a mere witness. As in a suspect. Now that I had learned that Deputy Commissioner Lane had been drugged with Rohypnol, I had to consider the possibility of a third party's involvement. I supposed he could have administered the drug to himself after shooting Letitia as a kind of quasi alibi or red herring for the investigation he was sure to know would follow, but I doubted it. The other alternative was that someone had given him the drug and that he was being framed for the murder. The list of three witnesses before me had to be considered as potential suspects in the frame-up and murder as well. But how could I consider a Royal as a suspect? And why would any of them want to kill Letitia Lane? And then there was the wild card of the DC's affair with his loyal secretary. Consuela Lettsome certainly wasn't a witness, but could she be a suspect? My head spun at the prospects. Best to get on with it and do something. Anything.

I decided it would be unseemly to appear at the Setting Point

Villa to interview the Royals at what many people still considered the breakfast hour. I thought that it would definitely be the breakfast hour yet for the aristocracy. How long did they sleep and how long did they linger when breaking the fast? I settled on eleven o'clock as an appropriate time to make my visit. That left the elusive Mr Watson as the only other incomplete interview on my list. There was no way I would be able to interview him today, given his absence from the jurisdiction, but I could at least begin by locating him. Or by hearing if some of my compatriots had done so.

The heavy sigh that was Inspector Rollie Stoutt's greeting for those bearing bad news, or, God forbid, requesting that he engage in the unhappy activity known as work, greeted me at the other end of the telephone line. I took the sound as Rollie's salutation and said, 'Good morning to you, too, Inspector.'

'Are there problems involving the Princess on Anegada?' I could visualize the look of dread on Rollie's chubby face and smiled to myself, knowing his relief when he learned the purpose of my call.

'No, sir. At least not that I am aware of.'

Another sigh, this one just a hair more upbeat. 'Good. Have you done your interviews with the Princess and the Viscount and determined that there is no longer any reason to ask them to remain in the Virgin Islands?' Rollie asked, hoping against hope that I had called to make the principal problem in his life go away.

'I haven't approached them for interviews yet. I plan to do so at eleven. You know, to give them some time to shake the cobwebs out of their eyes and enjoy some of Belle Lloyd's fried fish and johnnycake for breakfast. I'm calling about the other possible witness, Glenroy Watson.'

'Calling to see if he has been found yet?' Rollie said. 'No, not yet. No surprise, though, especially if he has escaped from the Virgin Islands. We both know that BOLO alerts to the other islands in the Caribbean get short shrift in most jurisdictions. You know they take care of any local problems before trying to help out on a case that has nothing to do with their home territory.'

'Is there something we can do to speed the search up?' I realized how naïve the question was as soon as it escaped my lips.

'You mean like sending out an enhanced BOLO? To tell everyone that we really, really mean it when we say to be on the lookout and detain a material witness?' Oh, sarcasm does not become you, Inspector Stoutt, I thought, but I guess I deserved the remark.

'OK, Inspector, I deserved that. It's just that I have so few potential witnesses to work with and it's frustrating to be unable to speak to the few that I have.'

'Hey, Constable, if you have a way to light a fire under the backsides of all the police agencies in the Windward and Leeward Islands, have at it. But I have no magic solution for your difficulties. Just keep me posted on the Princess and the Viscount. And I will ring you immediately if Mr Watson is picked up. Are we good then?'

'Yes, sir.'

Inspector Stoutt gave another sonant cue, this time what sounded like a grunt of satisfaction, and hung up. I was left to ponder if I was going to have to sit on my hands for days or weeks, hoping that some idle cop in Dominica or Barbuda would stumble on to Jubbie Watson. There had to be some other way. Then the obvious, if mildly uncomfortable, solution hit me. I had to ask a favor.

A favor from someone who didn't owe me one.

TWENTY-THREE

'Joint Interagency Task Force South,' said a voice on the line twelve hundred miles to the northwest, in Key West, Florida.

I recognized the voice, clear, professional, and a touch on the seductive side, from my last call to the JITFS several years ago. I also knew the drill to reach who I needed to reach, so I tried to shortcut the process. 'This is Constable Teddy Creque of the Royal Virgin Islands Police Force calling for Agent Rosenblum. And the next part is where you tell me that there was no one by that name at JITFS. And then I say to you, "Well, if there was someone by that name at your agency, I would give you my phone number and ask you to have him call me." And then I would give you my number, 284-494-3802 and you would say, very professionally, "Thank you, sir, but we have no one here by that name," and you would hang up. And then a few minutes later I would get a call from Agent Rosenblum. Would you like me to repeat the telephone number?'

'That won't be necessary, sir, as we have no one here by that name,' the coolly competent voice in Key West said.

'Thank you,' I said. 'I will be waiting for his call.'

The connection clicked off and I hung up the receiver on my office landline. I barely had time for a sip of my now-tepid Jamaican Peaberry before the phone rang.

'Constable Teddy Creque, sole representative of law and order on the crappy little island of – what is it? – Anegada. To what do I owe the honor of a call from the best lawman in His Majesty's Virgin Islands? One of those rambunctious feral cattle giving you a problem?' The voice at the other end of the line screamed both the Bronx and unbridled sarcasm.

'Agent Rosenblum, so good to hear your voice,' I said, and remembered that the first time I had heard it had evoked both fear and anger in me. Our relationship had evolved considerably since that day. I had grown to accept the DEA agent's twisted brand of humor and Agent Rosenblum had come to the realization that I was neither a backward island bumpkin nor a greedy grifting cop, unlike so many in the area south of the US border. 'And, no, the wild cattle on Anegada are not yet beyond my capabilities. But I could use some help. On an informal basis.'

'Informal basis. Kee-rist, Teddy, have we ever operated together in any other way?' I could picture Agent Rosenblum's dead-black shark eyes glittering with a predator's anticipation. 'So what is it this time? Not a hidden treasure of emeralds bought with embezzled funds or the smuggling of rare coral, I hope. We have already done those.'

'Nothing that exciting. I need to find a man.'

'That's it? Well, shit, Constable, I didn't know it was something with such a high degree of difficulty. I will put my eighty-year-old Aunt Tilly right on it.' Agent Rosenblum was always such a charmer.

'I know it is not particularly difficult to find an individual, but the problem for me is that he's probably out of my jurisdiction.'

'And the local cops where he is won't arrest the perp and ship him back to you? What am I supposed to do, kidnap him for you? Sorry, but we are not doing renditions any more. The weenies in Congress decided that it wasn't fair to the lowlifes to sneak up and snatch them out of their own beds.'

'Well, the man I am after really isn't a perpetrator. He is a material witness to a murder. I think.'

'Do you think there was a murder or you think he was a witness?' Agent Rosenblum sneered.

I countered the remark with an unseen eye roll. I was asking Agent Rosenblum to do something for me so I had to be some-what circumspect. 'I think he is a witness to a murder. The murder of the wife of a police officer, Deputy Commissioner Howard Lane.' I omitted the fact that the Deputy Commissioner was the prime suspect.

'Your superior officer, right? Big guy, by the book, polishes his uniform brass twice a day?'

'The same.'

'That's rough. OK, for a fellow cop's wife I can help. Wadda ya need?'

'The witness's name is Glenroy Watson. He goes by an alias

– Jubbie. He has an aunt in St Lucia. I think he might be there. The RVIPF put out a BOLO on him for the entire region but it hasn't produced.'

'When did the BOLO go out?'

'Yesterday.'

'Yesterday? Shit, Constable what do you want? Egg in your beer?'

'I could use some boots on the ground. Just to check out the auntie's place.'

'In St Lucia? Hell, I got guys there. I suppose we could make it happen. In fact, you should know the guys. They were with me when I came to Anna-whatever to clean up the corruption that wasn't there.' A sarcastic smile by Agent Rosenblum materialized in my mind's eye. 'You must remember. Two guys – twins – from Saint L. They wore camo all the time, and boonie hats. Carried matching AR-15s. Carlos and Charlie. One is the deputy chief of the local cops now and the other is a lieutenant, head of their narcotics division. They know every outhouse and whorehouse on the beautiful Helen of the West Indies. They should be able to find your boy in short order, if he is in St Lucia. I'll make some calls and get back to you.'

'Thank you, Agent Rosenblum. I knew I could count on you.'

'Hey, Constable, you know me. When the shit hits the fan, I'm either the one dodgin' it or the one throwin' it. Speak soon.' Agent Rosenblum hung up.

I sat back in my chair. I still didn't know the guy's first name.

TWENTY-FOUR

My RVIPF Land Rover, the survivor of a decade on the washboard-rough sand roads of Anegada, had seen better days. Its exterior was scraped and scratched from a thousand collisions with the Antillean scrub thorn vegetation that bordered most of Anegada's roads so closely that you couldn't open the window when passing. The RVIPF emblem on the driver's side door, with its *Beati Pacifici* motto, still carries the saltwater stain midway up its face from its immersion during Hurricane Leatha. Yet it stood with faded dignity outside the Setting Point Villa ready to transport a member of the Royal family seventh in line to the throne of the most famous monarchy in the world.

The Land Rover's readiness at the beck and call of Princess Portia, the Viscount of Newent and their modest entourage was the reason I had to walk partway from The Settlement to Setting Point. My trip by Shanks' mare was blessedly shortened when Alan Soares came along in his pick-up truck and offered me a ride for the final two miles.

'Are you going to see the Princess, Teddy?' Alan asked, informed of the Royal presence by the coconut telegraph like everyone else on the island.

'I don't know what you're talking about, Alan,' I said. 'You can drop me by the villa gate. No need to pull in.'

'No problem, Teddy,' he said, wheeling into the circular drive, neck craning for a glimpse of Royal flesh. When there was none to be had, a crestfallen Alan dropped me off and headed back to the road.

Before I could knock on the villa's red double doors, they opened and Anthony Wedderburn hustled me back out to the driveway, a finger to his lips.

'Soliloquies. Oaths. It is like a Shakespearean tragedy in there,' De Rasta whispered. 'The only thing that I haven't heard is the invocation of supernatural powers. But I have no doubt that a coven of witches will be the next affliction called down upon your head.'

'Not happy campers, eh?'

'Most decidedly not. Lord Sutherland has been cursing a torrent of obscenities since he was spirited on to the helicopter yesterday. He spent most of the night on the phone to his solicitors, er . . . attorneys, in New York, demanding that they come here and "free" him immediately. There was quite an explosion when they explained to him that they could not do as he asked because they had no license to practice in His Majesty's law courts here in the Virgin Islands. This morning he arose early and began working the telephones to England. There was an even larger explosion than the one with the lawyers when the Private Secretary to the Sovereign explained that His Majesty would be unable to immediately take his call and suggested scheduling a time on Wednesday.' Anthony's eyes twinkled in mischievous recollection.

'Well, I must talk to the man sometime,' I said.

'I wouldn't think now would be the time, old man,' Anthony counseled. 'The Viscount still has a considerable head of steam up. Why not wait until the afternoon? It's a rare man who can stay full on mad for an entire day.'

'What about Princess Portia? Is she angry too? Or, I suppose, the first question is, is she in any condition to speak to me at all?'

'She is.' Cat Wells called from the doorway in a voice just loud enough to be heard but not loud enough, I suspected, to register inside the villa. She stood where the morning sun caught her profile. The time in prison had not stolen from her natural beauty. She wore khaki shorts, sandals, and a gauzy white blouse, drifting easily back into island attire. 'She had a good night last night. She slept well, despite Jeremy's ranting. She didn't need a sedative. And she is certainly not angry. If anything, she wishes to help.'

'Will she speak with me now?' I said.

'Come in. Let's find out.'

Cat opened the door and led the way in. I nodded to the RVIPF officer just inside and spoke to Sir Roger, who was lounging, head back, on an overstuffed rattan loveseat. 'Good morning, Sir Roger.'

Sir Roger fixed bloodshot eyes on me. 'You have a bloody

nerve showing up here, policeman. I'd have thought your superiors would have removed you from this case by now, given the
cock-up you've made of it.'

'I am on the case until I hear otherwise,' I said. 'From someone
in authority.'

'Boys, boys, let's remember we are all on the same team here,'
Cat interjected.

'The side of the Royal family, you mean?' Sir Roger sneered.

'The side of justice,' I said, eliciting an eye roll from Sir Roger.
'Now, I am here to speak to the Princess and the Viscount.'

'The Viscount is on a telephone call which is likely to be
protracted,' Sir Roger said. 'As for the Princess, she remains
indisposed.'

'She is swimming.' Anthony Wedderburn pointed through the
French doors which opened on to a patio, the green lawn beyond,
and finally the white sand beach fronting the bay. There, Princess
Portia emerged from the aquamarine waters of the Caribbean
like a shorter, lumpier and much more pale version of Botticelli's
Venus. Except that she was clothed in a bikini so frumpy it looked
to have been designed by the Amish. And, of course, she wasn't
standing on a half shell.

'Cat,' I said. 'Will you go ask the Princess if she will see
me now?'

Cat was out the door and across the dozen steps of the lawn
before Sir Roger could protest, grabbing a towel from a chair
on the patio on the way. I watched as the two women spoke,
putting their heads together, Cat a head taller and two stone
lighter than the Princess. After a brief conversation, Cat waved
to me to join them.

I stepped on to the patio, realizing that I was about to have
an audience with a woman who might one day be the Most High,
Most Mighty, and Most Excellent Monarch, Portia the First, by
the Grace of God, of the United Kingdom of Great Britain and
Northern Ireland and of Her other Realms and Territories Queen,
Head of the Commonwealth, Defender of the Faith, and Sovereign
of the Most Noble Order of the Garter.

I had held her in my arms and comforted her short days ago.
Now I was terrified of her.

TWENTY-FIVE

Princess Portia padded, pigeon-toed, across the sand and green lawn toward the patio chairs and table where I waited. She wrapped herself in a beach towel and ran her fingers through her wet hair, combing it as she walked. Cat tracked two steps behind.

Sir Roger popped out the door and on to the patio at the moment the Princess arrived. 'I'm sorry, Your Royal Highness. This policeman has come here without following proper protocol. Shall I have him removed?' Sir Roger took my elbow, already preparing to implement an order should the Princess give it. I pulled it away.

'You are the officer who came upon me the night of that poor woman's murder, are you not?' Princess Portia's words brought Sir Roger's efforts to remove me to a halt.

'I am, Your Royal Highness. Constable Teddy Creque, Royal Virgin Islands Police Force, ma'am.' Not knowing how to properly conduct myself in the Royal presence, I bowed. Slightly. A halfway, unsure bow. The skin around the Princess's small dark eyes and the corner of her mouth crinkled into a barely discernible smile.

'And are you also the officer assigned to investigate the murder?'

'Yes, ma'am.'

'So you are the one who sought to prevent Lord Sutherland and me from leaving the Virgin Islands until we could be interviewed about the murder. I believe you actually had a warrant issued to detain us as material witnesses when we were about to depart.' She looked me evenly in the eye.

'Yes, ma'am.' At that moment, I wanted to shrink into a size suitable to crawl under one of the coral stone pavers of the patio. What would she think if she knew I was also considering her a suspect?

'I will remove him now, Your Royal Highness,' Sir Roger said.

The Princess raised her hand. Her stubby fingers were adorned with a diamond the size of a ground dove's eye. 'No, Sir Roger. I find Constable Creque's actions very appropriate. Jeremy would have had us depart had the constable not acted. He was being diligent in his duty. Indeed, courageous, I suspect, in the face of considerable pressure to allow us to leave, if I know my husband.' She turned to me. 'I admire such diligence and courage, Constable. I am just sorry you had to go to such effort to ensure that we spoke. And I am sorry that I was not in a condition to speak to you for so long. What I saw that night was alarming and gruesome. It was not something to which a princess is accustomed. I am afraid I took it rather poorly.'

'I can assure you that no one is accustomed to such things, ma'am,' I said. 'And your reaction to it was not unusual for those who experience what you did.'

'Thank you for your kind words, Constable. I am ready to speak with you about the event now. Sir Roger, you may retire to the house.'

'Ma'am, it is customary for a member of the Royal household staff to be present for—' Sir Roger began.

Princess Portia cut him off. 'I am sure that I am safe and that my delicate sensibilities will be protected by having both a police officer and Ms Wells here with me, Sir Roger. You may now retire.'

'Yes, ma'am.' Sir Roger scuttled back inside the house but not before tossing the stink eye in my direction.

'There are times, Constable, when I feel I need protection from my protectors. Shall we sit?'

'Yes, ma'am.'

I took out my notebook, a tool of my profession I use as rarely as my Webley Mark III revolver. I used it on this occasion to steady my nerves and to give me something to look at occasionally because Princess Portia had a habit of looking directly into my eyes and it unnerved me. 'I think it will be easiest, ma'am, if we begin with you telling me what you recall of the evening from the time just before you went out into the garden of Government House.'

'Well, I was upset, Constable. At Jeremy – Lord Sutherland – for misbehaving at the reception. He has made me the happiest woman in the world –' she smiled a winsome smile – 'but he can be a trial sometimes, like all men, I suppose. He has this knack for acting up in public, but he is so sweet and attentive when we are alone.

'In any event, he had gone out into the garden and had been a while, so I thought to go after him. To make things right. When I started for the door, that poor dear lady, Mrs Lane, who had been with Ms Wells in the ladies' trying to comfort me, insisted that she go ahead of me. For my safety, she said. I was upset about the earlier occurrences with Jeremy, and I was impatient to smooth things over between us, so I moved toward the door. I was certain the garden had been secured by the local police for the event, so I wasn't really concerned for my safety. Lord Wedderburn tried to stop me at the doorway but I dodged around him.'

'Quite handily, if I may say so, ma'am,' I said.

'Thank you, Constable. I was a passable hockey player in my school days. I suppose I still retain a few of my moves. In any event, I was searching for Jeremy when I heard a pistol shot. I recognized the sound because pistol shooting is a hobby of Jeremy's, one to which he has introduced me. I was concerned for Jeremy and I guess I just reacted. I ran in what I thought was the direction of the shot. It was very dark in the garden, as you know, with no artificial lighting and only the barest sliver of a moon. I was a bit frantic in my concern for Jeremy and I ran headlong, as fast as I could, despite the darkness. After only seconds I heard footsteps. Someone else was running nearby but it did not sound like they were on the path ahead of me.'

'Did you see the person you heard running, ma'am?'

'No, Constable.' The Princess's forehead wrinkled in a thoughtful frown. 'No. And as I think about it now, the sound of the footsteps was not moving in the same direction as me but rather away, perpendicular, to my path. Rather odd, isn't it? But maybe whoever was running was as confused as to where the shot had . . .' Princess Portia stopped.

'Ma'am?'

'I'm sorry, Constable. I really had not thought this through. I had just assumed that whoever was running in that garden was doing what I was doing. Trying to locate where the shooting had occurred. I thought it was probably a member of the security detail, and that they were confused, with the darkness, as to the direction from which the sound of the shot had come. But maybe they were running away from the shot.'

'Is there something about what you saw or heard that causes you to believe that, ma'am?'

'No. No, I guess not, Constable.'

'And there is nothing that you can think of that allows you to identify the runner?'

'Identify, no. But the footsteps were heavy. I am sure it was a man, from the, well, heavy sound of the steps. Definitely not a woman. And it was all very brief, you understand. I heard the steps for a second or two and then they were gone. And I was more concerned with the shot. I ran on. For some reason – irrational really, now that I think about it – I had the sense that if I found the location of the shot, I would find Jeremy.'

'Go on, ma'am.'

'Yes. Well, I ran a short distance further, maybe thirty feet, and there she was, poor Mrs Lane, on the ground. I stopped running when I saw her, pulled up short. Seeing her on the ground like that surprised me, I guess. It was unexpected although I don't know what I did expect. And then I saw the blood. There was so much blood, Constable, smeared across her dress and, I realized, pooling on the ground beside her. And her eyes. They were open, staring, and I knew that she was dead. And I screamed. I suppose I should have thought to call for help but it was all so horrible and the scream just came out. And then I saw him.'

'Him?'

'A man in a uniform, standing over Mrs Lane. I had not seen him or he wasn't there, just seconds before. But there he was, and I recognized him. It was Deputy Commissioner Lane. I had been introduced to him earlier, at the reception. He just stood there looking down at her. I felt faint. I dropped to my knees in the grass. And then I saw it. He had a gun in his hand, not holding it out away from his body but carried loosely, hanging down beside his leg, like he didn't even know that he was carrying it. I heard myself scream again, and again. I could not stop. It seemed like the sound was coming from outside my body, like it was not me screaming but I knew it was. I knew when I saw the gun that I should run, that it wasn't safe for me there. But I couldn't run. I couldn't do anything. I just knelt on the grass there and screamed.

'At first it was as if Deputy Commissioner Lane did not hear me, but then he turned toward me. I saw his eyes looking my way. I don't know any other way to describe it – his eyes were looking my way but I could tell that they didn't see me. They were blank, empty. And after a moment, he turned back to Mrs Lane and just stood there. And then you arrived, Constable.'

'Did you see or hear anyone else nearby?'

'No, Constable. Until you arrived, the only other person I was aware of in the area was the person running who I have already described to you.'

'And then, ma'am?'

Suddenly, we were interrupted by an enraged Lord Sutherland charging out of the patio door.

'What the bloody hell?' Though the Viscount was an American, he had adopted the English expletive, maybe as a demonstration of his Britishness. Maybe the wanker in him thought that such a demonstration would endear him to his new countrymen.

'Oh, Jeremy, you remember Constable Creque, the officer who brought me in from the garden on the night of Mrs Lane's killing?' Princess Portia remained placid despite the Viscount's stormy entrance; perhaps she was accustomed to such drama.

'You're damned right I remember him.' Lord Sutherland fully focused his outrage on me. 'Get out.'

'Jeremy, please,' Princess Portia said.

'Get the fuck out!' No more tepid English cursing. Lord Sutherland went full American, punctuating the crude profanity with a stabbing finger directing me off the property. Sir Roger appeared as back-up, tut-tutting and glaring at me from a safe distance. Anthony Wedderburn stepped out behind Sir Roger, slight amusement in his eyes at Sir Roger's effete support of the enraged Wanker.

'Jeremy!' Princess Portia's raised voice brought the escalating situation to a sudden halt. 'Constable Creque is merely trying to do his sworn duty. His sworn duty to His Majesty, the King.'

'He's an asshole and I won't have him talking to you any

more.' The Viscount was calmer when he addressed the Princess but still firm. 'I have lawyers coming.'

'Princess Portia has given her full statement to me,' I said. 'I won't need to speak to her again. She is free to return to England. If you give me your statement, and I see no further reason to require you to remain afterward, you would be free to return as well. But I do need your statement first, Lord Sutherland.'

Lord Sutherland leveled his eyes on me. 'Out.'

'Very well. Sir Roger knows how to reach me if you change your mind.'

'Out.'

TWENTY-SIX

'That went swimmingly, old man.' De White Rasta flashed me a grin designed, I supposed, to take the edge off his remark. 'I would say about as well as King Lear's estate plan.'

'Shakespeare and sarcasm. Oh, very nice, Anthony.'

'I said it with a smile and didn't drop the f-bomb. You have to admit that is better treatment than you received from my equal in the peerage just now.'

'I attribute that to his American cheek, Anthony. It's forgivable. Lord Sutherland will come around.'

'From what I have seen, he will come around when Anegada's wild burros sprout wings and fly,' Cat said, joining Anthony and me in the circular driveway of the Setting Point Villa. 'And that's an American's opinion.'

'Then may the gods deliver me from Americans with entitled attitudes.'

'So, Teddy, was the interview with the Princess worth all the effort?'

'Well, we learned about the unknown running individual. That is something. And her story confirms the DC's presence immediately after the shooting.'

'After? It seems more like during.'

'It is damning but it really is not surprising. It is something we already knew.' The finger of guilt pointed more strongly toward Deputy Commissioner Lane with Princess Portia's statement, I supposed. But it did little to eliminate the others on my list as suspects. Jubbie Watson was still in the wind and his known role in events was only what I had learned in my brief encounter with him. Consuela Lettsome still remained in consideration. Though there was nothing to place her at the murder scene, she had something the others did not – a motive. Lord Sutherland was also in the mix and his belligerence didn't help my view of him. But belligerence isn't fact, and cases are proved with facts, not the impressions of the investigating officer. And Princess Portia, despite my reluctance to consider a Royal as a suspect, could not be eliminated. She had mentioned Lord Sutherland's hobby of pistol shooting. Had she made a particular point of doing so to me? I suspected a frame-up of the DC. Was the real frame-up of Jeremy Sutherland by the Princess? Was that her way to get rid of her Wanker problem? It seemed far-fetched. But maybe it seemed so simply because I was reluctant to consider a Royal as a murderer. I decided all my suspects remained so. I didn't mention my suspicion of any of them to Anthony. I couldn't admit even to him, my closest confidant, that my list of suspects included both a Lord and a Royal Princess.

My cell phone chimed. It made me jump; I still wasn't used to the contraption. Checking the screen showed 'Caller Unknown' and displayed the caller's number as +1 (000) 000-0000. Another American, this one an American I had been hoping to hear from.

'Hello,' I answered.

'Keep answering "Caller Unknown" numbers and you'll be up to your eyeballs in offers for car warranties, Teddy Creque.' Agent Rosenblum's New York accent grated on the ear, just as his personality grated on almost everyone. 'Hey, what are you doing with a cell phone anyway? Don't they have to move through the regular telecommunications development process on your pathetic little island first? You know, smoke signals, pony express, string-and-can, and then cell phones?'

'It is a pleasure to hear from you, Agent Rosenblum. I thought the cell phone number with all zeros might be you.'

'Clever, huh? Some weenie at Homeland Security thought that would keep the taco benders and the coffee beaners from knowing who was calling. Anyway, I got some news for you on this Glenroy "Jubbie" Watson character you have an interest in. Carlos and Charlie, the camo boys in St Lucia, remember 'em?'

'How could I forget? They all but arrested me.'

'Misunderstanding. Anyway, they owed me, like I told you, so I called in the favor. They found your man Jubbie hiding in the crapper out behind his auntie's house. Cuffed him right when he stepped out the door. Right in front of his auntie. They said she seemed more upset than he was.'

'Did they have to do that?'

'Hey, you're the one who wanted him pronto. Besides, it's not like locking up members of the Royal family or anything. That's right, your little escapade detaining that Princess and her wanker husband have even made the tabloid newspapers up here in the States. So has the shit storm arrived yet?'

'Not yet. There are a few clouds on the horizon.'

'Take it from your old weatherman Rosenblum, it will arrive. It is only a matter of time where Jeremy Sutherland is concerned. The dude has skated plenty, from what my buddy at Treasury FINCEN says. The dude has an army of lawyers in NYC.'

'What's FINCEN?'

'The Department of the Treasury's Financial Crimes Enforcement Network. They track money laundering, mostly. Your next king of the British Empire was on their radar screen for quite a few years but he always lawyered up and managed to avoid indictment. And, now that he's on the Royal gravy train, I'm guessing there's no need for him to wash Benjamins for the Russian mob any more.'

'He won't be king, even if Princess Portia becomes the monarch. The husband of a queen is usually a prince consort, not a king.'

'Well, la tee da. Bad enough having a president and Congress in the States. I don't know how you Brits can put up with all the dukes, princes, earls and whatevers that you've had for the last thousand years. So Sutherland will be a prince consort if that princess becomes queen. Seriously though, the lady best keep her eyes on her wallet, whatever she calls him.'

'Was this information known to the authorities in England before the Princess and Lord Sutherland wed?'

'My FINCEN guy says that they let MI5 know and supposedly the info went all the way up the chain. But I guess love conquers all, because the wedding took place. All it is now is good gossip. Hey, you seem more interested in this than the delivery of Jubbie into your waiting arms.'

'Just interesting information, I guess, but no real use to my murder investigation. Unlike Jubbie, who I'm dying to get to talk to. I will arrange for his transport from St Lucia.'

'No need for transport. Charlie was so enthusiastic about repaying the favor he owed to me that he put brother Carlos on a LIAT flight to Tortola with your man. They should be arriving in two hours. You're welcome.' Leave it to Agent Rosenblum to layer on the sarcasm even when he's being nice and helpful.

'Thank you, Agent Rosenblum. I owe you one.'

'Actually, Teddy, we are about even. But don't hesitate to call, even if you don't have one in the favor bank. Your shit's more interesting than ninety-nine percent of what I do. *Hasta la vista.*'

The line clicked dead.

'It sounds, old friend, like you are about to move from questioning the Royals to questioning the most common of the *hoi polloi*,' Anthony said.

'And not a minute too soon. This mixing with the rich and famous is a bit much for a simple Anegada boy like me. And you are coming with me, Anthony.'

'But who will mind the Royals?'

'We have enough police around to protect them. As far as the other parts, Cat's got that. Don't you, Cat?'

'I think I can handle it. I can tell Princess Portia is a bit ashamed of the way Jeremy behaved just now. She will be cooperative. Jeremy's hands will be tied until the lawyers start arriving from who knows where. And Sir Roger has no authority over me. I'll just ignore him. And let's not forget, none of these people can fly out of here without me. And I'm not flying anywhere until I hear from you, Teddy.'

'Good. Anthony and I will take the Land Rover. No sense making it easy for Lord Sutherland to get to the ferry dock to pick up his bevy of lawyers whenever they arrive. I'm sensing that he won't be walking there, or anywhere. It just doesn't seem to be his style.'

'Very nice, Teddy.' De Rasta grinned. 'You may be the modern era's most capable imprisoner of Royalty. There might be a job waiting for you as gaoler at the Tower of London.'

'I just hope I am not headed for lock-up there myself,' I said.

TWENTY-SEVEN

The LIAT Bombardier Dash-8 taxied to the debarkation area at Terrence B. Lettsome International Airport on Beef Island, its white, orange and yellow fuselage brilliant in the midday sun. The flight from St Lucia was late, a confirmation of the reputation of the airline that was also a play on its acronym. Despite the failure of the air carrier's marketing department to recognize the unwise homonym created by the first letters of its name – Leeward Islands Air Transport – it was my experience that its planes were no more tardy than most commercial flights in the Caribbean. That is, they were infrequently on time, and nobody seem to care.

Camo Carlos and Glenroy Watson were the last two people to navigate the air-stairs on to the tarmac, the task of coming down the narrow steps made more difficult by the fact that they were handcuffed together.

'I remember you, Constable Teddy Creque,' Carlos said by way of greeting.

'I remember you too, Officer . . .' I said, though I had never learned his name.

'Soto. I'm a lieutenant now, thanks in part to my time with JITFS. Your case was one of the most interesting I had during my time there. And the unit commendation really helped my career.'

'Glad to oblige,' I said.

'And, sorry about the circumstances the last time we met. Everyone thought we had a dirty cop on our hands.' Lieutenant Soto seemed genuinely contrite. 'Glad you made it alive.'

'Me, too.'

'Anyway, I have for you here Mr Glenroy Watson, as requested.'

'Thank you, Lieutenant, for bringing him all the way to our doorstep. It really wasn't necessary. We could've had someone fly over and pick him up.'

'The personal delivery of the package is just my attempt to

make up, in some small way, for our last meeting. Now, who do I cuff him to?'

'I think we will dispense with the handcuffs from this point. Immigration is this way.'

Anthony and I had Lieutenant Soto and Glenroy Watson through customs and immigration in a trice. We loaded Jubbie into our Land Rover. Lieutenant Soto headed to the airport cafe for a Ting and a chicken roti before his flight home.

'I-mon do no ting,' Jubbie said as soon as we were alone, rubbing his wrists. I was seated next to him in the rear seat of the police vehicle. De Rasta drove. 'De camo dude na have be brothupsy. Him a mean un.'

'Sight. Yuh right nah,' I said.

Jubbie inclined his head toward Anthony. 'Wah bout de pale un. Him Babylon?'

'No, Mr Watson, I am not a police officer,' Anthony said. Jubbie's eyes widened. I guessed that Anthony's ability to understand his patois was not usual for a white Englishman in Jubbie's experience.

'Nonetheless, and for my benefit, shall we try to use the King's English?' Anthony said. 'My patois is a bit rusty, truth be told.'

'Mr Wedderburn is administrative assistant with the RVIPF. And, don't worry, we are not going to handcuff you any more, provided you agree to behave,' I said.

'I behavin'. I did no thing.'

'I know. You aren't in trouble.' *Unless you reveal to me otherwise.*

'Then why you have that camo lieutenant cuff me?'

'To bring you back here,' I said. 'Maybe Lieutenant Soto was a little overzealous.'

'Mebbe?' Jubbie shook his head as if to clear it. 'I'm think he belief me was public enemy number one.'

'Well, you did run. Why?'

'Bad stuff was goin' on among the big peoples at Government House. I just a waiter but mebbe I see things, things I don't know what those things mean. Then I think what if those things is not meant for no waiter to see? Or, if the shot I hear means something bad, which most shots is what they mean. What if they need someone to blame for the bad thing that happen from the shot? Who the best choice to blame? Some big beef? Na. Or the low waiter, who can't defend hisself? Yes, that who they blame. So, yes, Constable, I run. I was goin' wait till this thing blow over an' be gone. You do the same thing, you be the lowish waiter.'

'Maybe, Jubbie,' I said. 'Or maybe, if I had seen things, I would go to the police and tell them what I had seen.'

'I could not take such a chance. I a nobody. I afraid the big mon hurt me to save himself. My madda say "When de elephunks fight, the grass get trampled." I don't want to be no grass.'

'Nothing like that will happen to you, Jubbie,' I said.

'That so, Constable? Who the one arrive at this party in hancuffs?'

'I understand,' I said. 'But now you're here and no longer in handcuffs. I need to know what you saw and heard that night. You tell me the truth and I will make sure you don't end up like the grass beneath the angry elephants' feet.'

TWENTY-EIGHT

Jubbie looked me in the eye, narrowing his own to slits. I did not shake off his stare, and he said, 'My madda tell me "to look in the eye to see if a mon lie." I see now you not a lyin' mon, Constable.'

'Good,' I said, pleased that I had passed Madda Watson's test for truthfulness. 'Now can we talk about what happened the night of the reception at Government House?'

'Ya mon.'

'So, you were assigned your regular waiter's job for the reception?'

'No. I was not a regular waiter. I just start at Government House in the kitchen six months before, as a dishwasher. Miss Nibbs hire me in.'

'She's a tough one.'

'Ain't that the truth? She scare me, I kid you not. Anyway, she hire me to wash dishes an' sometimes I bus the table after the Governor an' his guests leave. But I never be in the room when the Governor is there. Miss Nibbs say I not ready to meet the big peoples yet. Then, on the day of the big reception for the Princess an' the Viscount, two of the regular waiters got sick. Got the flu. Miss Nibbs already have called in all the waiters she use to back up the regulars, so she was two waiters short an' don't have no more to call in. So she say to me "Glenroy, you just becomed a waiter. You go in the uniform storage an' get dressed in a waiter uniform." Then she had Sheb Markie, one of the regular waiters, show me how to serve drinks an' them likle bits o' food . . .'

'Hors d'oeuvres?' Anthony contributed from the front seat.

'That's right, hors derves, from the silver trays. An' jus' like that, I a waiter. I am more than a likle nervous, meetin' all the important people an' mebbe even Princess Portia. But Miss Nibbs, she brush up my waiter jacket, tell me to keep my shoulders straight and my eyes down, an' said, "You a waiter now. Do Government House proud," an' sent me off to the reception.

'First, one of the sous chefs give me a tray of hors derves to carry 'round, some caviar canapes, they call 'em. Ain't but fish roe on a salt cracker, like sumpthin' you feed the ole folks ain't got no teeth. I go out among the big people in all they fine clothes, men with medals and sash things on and the ladies all drippin' with jewels. I never see such a thing. At first, I just walked 'round with the tray an' no one stop me to take any of the fish roe crackers. All the peoples waitin' for the Princess an' the Viscount and don't pay no attention to me, a low waiter, like I don't even exist on the face of Jah's green earth. They all pay attention to this fat Babylon by the door with feathers on his hat callin' out the name an' title of each people when they arrive.

'Then Sheb Markie see no one is takin' my crackers an' he snag me over to a corner an' say, "Jubbie, you got to offer the food on the tray to peoples, don't just run around. Stop an' say, 'Canapé, ma'am?', 'Canapé, sir?'" an' after I start that, my tray empty fast. I go back for more but passin' the bar, the barman say, "Take this tray of champagne, Jubbie." I take them, the tall glasses all jiggly like they goin' to drop but now the big peoples don't wait for me to offer what on me tray, they chase me down to get it. I even got snagged by the Princess an' Viscount after they been announced an' come in. I was so nervous with the Princess I held my breath til I almost faint. But she smile at me, jus' plain Jubbie, when she take the glass from the tray an' I could breathe then.

'After the Princess arrive, an' with all the big people drinkin' champagne, the place get noisy and noisier. I workin' hard an' it hot an' the noise keep comin' up an' I stressin'. Need a likle time away from all the bustle. Not lymin' or nuthin' like that, just a short break.

'I near the door to the garden, so I just step out, quick like, for some air an' relaxin'. With no place to put the tray, I just carry it with me.' Jubbie hesitated. 'You sure I not get in trouble?'

'I am investigating a murder, Jubbie,' I said. 'Not what the Government House waiters did on their breaks, sight?'

'Ya mon.' Jubbie went on: 'I take some steps out in the garden, just to get away from the noisiness. An' while I there I take one glass of champagne an' drink it. It ain't like rum. It tickle me nose but got no kick. So then mebbe I burn a likle kali I have in my pocket. Jus' a puff or two, or three, not like I smoke the whole blunt. Just to take the edge off.

'An' then, just when I light the kali, the Babylon show up. I nearly die right there. I jus' off the pathway, under a strongbark tree, an' the big policeman I see at the reception, he go walkin' right by, not five feet from me.'

'Which policemen, Jubbie?' I asked.

'Him tall, in a fancy uniform, white jacket an' black pants. Not the police with the feather hat on, the only other one at the reception. Tall, tall an' big, big.'

'That had to be the Deputy Commissioner,' Anthony said.

'I don' know his name an' rank but him in a hurry. Walk fast right by me. Maybe he didn't see me but he sure had to smell the kali. Him jus' keep on, fast, until him gone from eyesight. But I not alone long. No more than a minute later, the Viscount come along the same path. But him look right at me, just as I take a big drag on the kali, an' him do the strangest thing.'

'What was that, Jubbie?'

'Him not say a word. Him just reach over to where I have the tray of champagne sittin' on the grass, an' take two full glasses. Then he walk down the same path as the policeman just go down. Him never say nuthin' to me an' never look to me, just like I was invisible.'

'Did you say anything to the Viscount?'

'No.'

'What happened then?'

'I stay hid 'neath the strongbark tree tryin' to figure if I be in trouble now the Viscount see me. Then I hear two voices talkin', down the same path where the policeman an' the Viscount have walked. Men voices. I think it them, the policeman an' the Viscount, but since I never hear either of them talk, I not for sure.'

'Did you hear what the voices said?'

'No. They all mumbly-like.'

'Not loud or agitated?'

'No. Low an' calm.'

'How long did they talk?'

'Not long.'

'Then what happened?'

'I hear the glasses clink.'

'Like what? Like the glasses were breaking?'

'No, like when the big peoples touch the tall glasses together an' then drink.'

'You mean a toast?'

'Yeah, a toast.'

'Did you hear anything after the glasses clinked?'

'No. No more talking, if that what you ask.'

'Anything at all, other than talking?'

'Next thing I hear was the shot. A gun shot.'

'How much time passed between the glasses clinking and the gunshot?'

'I don' know. Not long. A minute. Two minute. Three minute.'

'Think hard, Jubbie. This is important. How much time?'

'I don' have no clock on it. It a short time, all I know. I not even have time to leave my restin' place under the tree. An' when the shot come, I freeze, not knowin' what to do. Then I hear one set o' footsteps, walkin'.'

'In which direction? Toward you? Away?'

'Away. But not up the path. Out to the sideways.'

'Perpendicular to the path?'

'Yeah. Perpledickaly. Quick like, but not runnin'.'

'A man or a woman?'

'The steps heavy, like a man, but no way to tell for sure. I not see who make the steps. But I did see the Princess not but seconds after I heard the steps goin' 'way. Princess Portia, she come chargin' down de path, from the same direction, from the Government House patio, that the policeman and the Viscount come before the shot. An' the Princess, she runnin', her gown all white in the moonlight like a duppie, flyin' down that path fast as she could go. She run right by me an', when she out my view, she scream. She scream, an' scream, an' scream. That is when I head tother direction, startin' up the path toward Government House. I knew no waiter, no Jubbie, want to be anywhere near where the Princess screaming. I get a dozen steps up de path an' I run smack into . . . you.'

'I remember.'

'An' you tell me to go back to Government House an' I head in that direction. But then I stop, part the way there, an' think, 'bout the Princess screamin', the policeman, the Viscount, and the gun shot I hear. An' the elephunks trampin' the grass. An' I know this is no place for Jubbie, so I light out through the garden to the side, climb a fence at the edge, an' then I out on the street. You know the rest. I run, all the way to St Lucia.'

'Is there anything else you saw, or heard, or remember, that you haven't told me, Jubbie?'

'No, Constable. Can I go now?'

'I'm afraid it is not quite that easy, Jubbie,' I said. 'You ran once, and ran far. And what you saw and heard is important. It may be that we will need your testimony in court one day. I cannot have you running off again, to St Lucia or maybe some place even further away.'

Anthony had been driving us west, from Beef Island over the little bridge to Tortola, and along the southern coast of that island to Road Town. We were approaching Wickams Cay but De Rasta turned on to Station Avenue, away from the water.

'Where are we goin'?' Jubbie's body language confirmed that he was no hard case; perspiration beaded his forehead and his eyes swung side to side in panic.

'His Majesty's Prison,' Anthony said, following my instructions from before Jubbie had deplaned.

'Don' take me to the prison. I done no thing wrong, sight? I not do well there. I need the fresh air, the sun, the birds singin'.'

'We have to keep you in custody because you ran,' I explained.

'I not run no more now. I promise. Please don' take me behind the walls.'

'But we have no place else to take you, Glenroy. I genuinely wish I did.'

'You take me home. I'm not run from there.'

I felt for the young man. He truly had been thrust into this situation through no fault of his own. His interview convinced me he was no longer a suspect, only a witness. 'Even if I put you back in your home at Long Trench, I have to have someone providing . . .' I searched for the most neutral term. 'Security for you. I have no one to do that.'

'That may not be entirely correct,' said De Rasta's voice from the driver's seat.

'What do you mean, Anthony?'

Jubbie's eyes pinballed between me and Anthony, hopeful.

'There is someone who could provide the needed security if Mr Watson wants to stay in his home instead of going to prison.'

'And who might that be, Anthony?'

'Boss Claudie.'

'I stay there,' Jubbie volunteered.

'Anthony, are you suggesting we place Glenroy here in the charge of a retired Jamaican drug lord instead of taking him to prison?'

'Just helping you to explore the possibilities, old man.'

'And why would Boss Claudie do something like that for me?'

'He wouldn't.' Anthony turned toward the back seat and shot Jubbie and me his Cheshire cat grin. 'For you. But he would for me.'

'Why?'

'Old times. Favors owed.'

I held up a hand. 'Forget I asked.' I pondered. 'This is all frightfully irregular.'

'No more irregular than keeping a witness in a safe house.' Anthony lowered his voice. 'No more irregular than the set-up with Princess Portia and Lord Sutherland.'

Anthony had a point. Ten minutes later, we were at Boss Claudie's door in Long Trench, speaking to the old gangster under the watchful eyes of half a dozen of his nephews and cousins. Twenty minutes after that, Glenroy Watson was ensconced in Claudie's ramshackle shack high in the hills overlooking Road Harbor, with two of the Boss's hulking nephews lounging outside his door. This is, after all, Great Britain, where a princess and a dishwasher have the same rights in the eyes of the law. Or do they?

TWENTY-NINE

'Now, Teddy, that you have most of the witnesses in your case under guard in hospital, or under guard in Long Trench, or under guard in Anegada, where does your investigation go from here?' Anthony asked as he navigated the police Land Rover down the convolutions of Great Mountain Road toward Road Town.

I opened my mouth to reply and then clapped it shut, again at a loss. I had been so busy corralling witnesses that I did not know my next step. I did not have a next move, let alone a strategy for checkmate. Then something that Anthony had said hit me. 'Most of the witnesses?'

'What, Teddy?'

'You said "most of the witnesses," Anthony.'

'Yes.'

'Who else is out there?'

'I thought maybe you had a strategy, Teddy. That you had a time selected in your mind to speak to her.'

'Who, for God's sake, Anthony?'

'Consuela Lettsome, of course. You told me that the Deputy Commissioner himself had described her as his paramour. That means she had a motive; what mistress would not like to see her lover's wife out of the way? And you don't know where she was or what she was doing on the night of Letitia Lane's murder.'

Anthony was right. The DC's loyal, long-time assistant and, as I had recently learned, lover, was a vital person with whom to speak. He shouldn't have had to remind me of this fact. She should have been on my list of interviewees from the moment the Deputy Commissioner had confessed their affair to me. And not just as an interviewee, as a suspect, though I couldn't place her at the scene of the crime as yet. I settled back into my jouncing seat and took a deep breath. My investigation had become sloppy, all action and no thought. It was being driven by third-party witnesses and a perceived urgency that had little, if anything, to do with learning who had killed Letitia Lane, and much to do with accommodating the Royals. And my own desire to quickly find a way out of confinement, and dishonor, for my mentor. He would hardly be proud of the way I was approaching this case. I could feel his eyes upon me, looking over the edges of the half-moon reading glasses he had taken to wearing, questioning why I hadn't spoken to this most obvious of witnesses.

'Of course, you are right, Anthony. Let's go to headquarters and speak to Ms Lettsome now.'

'She said she was going to take a couple of days off, Constable.' Sheila Colwood, who shared a small anteroom in the police headquarters administrative wing with Consuela Lettsome, and who I had met one time while sweating out an impending dressing down from the Deputy Commissioner, smiled warmly in my direction. I was flattered and began to smile back when I realized she was actually looking over my left shoulder to where Anthony Wedderburn stood. The man, without doubt, is a chick magnet, but all the flirting and long looks make traveling with him tough on the ego.

'Do you have her address, love?' De White Rasta reciprocated the smile and Ms Colwood practically fell over herself getting the address. She gave Anthony a little wave of her fingers when we departed.

'Must you really do that every chance you get?' I asked, when we were on our way to the address in Horse Path that Ms Colwood had given us for Consuela Lettsome.

Anthony was oblivious. 'Do what?'

'Slather on the charm like Irish butter on an oatmeal scone.'

'I just asked for an address.' De Rasta feigned pique. 'Isn't that what an administrative assistant is supposed to do?'

I was still trying to formulate a response when we rolled to a stop at the address on the sand road in Horse Path where Consuela Lettsome lived. A break in the overgrowth of vegetation at the roadside opened to a stone walkway leading to a wood-frame house built in the old Virgin Islands style. The rusted hip roof gave way to lemon-yellow scallop-and-dentel clapboard siding atop a coral stone foundation. Blue-painted hurricane shutters provided a pop of color contrast to the yellow siding. The cottage was neat and compact, its front yard domin-ated by a large kapok tree. In the shade of the kapok sat an old woman, as neat and compact as the house. She did not rise as we approached.

'Good afternoon, ma'am.' I would do the talking here. While Anthony might have it over me with the younger ladies, I was the master when it came to the geriatric set.

'Good afternoon, Constable,' the lady said. 'I haven't had a uniformed lawman visit since my Joseph, rest his soul, came courting fifty years ago. He was with the British Leeward Islands Police. A constable, too. That is why I recognized the insignia. I am Alicia Lettsome.' She offered her hand but still did not rise.

'I am Constable Teddy Creque and this is RVIPF Administrative Assistant, Anthony Wedderburn.'

'Ms Lettsome.' De White Rasta took the offered hand.

'What can I do for you, gentlemen?'

'We are here to speak to Consuela Lettsome.'

'Oh, my daughter. My heart.' The old woman smiled, revealing perfect teeth. 'She is at work. Obviously, you were not aware. I'm sorry you made the trip up here when you could have seen her right at the station.'

Were all the witnesses in this case going to be elusive? Something told me not to mention Consuela Lettsome's absence from work to her mother. 'When does she usually return home from work, Mrs Lettsome?'

'She works very long hours, Constable, owing to the nature of her position. Sometimes she doesn't return home until seven or eight in the evening. But on regular days she is home by six o'clock. Of course, today, she said she had a special assignment, one that would take her out to one of the sister islands. She packed an overnight bag. She said she might not be home for several days.'

'I see,' I said, though I really didn't have any idea what was happening with Ms Lettsome. Was she another runner, like Jubbie? Or something more? 'Well, we will probably locate her to speak with her at headquarters, but in case we do not connect, here is my card. Please have her give me a call.'

*   *   *

'Do you think she is running?' Anthony asked as he wheeled the Land Rover downhill toward Road Town. 'Or is it some kind of a mix-up?'

'I don't know, Anthony. I don't know why she would want to run. She merits some consideration as a suspect at this point, but we do not have a shred of evidence placing her anywhere near the murder scene. She hasn't done anything legally wrong that we know of. The last I heard, moral failings that are not a crime are no reason to run from home or hide from the police. And the affair between her and the DC is just that – a moral failing that isn't a crime.' Saying the last part brought me back to my bygone moral failing of the same nature, and all the crime that it begat.

'Does that mean we don't try to find her?' Anthony asked.

'No, we try to find her,' I said. 'Something tells me it should be our first priority.'

'Where to, then, old chum? Not at home. Not at work. Where can the woman be?'

We both spoke in unison. 'The hospital!'

Nurse Rowell looked up from where she was working on her charting in the Peebles Hospital ICU. 'Constable Creque, I didn't expect to see you here, now that your Deputy Commissioner had been cleared and released from custody.'

'What?' I said. 'Cleared and released from custody? When? By whom?'

'About an hour ago. A good thing, too, because Dr Patel was struggling with keeping Deputy Commissioner Lane here any longer, his condition has improved so. Last night he told me that he couldn't justify keeping . . .'

'Who authorized the release of the Deputy Commissioner?' I interrupted.

'I don't know exactly, Constable. The officer assigned as a guard checked the paperwork. Dr Patel authorized a medical discharge as soon as I contacted him after I learned that the Deputy Commissioner was free to go.'

'Where did the paperwork releasing the Deputy Commissioner come from?'

'A lady brought it in. An administrative assistant, I'm guessing.

She went right up to the officer on guard, spoke to him and handed him the paperwork. He signed whatever it was that she brought in, and left. I assume he left because Deputy Commissioner Lane was released from custody.'

'Did you speak to the lady who brought in the paperwork? Did she give you her name?'

'Yes. She confirmed that Deputy Commissioner Lane had been released from custody. I didn't think to get her name. I was just pleased that the Deputy Commissioner had been cleared.'

'What did she look like?'

'She was medium height. Black, but with a light complexion. Black hair, relaxed. Dark eyes but I really did not see the color. Middle-aged, maybe in her late forties. Well dressed, wearing a dark suit and high heels.'

Consuela Lettsome.

'Did the Deputy Commissioner leave with the woman?'

'Yes. They left about an hour ago. It took me about fifteen minutes to complete the paperwork for the hospital discharge after the officer left. They waited in the room together. Is there something wrong, Constable?'

Urgency made me ignore her question. 'Did they say where they were going?'

'No.'

'Did they seem to be in a hurry?'

'No. No more so than anyone being discharged from the hospital is. They walked out just . . . normally, once I had completed the discharge papers and given the Deputy Commissioner his home-going instructions from Dr Patel.'

'How did the Deputy Commissioner act? Confused? Surprised? Happy?'

'Just very normal.' A dark cloud passed across Nurse Rowell's face. 'Again, is something wrong?'

'Yes,' I said. 'The primary suspect in the murder of Letitia Lane and his accomplice just escaped police custody.'

THIRTY

The days when our eyes are opened are few and far between. They may be only a handful of days in an entire lifetime. But what they lack in frequency they make up, tenfold, a hundred fold, a thousand fold, in trauma. The morning you learn of your lover's unfaithfulness, the evening of your betrayal by your best friend, the dusty afternoon your dream of wealth, or fame, or heroism is crushed, the black night your model and mentor reveals himself to be a mere man, and a failed one at that, all pack a punch of heartache no physical wounding can match. I had suffered a few of those days in the past – the twice-in-one-night betrayal by my wife and then my lover in the sunset hour beside a hidden well on Anegada's East End will always come first to mind – but the shock of the man I most admired fleeing custody and by such flight all but admitting to murder, that most heinous of crimes, was almost more than I could stand. Almost.

'Drive,' I said to Anthony. 'I'll call it in.'

And De White Rasta drove, gunning the police vehicle along the high street of Road Town's waterfront toward RVIPF headquarters without asking me for a destination.

And I called the escape in, or began to. I got as far as giving our unit number, and the dispatcher's acknowledgement to 'go ahead' before allowing something – my loyalty, my heart? – to overrule my head.

'Disregard,' I told the dispatcher, in response to her third stated 'go ahead.'

'What?' Anthony exclaimed, eyes still fixed on the road, pushing hard on the accelerator. 'What are you doing, Teddy? You must call this in.'

'I . . . can't, Anthony.'

De Rasta braked and pulled to the curb, leaving the engine running. 'The man has escaped custody. Escaped with an accomplice or, at the least, an accessory after the fact, or whatever she may be called. He was being held on a charge of murder. A charge, I might add, which had been brought by you and for which you are the arresting and investigating officer. You cannot ignore those things, Constable Creque.'

De White Rasta's last reference to me by my formal RVIPF rank was intended to remind me of my duty and the obligation of my oath. To remind me that I was, first and foremost, an officer of the law. A cop.

But I am not now the cop that I was before, mediocre and untested. I put in twenty years that way, going through the motions. Events have jolted me away from being that slack second-rater. I count myself a good cop now, experienced, capable and, most importantly, endowed with that which had been so elusive to me in the past – good cop intuition. The veteran officer's ability to know, in his or her gut, the right move to make, who to trust, and what to find believable or doubtful. Now was the time to put my good cop intuition to the test.

'I am not calling it in, Anthony,' I said, not believing the words even as I spoke them. 'We will find him without notifying headquarters. We will take him into custody ourselves.'

'But . . . why?'

'Because I don't believe he killed his wife.'

'Fine. Good, Teddy. Investigate the crime. Find the true killer. Exonerate Deputy Commissioner Lane. But you still need to keep the man in custody. You still need to locate him because he has escaped.'

'You're right, Anthony. So let's find him. It can be done without the entire RVIPF chasing him down. We can do it.' Hearing the 'we' coming from my own lips gave me pause. 'No, wait. That is not fair to you. I can't ask you to help with this.'

'You are not asking me to commit a crime,' De Rasta said. Then doubt crept into his tone. 'Are you?'

'No, of course not. I was asking only that you help me find the Deputy Commissioner on our own. In our own way. But doing it our own way may cost you your employment. I cannot ask you to do that.'

'My employment? You mean my job making coffee when Pamela Pickering's cup is empty? That employment?'

'All right, so it is a tad menial at times. But there is the salary.

I don't want my bad choices to put you back to sleeping on the beach and cadging leftovers from the Cow Wreck Beach Bar & Grill like in the old days before . . .'

'Before what? Before I cleaned up my act? Not to worry, my friend. True, I am making my way quite handily on my government salary, but there is always my living if it disappears.'

'Your living?'

'Ah, you colonials. So naïve about the workings of the mother country. I have a living as the Viscount of Thetford. A stipend, if you will.'

'But is that enough? In the worst case?'

'Well, let me see. There is the family estate. The castle itself does not generate any income but the ninety thousand acres surrounding it does quite well, according to the estate manager. And since I am sober now, I could always sell off some of my late father's wine collection. Twenty thousand bottles, with vintages as far back as 1870. Selling a case of the '47 Cheval Blanc ought to set me up nicely for three or four decades, given the current market price and Anegada's cost of living. But then there's the rent from the office buildings in Holland Park in London, so no real need to sell any of the wine. Oh, and there's the art collection. I could always auction a Renoir if the situation becomes desperate.' De Rasta flashed one of his patented dazzling smiles for emphasis.

'Right, then. Gotcha. You are bulletproof, financially,' I said.

'Comfortable, anyway,' Anthony, master of understatement, allowed. 'So I'm in. How do we carry out this folly?'

'We think. Before acting. Instead of just acting, like we have been doing. You can take the car out of gear and turn off the engine.'

'Done.' Anthony pocketed the key. 'Now where do we find Deputy Commissioner Lane and Ms Lettsome?'

'The first question is whether they are attempting to leave the Virgin Islands or are they trying to hide somewhere in the territory?'

'This is a small spot, Teddy, but there are places to hide. I know. I've hidden in them.'

'You hid in them when you were a dreadlocked, ganja-smoking drifter whose biggest crime was recreational drug consumption.

You hid with, or were hidden by, people like you. Do you think those same people are going to welcome a brass-bound Deputy Police Commissioner and his equally buttoned-up girlfriend? Do you think, even if they let our two fugitives in, that their hosts will let them stay around for even a second if they find out that there's a murder charge in the mix?'

'Good point, Teddy,' De Rasta allowed. 'The people I was thinking of would give the ten-foot-pole treatment to anyone in those circumstances.'

'And I don't think there is a willing relative for either of them to hide with. The DC has no kids and no living parents, as far as I know. I think we visited Consuela Lettsome's only relative earlier today and she doesn't strike me as the type who would harbor a fugitive, even if the fugitive was her daughter.'

'Very well then, it's flight we will be looking at. Literally?'

'I don't think so,' I said. 'Whether it's the DC or Ms Lettsome who is the mastermind, both are too sophisticated to try to escape by air. The airport is too easily watched.'

'By sea, then.'

'Yes. There is so much coastline and so many boats.'

'We can't begin to watch the entire coastline or stop every boat. Maybe we should rethink your desire to go this alone, Teddy.'

'I don't believe so, Anthony. I do believe that I know exactly how they plan to leave, and when. I hope that I am right.'

Because I was betting my badge on it.

THIRTY-ONE

Anthony and I waded against the flow sweeping across Tortola Pier Park like a comber colliding with the Horseshoe Reef. This flow, however, was not the deep blue water of the Atlantic. Its color was predominantly white – white socks, cheap white sneakers and much, too much, pasty white skin. The surging crowd of cruise-ship tourists coming off the massive floating hotel-cum-gambling-den-cum-amusement park tied to the pier had the once quaint, now jaded, Road Town waterfront as its destination. The waterfront's sailboat chandleries and laid-back rum bars had been replaced by ice cream parlors and cheap T-shirt shops selling genuine, made-in-China souvenirs of the BVI. It was like this every day now when a cruise ship visited on its round of the eastern Caribbean.

The throng thinned the closer we got to the ship, the stragglers navigating with canes and walkers, or nursing hangovers and sunburns.

Anthony halted me fifty feet from the gangway on to the ship. 'Just curious, old friend. How do you think the Deputy Commissioner and Ms Lettsome are going to escape by boarding a cruise ship in the midst of its port calls? This isn't the days of yore, where one could just buy a ticket to the next port. There are maritime conventions and such, which to my understanding prevent mid-cruise boardings. All passengers must board at the home port of the vessel and must return to that port. Passengers are permitted to do port calls but no new passengers are allowed to board at the port calls.'

'All correct, Anthony. But they won't be boarding as passengers.'

'Stowing away?' Anthony's face failed to conceal his skepticism. 'Do you see the security one must get through just to set foot on the gangway? An identification check plus a metal detector and a luggage X-ray. Again, Teddy, these are not the days of yore.'

'They are not boarding as stowaways, either,' I said. 'They are going to walk aboard, show their real passports, and be welcomed with open arms by the crew. Specifically, by the human resources director for the ship.'

'Please enlighten me.' De Rasta now exuded doubt.

'Do you remember my cousin, Victoria Creque, from Barbados?'

'Visited you last year, didn't she? Tall girl, too much make-up?'

'One man's too much is another man's just right. But, yes, that's her.'

'And she has to do with our escapees . . . what?'

'Her, nothing. Her job, everything. She works on cruise ships, all around the Caribbean, as a temporary employee. If a steward, or a cleaner, or a dishwasher jumps ship, or, more often, takes ill in the middle of a cruise and needs to be replaced, she is the replacement. She gets variety in her work and the cruise lines pay a wage premium for her willingness to pick up and leave home on short notice. And I think the DC and Ms Lettsome are more than willing to pick up and leave the BVI on *very* short notice. My guess is that Ms Lettsome watched on-line for crew replacement requests and made her move when two replacement jobs opened. And she didn't have the time, or maybe even the capability, to get a fake passport for her and the Deputy Commissioner on such short notice. So they are taking a chance by traveling under their own names, hoping that they get away before their escape is even found out. This is the only cruise ship in port today, so this is the ship they must take to escape.'

'Marvelous. Astute. Astounding. What if you are not right?' Anthony tried to make the question sound casual.

'Then they will get off island on a small boat leaving out of an isolated bay in the dead of night,' I said. 'But the DC is a land cop, not a waterman, and Consuela Lettsome is comfortable with forms, desks and typewriters. I'm guessing neither of them would have much enthusiasm for a small boat sea crossing to the USVI or further, in the dark, when the alternative is a big safe floating castle that doesn't sway an inch in a hurricane. Let's find out if I am right.'

I led the way up the gangway, showed my badge and

identification to the ship's officer in charge, and received a crew escort to the shipboard human resources director for myself and Anthony. In minutes we were in a spartan office deep in the bowels of the vessel, seated across from Rachel Mueller, the ship's human resources director.

'So what is it that I can do for you, Constable Creque?' Ms Mueller asked after introductions.

'We believe two fugitives from justice, an escaped prisoner and his mistress, will seek to sail with your ship as temporary employees when it leaves this evening,' I said.

'I would be surprised if we were getting those types of individuals aboard as temporary employees.' Ms Mueller, in her crisp uniform, long blonde hair in a loose chignon, radiated competence. 'We vet all potential employees, including temps, before they are offered a position. They would never have a chance to set a foot on board if their background check turned up a criminal record.'

'Do your background checks include arrests without conviction?'

Ms Mueller colored slightly. 'Convictions only. Arrest searches are unreliable in the Caribbean and, frankly, too expensive.'

'Are you taking any temporary crew on today?' I thought I might as well cut to the chase.

'Yes. Three.' She shuffled files on her desk and read from a paper she picked out of one. 'A casino dealer, Jasmine George. Consuela Lettsome, a housekeeper. And Howard Lane, a dishwasher.'

'Eureka!' Anthony Wedderburn's exclamation, exceedingly in character for his aristocratic roots and Eton-Oxford education, prompted a what-kind-of-nerds-am-I-dealing-with-smile from Ms Mueller.

'The last two you mentioned are our fugitives, Ms Mueller,' I said. 'Are they already on board?'

'No. The first thing we do with temporary crew is to have them escorted from the gangway to my office to sign paperwork. They have not been here yet. We tell all temps coming aboard to arrive between three o'clock and four o'clock in the afternoon.'

I checked my watch. It was quarter after three. 'I'm sorry but we will be arresting both Ms Lettsome and Mr Lane when they appear.'

Ms Mueller, apparently unfazed by anything, had a request. 'Can you do it away from the ship? We don't like the passengers to see such things while on vacation. Dampens the vibe, you know. I'm sure you understand.' It sounded as if this arrest was not Ms Mueller's first rodeo, as the Yanks say.

'There is too much risk of losing them in the crowd on the pier,' I said. 'We would prefer to wait until they are in your office. You, of course, would not be here. Is there a place where we might wait nearby?'

'The purser's office is right next door. She is busy on deck and will be until we get underway. You may wait in there.'

'Very good. Thank you,' I said. 'We must ask that you vacate your office so we can prepare. Is there anything else you would like to know before we begin?'

'Yes. Do you know where I can find a dishwasher and a housekeeper on short notice?'

THIRTY-TWO

Anthony Wedderburn was seated behind Rachel Mueller's desk when a crewman ushered Deputy Commissioner Lane and Consuela Lettsome into the human resources office. Ms Lettsome, unacquainted with Anthony, held out her hand to introduce herself to the faux human resources director.

Seconds before, the two fugitives and the crewman had passed by the slightly ajar door to the purser's office, where I waited. I overheard the DC asking, 'Why are we going here, Consuela? I thought this cruise was our getaway to celebrate, but this doesn't look like we are going to a cabin.' Ms Lettsome's reply as they passed along the corridor was unintelligible.

I did clearly hear the next remark coming from the couple. Deputy Commissioner Lane said, 'Mr Wedderburn, what are you doing here?'

I stepped from the purser's office and entered the human resources office behind the two fugitives. 'You are both under arrest, for escape, and aiding and abetting escape and harboring a fugitive,' I said.

'He didn't know.' Consuela Lettsome immediately turned to me with pleading eyes. 'He thought he had been released. I told him that he had been cleared, and that we were getting away for a few days for him to rest. Please.'

'Didn't know what, Consuela?' The Deputy Commissioner's question was meek, his normally resounding voice a near whisper, his towering stature still shrunken to old-man size by the emotional strain and physical damage from his recent tribulations.

Ms Lettsome took a long moment to look at the floor and then brought her brimming eyes up to look directly into the DC's. 'Didn't know that I had planned your escape from the hospital and our flight out of the country. Didn't know that I lied to you when I told you that you had been cleared. Didn't know that I had forged your release papers. I am so sorry, Howard.' She reached for his hand but he pulled it away.

I took out handcuffs. 'I have no choice,' I said to the DC.

He held out his hands to accept the manacles. 'Not for her, please,' he begged.

'I must,' I said.

'It's all right, Howard.' Ms Lettsome held out her hands for the cuffs.

De Rasta persuaded a couple of hand towels from one of the ship's housekeepers and we placed them over the handcuffs as we walked our prisoners to the RVIPF police vehicle, with the next stop being His Majesty's Prison.

Deputy Commissioner Lane sat in dejected silence in the caged rear seat as we made slow progress through the late-afternoon traffic on Waterfront Drive. Consuela Lettsome leaned forward, her face almost against the cage between the rear and front seats. 'He cannot go to prison, Constable Creque. Please don't put him in prison. His body is weak. His soul is even weaker. I beg you. Put me where you must. I am the one who thought of this. I am the one who arranged this. I am the one who is guilty. I deceived him. He had nothing to do with it. If you put him in prison now, it will kill him. I cannot bear the thought of it. And you know what I say is true, Constable. Please. Anywhere but prison.'

RVIPF policy prohibits speaking to prisoners being transported except for providing them with instructions or in emergency situations. An interrogation in a vehicle is useless; there is no way to record it. And trying to reason with a prisoner upset about going to jail is almost always futile. I did not follow RVIPF policy in this instance. Why? Because in my heart, I knew that what Consuela Lettsome was saying was absolutely truthful. 'You know I must take you both to jail. Even if what you say is absolutely truthful, Ms Lettsome. I have my duty.'

'Bah, duty.' Ms Lettsome practically spit out the words. 'Is this Howard's reward for doing his duty all these years, these decades? Is he to receive no consideration?'

'It is not a matter of consideration . . .' I began.

Ms Lettsome interrupted me. 'I have confessed. It was all my doing. You saw his reaction. He did not understand what was going on. He did nothing.'

'He is charged with murder.'

'And you managed to keep him in the hospital, safe, even though he was charged.'

'But he was still in custody,' I said, even though there was little doubt that any one of us in the vehicle was keen on seeing the DC in His Majesty's Prison. 'Besides, even if I agreed, I have no place to keep him in custody now. Returning him to the hospital is out of the question. You have seen to that. Where am I to put him?' This last question was directed out into the heavens rather than to Ms Lettsome.

'I can think of a place.' Anthony Wedderburn's statement brought the discussion in the Land Rover to a halt. 'He will be safe there. And he won't be able to leave. He will be in custody. But he will not be in prison.'

There was a clamor of comments from the cage in the rear seat, which I overrode. 'And where would that be? You are not thinking of placing him with Boss Claudie, are you? Are we turning a drug dealer into our own private prison warden?'

'He is not a drug dealer, old man. He is simply a retired individual. A retired individual who has more than a qualm or two about his past role in society. A man who owes me, still, for things that I did for him in the past. In my past. He would keep the Deputy Commissioner safe and well treated. He would make certain that the Deputy Commissioner stayed where he was supposed to stay, until he's released to you.'

'Are you out of your mind, Anthony? This is not just a material witness, like Jubbie Watson. This is a man charged with the most serious crime there is. And it doesn't matter whether Claudie is a former drug dealer, a current drug dealer, or the King of Sweden. He is not acceptable to hold a charged suspect in custody.'

A gaggle of tourists stepped from the curb in front of the police car, a half block from the nearest crosswalk. De Rasta calmly braked to a stop, gave them a brief wave, and flashed his patented smile. They waved in return, oblivious to the fact that they were jaywalking in front of the police. Good Lord, is my entire country rife with lawlessness? Including my friend and administrative assistant, proposing what he had? And what about me for considering the proposal?

Because I was considering it. After risking my career as a police officer by not reporting that the DC had escaped, and having the good fortune to recapture him, was I now going even further into the realm of risk by not returning the escaped prisoner to custody? Well, anyway not normal custody. Not His Majesty's Prison. But wasn't that my unconscious plan all along? Why else hadn't I reported the Deputy Commissioner's escape, if not to keep him from prison when he was re-captured?

Still, there were issues I could not ignore. 'How can I justify putting him with Boss Claudie when the time of reckoning comes? And it will come, Anthony. The reckoning always does. I know.'

'He just needs to be in police custody, doesn't he, Teddy?' Anthony asked. 'It doesn't necessarily need to be in a jail or at His Majesty's Prison. I mean, the Deputy Commissioner is in police custody now.'

'That's right, Anthony. Our situation is currently within regulations because he is in this car with an officer of the RVIPF. Me. Do you have a police officer in mind who will be present to guard him while he is up in the hills at Long Trench?'

'Yes,' De Rasta said. 'Me.'

'You? May I remind you that you are not an RVIPF officer.'

'But I am an RVIPF *employee*.' Anthony was in full hair-splitting mode.

'And what does that do to resolve our situation?'

'An RVIPF employee who is not a police officer can guard a prisoner. I was asked – by you – to guard Queen Ya-Ya on Anegada during Hurricane Leatha.'

'Which resulted in her escape, as I recall, Anthony.'

'Not to be rude, old chum, but you didn't do any better with her in the end.'

'All right,' I said. 'Point taken. But those were extraordinary circumstances.'

'I will not escape.' Deputy Commissioner Lane's once-forceful voice, returned now to half level, was still loud enough to silence the exchange between Anthony and me. 'I will not try to escape. I will not leave whatever place you take me to without your permission. You have my word.'

THIRTY-THREE

I could not think of a time since I had known him that Deputy Commissioner Howard Lane's word had not been good. Now, if I took his word, my career as a police officer would be on the line. But it had been on the line before. I had taken risks before, much greater risks than accepting the word of the Deputy Commissioner. So I decided that his word was good enough for me now.

The nephews and cousins loitering outside Boss Claudie's house came to languid alertness on the approach of the RVIPF police vehicle. Unlike our last visit, Claudie almost instantly appeared, De White Rasta having made himself highly visible by rolling down the driver's side window as we approached.

'I would have had a good meal prepared for you today had I known you were going to visit.' Boss Claudie looked cool and collected in retro Ray-Bans, Gucci loafers, a blue linen shirt and razor-creased black slacks, standing on his front stoop. Seeing his welcoming mood, the nephews and cousins returned to their ease. 'I must admit, though, I didn't expect our confabulations to become a regular occurrence. To what do I owe the pleasure of your and Constable Creque's company today, Anthony?'

'We have come to ask a favor, Claudie.' Anthony, equally cool, responded as if he asked retired drug kingpins for favors on a daily basis.

'We?' Boss Claudie cocked an eyebrow.

'Constable Creque and me.'

'What about your two passengers in the rear seat of that Babylon bus, as my nephews call it? Are they also here to ask a favor?'

'Not of you, Claudie, but they are part of the favor we ask.'

'Let me see them, then, so I may fully evaluate your request when it comes.'

I opened the rear door of the car and helped the DC and Ms

Lettsome out. They both remained in handcuffs. I noticed Boss Claudie's eyes register the fact.

'I see some of us are not here on a voluntary basis,' Claudie said. 'Just like with Jubbie. I guess you are making a habit, Anthony and Constable Creque, of bringing me people who are, or have been, in handcuffs. The gentleman has policeman written all over him. And the gentlelady by appearance seems even less likely to be acquainted with the criminal life.'

'No need to concern yourself with the lady, sir,' I said. 'She will be leaving with us shortly.'

'And the corollary of that statement is that you expect the gentleman to remain here, with me, when you depart.' Claudie's tone made his statement into a question. His eyes directed the question to Anthony.

'That is correct, Claudie,' De Rasta said. 'We hope to leave him here in your care, as we did with Jubbie Watson.'

'Until this week, I was unaccustomed to the role of caretaker, Anthony. And those handcuffs tell me my duties may be more like those of a warden. This is a bit of a different situation than with Jubbie, a mere witness. Doesn't the Royal Virgin Islands Police Force have personnel and facilities more suited for such things than me and my humble home?'

'There are reasons he cannot go to those facilities,' I interjected.

Claudie turned to me. 'Is this man a protected witness?'

'No,' I said. 'He is a prisoner, awaiting trial.'

'And the charge is something tame, I trust. Embezzlement or some other type of financial crime? Something else non-violent?'

'No. Murder.'

'Well, why not go the whole hog if you are going to ask a favor?' Claudie chuckled.

'Why not indeed?' Anthony said, good-naturedly, and the two dissolved in laughter.

Boss Claudie stopped laughing and turned serious. 'I suppose I do not need to know the precise reason for this. Probably the less I know the better. But I need the absolute truth – we are not talking about committing crimes here, are we, gentlemen? Because I have given up that life. I would be very angry to accidentally restart it by doing an old friend a favor. No one will accuse me of, say, kidnapping, if I do this favor?'

The Deputy Commissioner's voice boomed out, carrying more than a hint of its old strength. 'Kidnapping occurs when one is held against one's will. I can assure you, sir, that this is being done with my consent. I am prepared to confirm that to anyone who asks.'

Boss Claudie considered the Deputy Commissioner's statement a minute and said, 'Reassuring as the word of one charged with murder is, sir, I will need to hear it from those currently in control of your future. Anthony? Constable?'

'There will not be a fall to be taken, but if there is one, I will stay with you, Claudie, and take the fall,' De Rasta said.

'Well, the guarantee of a convivial cellmate puts my mind as at ease as it can be in the circumstances. All right. How long will the gentleman be staying?'

'A matter of a few days. A week at the most,' I said, giving myself a deadline which, as far as I could tell, had no reasonable basis in fact. 'Longer than that and I will take him off your hands, Claudie.'

'Fair enough.' Boss Claudie's demeanor turned breezy. 'Your gentleman will find this an amiable bridewell. I know I do. There are plenty of books. And the food is top-notch. Just ask any of the boys.'

'Thank you, Claudie,' Anthony said.

Boss Claudie turned a stern eye on De Rasta. 'There is just one thing, Anthony. This wipes the slate clean. Agreed?'

'Agreed, Claudie.'

I wondered what De White Rasta had done to entitle him to such a debt of gratitude from someone who had been one of the biggest drug lords in the Caribbean. But maybe, just as Boss Claudie had been about our request, I was better off if I didn't know.

THIRTY-FOUR

'What about Consuela?' Deputy Commissioner Lane's voice, so often reminiscent of Zeus or James Earl Jones playing Zeus, dropped into Lou Rawls mode. Soothing. Mellow. Friendly instead of fearsome. 'Surely if I can stay here, so can she, can't she?'

'I can't . . .' I began.

'No, Howard,' Consuela Lettsome interrupted. 'Constable Creque cannot keep me here. There is a difference between my situation and yours. I have committed a crime. I prepared for it, and did the crime with full knowledge and intent. I have confessed to the crime. I am guilty. I deserve to go to prison.'

'But . . .' The DC began to object.

Ms Lettsome brought her cuffed hands up to the DC's chest, placing them over the big man's heart. 'No buts, Howard. Your situation is different. As a police officer, prison is especially dangerous for you. You know that. But there is a more compelling reason: what you told me as we drove to the ship, before we were arrested. Tell Constable Creque.'

Deputy Commissioner Lane looked me squarely in the eye. 'There is so much I don't remember about that night, Teddy, the night Letitia was killed. There was so much doubt in my mind. I spent the days in the hospital asking myself if I really could have done it, if I really had killed her. For days I didn't know the answer to that question. It haunted me. I tried and tried to remember but that evening wouldn't come back to me. It just wouldn't come back. But in the last day something has changed. I still cannot remember anything about the events that took place in the garden at Government House that night. But now I know. Somehow I just know. I know that I didn't kill Letitia.'

The DC straightened and stood tall. 'Before, I wanted justice. For Letitia. Even if justice meant that the evidence showed that I was her killer. Now I know that justice means finding who it was that killed her and bringing him to account. Find her killer, Teddy. Letitia's killer is out there, somewhere. Find him.'

Anthony and I booked Consuela Lettsome into His Majesty's Prison on a charge of aiding and abetting escape and harboring a fugitive. As the matron took her arm to lead her away, she wiped a tear from her eye and said, 'Thank you, Constable. Find the real killer and save my dear Howard. I cannot be saved now but he must be.'

Walking out of His Majesty's Prison afterward, De Rasta was upbeat. 'That worked out much better than I expected, old sport. Just two broken lives and still no killer in custody. So what other fun do we have planned for today?'

'Now we go report the Deputy Commissioner's escape, apprehension, and the apprehension of Ms Lettsome.'

'What?' Anthony's jaw dropped. 'We jump through all those hoops just to make sure the Deputy Commissioner doesn't end up in His Majesty's Prison and now we are going to make a report that will most decidedly end with him in that very place? I don't understand, Teddy.'

'Just have some confidence in the chain of command, Anthony.'

'Jeezum, Teddy, you did what?' Inspector Rollie Stoutt's ample jowls trembled like butterfly wings. 'You always were anything but by the book but this really takes the cake. And why are you telling me this? So you have someone to sit next to you at the disciplinary hearing? I don't want to hear any more. I don't want to hear any of this.'

I expected Rollie to cover his ears with his hands next. Instead, he just stared at me like I was a bad dream that he somehow expected would go away. I did not go away. I did give him my reason for reporting to him. 'You are my immediate superior for this investigation, Inspector. I am following procedures and making my report to you.'

'Oh, jeezum. Jeezum!' The tremor in Inspector Stoutt's cheeks increased in frequency, its lazy butterfly flutter rising to a shudder that threatened to detach the poor man's head completely. Suddenly, he placed both hands on the uncluttered desk in front

ОбÉ

of him and, through what appeared to be a Herculean physical effort, calmed his shuddering jawline to a complete standstill. 'You've got to take the DC to prison now, Teddy.'

Rollie tried to speak with authority, with conviction, even with command. He tried to be like Deputy Commissioner Lane, a man we both feared and admired, and who we could never overtly disobey. But Inspector Stoutt didn't have it, that certain *je ne sais quoi*, that made for an unquestioned leader of men. His voice had the slightest inflection of request, rather than decree. His eyes would not meet mine. He leaned back, not forward, and his rearward inclination was not one of assurance, but of reticence.

I sensed an opening. 'One week is all I ask,' I said.

Deputy Commissioner Lane's answer to such a request from me would have been an unequivocal 'no' roared at a volume loud enough to rattle his office windows in their frames. When Rollie said, 'What if someone finds out?', I knew we were in a negotiation. That was what I had counted on.

'No one will find out,' I said. 'You are my superior, and you won't raise an issue. The Commissioner does not bother to check on the location of prisoners; at most he will ask the status of my investigation. You can tell him, truthfully, that I am working on tying up loose ends and expect it to be completed in a week. And, if the Royals raise a fuss earlier than that, I will bring him in. Immediately. No argument.'

'Why do you do this to me, Teddy?' Rollie shook his head, trying to clear cobwebs when there were none there.

'Just one week.' I made my request barely audible, just enough to push the Inspector across the line.

He surprised me. 'Three days, Teddy. Not a second more.' I had thought Rollie Stoutt was a teddy bear, if teddy bears were stuffed with johnnycake, fungi, conch fritters, and roti. But there was a spine in there somewhere.

I took the three days and counted it as a win. 'Yes, sir, three days and I will have Letitia Lane's killer in custody.'

'And do not come back asking for more time, Constable. Not a second more, do you understand?'

'Yes, sir. Thank you, sir.' I snapped out my best police academy salute – fingers together, palm out – and turned on my heel for the door. As I crossed the threshold, I increased my pace, De White Rasta matching me stride for stride. We were almost out of earshot when I heard Rollie's voice behind me.

'Jeezum!'

THIRTY-FIVE

One drawback to the otherwise unparalleled beauty of the tropics is the sunsets. Wait, you say, you've been to the tropics, to the Caribbean or to the equatorial Pacific Islands, or to the Maldives, and the sunsets while you were there were stunning, glorious, beyond compare, a palette of all the colors of the sky against the many hues of the sea. But there is a drawback, though most visitors to the tropics almost never notice, being at least two and a half sheets to the wind from the consumption of painkillers, or margaritas, or gin and tonics, or, in Anegada, rum smoothies.

The drawback is that the sunsets are short in duration. Quick, like the snapping shut of a shade or the flicking off of a light switch. I know, you've solved that issue easily – you drink that sundown libation, or two, or three, fast, to compensate for mother nature's rapid lights-out. Problem solved. Were it as easy to solve mine when we emerged from headquarters just as the lights went down on another flawless island day.

'What now?' Anthony always came up with penetrating questions.

I didn't know the answer so I began with my default response. 'We go home, Anthony, get a good night's rest and . . .'

Ping.

'What was that sound?' As soon as I asked the question, I realized the sound had come from me. From the pocket of my uniform pants. The pocket where I kept my cell phone.

'You most certainly jest, Teddy.' De Rasta's voice had an inflection that told me that the joke I was making was not even remotely funny. Then, 'Dear sweet Petula Clark, you don't know, do you?'

In my defense, much of the communication I'm involved in on Anegada still takes place on marine radio. Channel 16 is still the party line of the island and still the source of most of the police calls I receive there. The landline telephone at the station is the medium of most of the rest. But like many on our home island, I now own the cell phone and occasionally make and receive calls on it. Calls, where you punch in the number and speak to people, or people punch in the number, the cell phone rings just like my office landline, and I press a button and speak to people. That is how I use a cell phone and that is how the fine people of Anegada use theirs. The pinging sound that came from my cell phone was completely new to me.

'You have never heard that sound from your cell phone before?' De Rasta was gobsmacked. 'And I thought I was the one who was off the grid and out of touch when I was sleeping on the beach most nights and doing my daily ablutions in the shallows at Bones Bight. It's the tone for a text, Teddy. Someone has sent you a message. Look at the phone's screen.'

I looked. The screen read:

NEED 2 C U ASAP. PRIVATELY. WAYN. C

I was completely baffled. Above the incomprehensible letters was a US telephone number that I recognized as belonging to Cat Wells. But the message was baffling to me. I stared at the screen, unable to make heads or tails of it.

'Here, old chum, let me.' Anthony took the phone. 'Oh. Ms Wells needs to see you in private.'

'Now, what do I do?'

'You mean do you see Ms Wells in private?'

'No, Anthony. I mean how do I say yes to her?'

'Really, Teddy?'

'Really.'

'What do you want to tell her in response?'

'I cannot see her right now because we are on Tortola. I could see her tomorrow morning if that is soon enough. And if she wants it to be private, I can't come to the Setting Point Villa. Where does she want to meet?'

Anthony's thumbs flew over the phone's tiny keyboard like a crazed chimp who had just learned he had opposable digits. A message appeared as he typed:

ON TORTOLA. TMW OK?

Anthony hit the arrow beside the message and it changed color
with a whooshing sound. Seconds later, another ping.

Y. 9 AM. USUAL PLACE.

'She wants to meet you tomorrow at nine o'clock in the
morning at the usual place, Teddy. Do you know what she means?'
My thoughts flew back to the days, years ago, before crime
and death and prison intervened, to Cat's and my meetings at
our usual place. To the long looks between us that preceded the
lovemaking on a blanket under a seagrape tree. To the naked
swims in the crystal waters that followed. To the between-lovers
patter, the hiding of our assignations, the guilt, the lust, the thrill.
I thought I had put it all behind me, buried it for good, and
cleansed it from my soul with the goodness of Jeanne Trengrouse
and our good life together. But it flew back, it roared back,
unbidden.
'Yes, Anthony. I know the place. I will be there.'
De Rasta's thumbs danced briefly on the phone's face.

OK

The woosh, or swoosh, or whatever sound it was supposed to
be, sounded, and I was back there, back again, meeting Cat Wells,
tomorrow, alone, in the place where we had done the deeds that
had almost destroyed my life.

Jeanne Trengrouse groaned and turned away from the window
where the morning sun cut bright lines around the Bahama
shutters of our bedroom. She had been in bed last night, still
awake, when I arrived late from the cross-water trip home from
Road Town. We had whispered the news of our respective days
to each other, and then followed with a session of silent, the-
kids-are-in-the-house lovemaking and finally drifted off to sleep
as the moon was about to set outside our bedroom window.
I rose, dressed, and headed to the kitchen to make coffee,
a nagging voice inside my head asking why, when we had

whispered to each other in the night about the Deputy Commissioner's escape, and Tamia's grade card, and Jemmy's budding enthusiasm for track sports, I had not mentioned my upcoming meeting with Cat Wells. I silenced the voice by telling it that I would correct my oversight the first thing this morning, and put my energies to making coffee.

The burble and hiss of steam from the coffee maker had just ended when Tamia walked in. 'Good mornin', Dada.'

'Good morning, Dawta.'

Tamia responded with a hug. Already dressed in her school uniform, I was struck by how out of place she looked in it. At first I couldn't put my finger on the reason, but then it registered with me – the uniform looked out of place because she was becoming a young woman. Jeanne had mentioned that some of the older boys from school had been coming around to visit, a bit of information I had mentally discounted as an overprotective stepmother's unfounded concern. Now, though, I had a father's vision of why those boys were coming around, and vowed a terrifying interrogation of the next young swain who arrived at our door. Perhaps I would clean my Webley during the questioning, to add emphasis and to make certain that the unlucky gallant would spread the word among his contemporaries.

Jemmy was in next, silent after his 'Good morning, Dada,' but beaming over a new pair of running shoes that had arrived in the most recent shipping container to come from Tortola. Kevin followed, chatty as always, joshing Tamia, and earnestly planning a snapper fishing expedition with Jemmy for after school.

I leaned against the counter, sipping the rich black liquid just brewed, and watched the happy by-play among my children, thinking how lucky I was.

'Mmmm, that coffee smells good.' Jeanne strolled in, barefoot, long tawny legs disappearing into the blue silk robe with Chinese characters on it that was her present from me last Christmas. She nuzzled against me. 'Good morning, my man.'

A quick peck of a kiss – no excessive displays in front of the children was our rule – and I poured her a cup of coffee. Jeanne sipped while she made a breakfast consisting of a mountain of scrambled eggs, johnnycake and fried yellowtail snapper, and joined in the kids' repartee. Before I knew it, it was time for school. The family routine was that I walk with the kids to the Anegada School, and from there on to the police station.

'Off you go,' Jeanne said, hurrying the three children out the door. Once they were out, she drew the door shut for a moment and flung her arms around my neck. 'I can't let you leave without a proper goodbye, lover.'

Jeanne's proper goodbye had the combined effect of leaving me weak in the knees and in need of a cold shower. When she finally separated her body from mine, she looked down, laughed, and said, 'You can't take your children to school like that, Teddy Creque.'

I glanced down and felt my neck flush hot.

'Cricket,' Jeanne said.

'What? What about cricket?'

'Think about cricket, Teddy. Batting averages, nervous nineties, five-wicket hauls, asking rates, blockers and biffers.'

'Where did you learn all that?'

'I played a few innings when the local lads were shorthanded when I was growing up.'

'Loved to have seen that.'

Jeanne looked down and smiled. 'You're fine to go now.' She pushed me out the door.

In the yard, Kevin and Jemmy met me with fake-mooning eyes. Tamia looked wistful and placed a hand over her heart. I hustled the group off to school.

It was only when I was alone and approaching the station that I remembered I had not told Jeanne about my meeting with Cat. I thought about returning home but it was almost nine.

THIRTY-SIX

The milk-white strand at Windlass Bight was deserted, though it was the picture of the idyllic beach in the mind of every auto worker staring down the dark days of a Detroit winter and every Minneapolis banker driving through another slush-burdened commute. Windlass was near-perfection on an island of perfect beaches. It was the just-pretty girl on stage with the stunning bodies, perfect hair, and fetching smiles of the contestants at the Miss Universe Pageant. The sand at Windlass was sugar soft but no match for the amazing pink hue of the powdery strand at Cow Wreck Bay. The snorkeling at Windless, on a patch of reef a hundred feet from shore, would be a top-ten attraction in the Bahamas, Belize or Bonaire. In Anegada, it paled beside the wonders of the Horseshoe Reef. In short, Windless Bight was merely beautiful on an island where voluptuous perfection was the standard.

Because it was merely beautiful, Windless Bight was usually empty. Its emptiness made it attractive to lovers seeking privacy. Hence, Cat Wells' and my penchant for using it for our liaisons so many years ago and for our rendezvous on this morning. I arrived first, driving the Land Rover down a sand path among the seagrapes until it was hidden from view. I got out and walked the dozen steps to the bower where Cat and I used to spread our blanket and make love. It was as it had always been, shady, secluded, and silent save for the muffled sound of the waves against the shore and the chitter of a bananaquit feeding on the seagrape fruit.

'Hello, Teddy,' Cat said. She padded in on bare feet, wearing a yellow sundress, tall and regal, a slight sheen of perspiration on her perfect skin. Seeing her, in this place, brought a rush of memories, sweet and guilty.

'It must be important if you walked all the way here,' I said, trying to push back the memories and keep to our business.

'Wendell George was driving to The Settlement. I caught a

ride with him for most of the way.' Our conversation was mundane but I could read in her eyes that she was dealing with memories, too. I wondered if they were sweet and guilty for her too.

'Why are we here?' The question sounded odd, fraught, when I asked it.

'Shall we sit?' Cat gestured to the very spot where we used to make love. We sat, an arm's length away from each other.

'Now, then, what is happening at the villa?'

'The Princess is fine,' she said, addressing the primary object of both of our concerns. 'Maybe better than fine. She seems to be enjoying her stay. She swims a lot. Sunbathes in the morning. She has a glow about her that she didn't when she first arrived.'

'And?'

'It's Jeremy Sutherland. He has been like a caged animal since you were last there. He snaps at Sir Roger all the time. Spends hours on the telephone to England, raving. And on the phone to his lawyers in the States, at all hours of the day and night.'

'That was going on before. And, of course, there is an easy solution to his problem if he would only take it. Is he getting anywhere with England?'

'Not that I can tell. But that is not why I wanted to meet you. It's about his calls to the United States, to New York. I overheard one yesterday . . .'

'Overheard?'

'Yes, Teddy, overheard. I'm making sure I overhear as much as possible. Isn't that what you wanted me to do? Isn't that why you brought me here to Anegada?'

'I wanted you to care for Princess Portia, to make certain she is well and comfortable.'

'Then you got a bonus. A spy.'

'You sound as though you resent it, Cat. I didn't ask you to spy.'

'Do you want to know what I heard or not?'

'Of course. Sorry. What did you hear?'

'Lord Sutherland asked for an American lawyer to come here.'

'Here? You mean to Tortola.'

'No. Here.'

'To Anegada? There is no court here. And an American lawyer

will be of no use here. They aren't even licensed to practice in BVI courts, if there was a court on the island.'

'I don't know why Jeremy wants a lawyer here but that's not the best part. He was on the phone to his regular lawyer, a slime-ball fixer named Joe Rizzo. Rizzo is a real-estate lawyer, known for his ability to bribe planning commissions and building inspectors. He is out of his depth on anything where he can't arrive with a brown paper bag of cash and depart with a permit with "approved" stamped on it.'

'So this Attorney Rizzo is going to come here with his bag of cash? That simply won't work here. Not with me. Not with Rollie Stoutt. Certainly not with Dr Shapiro.'

'But it's not Attorney Rizzo who is coming, Teddy.'

'Who is, then?'

'I don't know exactly who it is. But I know what. A criminal lawyer is coming. That is what I overheard. Attorney Rizzo has a colleague, a real criminal law hotshot, who he said he would have on an airplane last night and on Jeremy Sutherland's door-step within twenty-four hours. As in today, Teddy. Why would Lord Sutherland need a criminal lawyer? He might be a *witness* to a crime but he has nothing more to do with the crime than that. Why do you need a criminal lawyer when you haven't committed a crime and are not even a suspect?'

'I don't know,' I said. 'Maybe it is just because the Viscount is an American. I've heard that they don't even get out of bed in the morning in America without consulting their lawyer. Maybe it is just a cultural thing.' That is what I said but I didn't believe it for a second. 'Whatever it means, I think I will have a word with that lawyer when he arrives.'

'She.'

'The hotshot criminal lawyer from America is a female?'

'That was what I overheard and, man, did I overhear a lot about it. Jeremy pitched a fit when Rizzo mentioned that the hotshot was a woman. He practically screamed "I don't need some damn woman in charge of my fate. With Portia and the other one here –" me – "it is already a damn estrogen-fest around this place. I need a pit bull, Rizzo. A male pit bull."'

'So why is the lawyer who is coming a woman?'

'Good question. I don't know the answer. What I do know is

that, after Jeremy threw his chauvinistic fit, he stopped ranting long enough for Rizzo to tell him something that shut him up about wanting a man lawyer.'

'There are female pit bulls, I suppose. Nevertheless, I will speak with her when she arrives. I'll put her at ease about letting me interview Lord Sutherland. She may actually be helpful once she hears what I intend to ask. Do you know how she is traveling?'

'I heard it mentioned that she was flying into St Thomas this afternoon. I took the liberty of calling a friend at VI Birds. There are no charters scheduled from St Thomas to Anegada today. I also checked with Charley's Charters and Island Air. It's a good thing my pilot friends there haven't moved on from those places because the receptionists weren't really forthcoming. But no air charters inbound to Anegada from those two air services either. My best guess is that Ms Pit Bull will be arriving on the afternoon ferry from St Thomas today.'

'Wow, Cat. You really dug into this. This is very helpful.'

'I'm just trying to make sure Princess Portia doesn't get hurt. And I have an inkling that the sooner this is over, the better it is for her.'

'Still, thank you, Cat.'

'You're welcome, Teddy.' Cat shook her head like she was trying to rid it of an offending thought. 'Damn, that was excessively formal.'

'Just polite. For all of our failings, we are two polite people.'

Cat pushed her lips together, making a mouth, and looked into my eyes. 'Damn. Oh, damn.'

'What is it?'

'This place. You remember about this place. Don't tell me you don't.'

'That was a long time ago.'

'Not so long, Teddy. Not so long for me.'

'I have a . . . different life now, Cat.'

'So do I, Teddy. But that doesn't mean that I don't think about us. And now, coming back to Anegada, back to this place, seeing you . . .' She lowered her eyes. 'Don't tell me you don't ever think about me. About us. About what we had. About having it back.'

The breaking waves, coming from Africa three thousand miles away, thundered against the reef just offshore. I felt the rumble deep inside my chest, my soul, and then the weakness, the sickness, the aching need that I thought had been banished, exorcized from me in that twilight arbor beside the spring at Spanish Camp, with my life blood leaking from me and Cat, so serene, so exquisite, walking away from me, a bag heavy with emeralds in her hand and not an ounce of concern in her heart. I thought that burning longing has been erased, never to return. And yet here it was. And here was the woman who was its source, in this place, with me, alone.

Cat reached a hand out to touch mine, slender fingers, scarlet nails, a caress no more than a butterfly alighting. I pulled my hand back reflexively. I had touched the hot stove before and my body remembered.

'Teddy . . . what we had.'

'What we had wasn't much beyond lust, and whatever we had is gone. We are better people than that now. Both of us are.'

'Are we?' Cat's deep green eyes turned wistful. 'You are. I can see that. I wish I could be. Sometimes I am. And sometimes, as you can see, I lapse. I'm sorry, Teddy. It was a weak moment, the kind of weakness I spent the last seven years in prison vowing I would never allow to happen again. Oh, well, you can't fault a girl for remembering the most exciting days of her life, can you?'

Surprised, I said, 'I guess not.'

Cat touched my hand again, this time a sisterly pat. 'Thanks, Teddy. Anyway, you have your work cut out for you today with the pit bull lawyer that's coming. We had better go. Give me a ride back to the villa?'

THIRTY-SEVEN

At the intersection of the Airport Road and the unnamed main road from The Settlement to the West End, the Lions Club, Anegada's only civic organization, has placed a garden. Because of the configuration of the roads, the intersection isn't at a right angle and the garden is in the shape of a wedge. The original garden was just some plantings that were almost immediately eaten by the goats and feral cattle which roam the island. The Lions Club, undaunted, erected a waist-high white picket fence around the plot and replanted. As a result, the intersection has a blind spot and is the only one on the island where you must actually stop and look around the flowering trees and hibiscus bushes for oncoming traffic. At one time I had considered asking the Public Works Department to erect Anegada's first stop sign there, but everyone knows about the blind spot so there was really no need to clutter up the view with an ugly street sign. To date, Anegada's few roads remain free of any traffic signs. We like it that way.

The route from Windlass Bight to the Setting Point Villa took Cat and me through this major intersection. I was stopped, edging out to look around the foliage, when I saw a truck approaching. Saw *my* truck approaching. Before, both married and single, I had gotten along with one vehicle, my police Land Rover. Back then, a boat was more important and that was the private transportation I had owned. But Jeanne Trengrouse was the land-bound sort. When she and Jemmy moved to Anegada to be with me, we had purchased a classic of island transportation – a used Toyota pick-up truck. Now that same truck came bounding along, Jeanne in the driver's seat and Marie Benoit, of Pomato Point Restaurant fame, as a passenger.

At the sight of my Land Rover, Jeanne slowed. Normally we would stop in the road and talk. But then she recognized my passenger. The Toyota accelerated, Marie flashing a friendly wave as it sped up, Jeanne's face looking like she had just smelled, or seen, or heard, something very unpleasant. I thought about following the pick-up to Pomato Point and making the explanation I knew I needed to make, but the time for the landing of the ferry from St Thomas approached and I didn't want to miss the arrival of the pit bull lawyer. Indeed, I had to be present for the ferry's arrival to fulfill my duties as Anegada's customs officer. My explanation, or apology, to Jeanne would have to wait. I hoped it wouldn't allow Jeanne's imagination too much time to fester.

The fast ferry churned a frothing wake across the pale green waters inside the Horseshoe Reef and eased to the concrete government dock at Setting Point. A handful of noisy passengers disembarked – belongers with boxes and bags, greeted by relatives; tourists in beach gear, met by one of the staff from the Reef Hotel; and anglers in tropic-weight fishing clothing, with tubes of rods and tackle boxes filled with the latest bonefish flies. As the small crowd dissolved and the individuals went their separate ways, a single figure remained at the base of the ferry gangway. Her blonde hair was cut in a pageboy, the bangs plastered to her head with perspiration. The perspiration existed, despite our genial climate, because the figure wore a coal-black Armani pencil skirt and jacket, hosiery, and the highest pair of heels ever to catch and stumble along the irregular surface of the concrete quay. She wore glasses, not sunglasses, but thick metal frame spectacles which made her already severe appearance seem even more off-putting. As a testament to this, not one person on the boat or dock offered to help with her bag or to give her transportation, a very un-Anegada-like circumstance indeed. The pit bull lawyer, obviously, had arrived.

She walked gingerly along the ferry dock, her wheeled suitcase trailing from one hand, a black briefcase clutched in the other. She stopped at the land end of the dock near where I waited, the wheels of the suitcase rendered ineffective by the sand road, and looked both ways.

'Can I help you, Miss?' I asked.

She frowned. 'Not miss. Ms.'

'Then can I help you, *Ms*?' I'm as enlightened as the next man.

'This place has taxis, doesn't it?'

'A taxi. Charlie George's.'

'Well, where is it? I need a ride. Now.'

'He just left. Picked up his auntie from the ferry. She is visiting for a week from Saba.'

'And when will Charlie George and his taxi be available to take me where I need to go?' Her voice dripped with indignation at being stuck in this jerkwater hole.

'Charlie usually takes the week off when his auntie visits. So it will probably be a while. In fact, it will probably be a week. Can I give you a ride somewhere?' And, unsaid, can I take this opportunity to find out just what you intend to do on Anegada, when it is thirty miles as the pelican flies from the nearest law court?

The pit bull looked me up and down, trying to determine how much disdain she could heap on me. 'You're a cop. I don't ride with cops. I don't talk to cops. I don't like cops.'

Apparently she had no problem dishing out disdain in large portions. But I had the upper hand known as local knowledge. 'Suit yourself, Ms. But unless you are going to the Reef Hotel, which is just a few hundred feet down the road and to the left, walking anywhere on Anegada in those shoes, pulling that suitcase, is going to be a long, uncomfortable trek.'

A bead of sweat chose that very moment to drip from the tip of the pit bull's snubbed, squarish nose. She swiped the back of her hand across her face. It came away glistening with moisture, which the lawyer stared at like it was some alien substance. 'OK, I'll take the ride.' Her acceptance was grudging.

'Fine,' I said. 'Where are you headed, Ms . . .?'

Conceding that acceptance of a ride obligated her to surrender her name, she said, 'Racey. Attorney Susan Racey. I'm going to something called the Setting Point Villa.'

'Pleased to meet you, Susan,' I said.

'Attorney Racey.'

'Attorney Racey, then. I'm Constable Teddy Creque of the Royal Virgin Islands Police Force. I know the Setting Point Villa well. But I must tell you, it is currently occupied with no additional room for guests. What is it that takes you there?'

'Really, Constable? I am not going to play twenty questions with you.'

'I have charge of a special guest at the Setting Point Villa and have an interest in who goes there. And besides, I was just trying to make conversation, Attorney Racey. It's what we do here on Anegada. You'll find Anegadians are all very friendly and curious.'

'I knew I didn't like the looks of this place. Is that your car?' She pointed to the RVIPF Land Rover across the sand road, parked in front of Potter's by the Sea. Without waiting for a reply, she dragged the wheeled suitcase through the sand, placed it in the backseat of the car, and got in on the passenger side.

'So you must have an invitation to the villa?' I asked. 'Not as a matter of curiosity or conversation, but because there is a security issue.'

'I have an invitation from Lord Jeremy Sutherland. Does that satisfy you and your security issue, Constable? If not, I'm sure Lord Sutherland can make a few calls and see to it that your supervisor rips you a new bodily orifice.' The pit bull glared at me with angry eyes.

'No orifice ripping necessary, Attorney Racey. An invitation from Lord Sutherland is more than enough for my purposes.'

The ride to the villa was silent. The pit bull kept up her cold façade but I caught her glancing out the window with a where-the-hell-am-I expression when we passed a feral cow standing in the road, nursing her calf.

Sir Roger, with the unsettling prescience of his ilk, stood waiting on the villa's entrance step when we arrived. 'Attorney Racey, right on time. I am Sir Roger Chamberlain. Welcome to the Virgin Islands. I trust your journey was pleasant.'

'Who the hell are you?' Attorney Racey, it seemed, did not restrict her charm campaign to policemen alone.

Sir Roger, only momentarily taken aback, gave a concise description of his duties to King and country.

Duly impressed, the pit bull said, 'OK, Roger, why don't you pay off Barney Fife here for my ride. I didn't have time to pick up any of the local coin before flying out.'

'The local coin in the British Virgin Islands is the US dollar,' I said. 'But there is no need for payment. The RVIPF regularly extends courtesies to non-belongers. Or, as you might call them, visitors. We find it benefits all involved.'

'Yeah? That wouldn't cut it in the Rotten Apple. The only courtesies extended to visitors there are relieving them of their cash and allowing most of them to escape with their lives.' The lawyer turned to Sir Roger. 'Where is my client?'

'The Viscount is on the oceanside patio,' Sir Roger said, swinging the door open.

'You represent Lord Sutherland?' I couldn't let this opportunity go by.

'Not that it's any of your business, Constable,' Attorney Racey said. 'But I guess I have to tell you I represent him to tell you to stay away from him. So, yes, I represent Mr Jeremy Sutherland. And you and your inquiring mind are to stay far, far away from him.'

'Unless you are present, as I understand the rules, Attorney Racey.' I gave her my warmest smile. It took an effort.

'Unless I am present and I give you permission to pick my client's brain, which isn't happening in this lifetime.'

'Perhaps. But maybe if you heard my reasons you would feel differently about withholding permission.'

'Possibly, but I doubt it.'

'There is only one way to find out, counselor.' The warmest smile from me again, plus a coaxing challenge with the eyes.

'OK, Constable, try me. And save the smarmy smile and googly eyes for someone who gives a flying flip about helping the cops.'

Sir Roger had remained holding the door open until now, but he allowed it to swing shut and assumed a spot in the shade of the entryway, waiting for Attorney Racey to deliver my comeuppance.

'First, Attorney Racey, Lord Sutherland is only a *possible* material witness to a homicide. He is not a suspect, nor, as law enforcement in the United States now so coyly phrases it, a person of interest. There is currently a suspect in custody, a high-ranking officer of the Royal Virgin Islands Police Force, and the circumstantial evidence points strongly to that officer's guilt . . .

'So you've got your man. Why keep jacking Lord Sutherland around?'

'Because I believe the suspect in custody is not guilty.'

'Why, is he a pal of yours? You cops all stick together and

you'll screw anyone over, even a member of the Royal family, to protect your own.'

I resisted pointing out that the Viscount wasn't really a member of the Royal family; you can't just marry in and become a member, though lots of Americans like Jeremy Sutherland would love to think they can. 'I will go where the evidence leads, even if it confirms the guilt of the current suspect. I am merely seeking an interview with the Viscount to determine what he saw and heard while he was in the garden at Government House on the evening of the murder. Surely that is not too much to ask. Even Princess Portia has given a full statement, though she was deeply upset by what she saw. All I ask is that the Viscount do the same.'

'The Viscount will not do the same. I will counsel him to not speak to you. And I will have him freed from the ridiculous warrant that you obtained, and back to his home, in short order, even as you are kissing your pathetic career in this godforsaken sandbox goodbye.'

Attorney Racey turned to the door. Sir Roger popped from his resting position to open it. The pit bull swept inside. Sir Roger's eyes crinkled at their corners with – what? – glee, vindication, malice? Or maybe all those things.

THIRTY-EIGHT

Rare is the man who hasn't walked into what he believed was his happy home, only to be disabused of that notion by what can only be described as The Chill. The Chill does not blow in from Canada, or Siberia, and it doesn't infect only the northerly climes. The Chill emanates from within, unexpected, or at least, unbidden.

I had almost forgotten about Jeanne's sighting of me earlier that morning, but The Chill immediately brought the moment back to me, its icy fingers reaching out from the kitchen as I received my regular evening greetings from the children.

'Dada!' Tamia hugged me.

'Dada,' Kevin said, with near-teen solemnity.

'Hi Dada.' Sir Winston Churchill, frilling his neck feathers, said in perfect mimicry of Jemmy's voice, pre-empting the boy's greeting but not the smiling hug he had for me.

It was at this point that Jeanne usually emerged, a sunny smile on her face, a dapple of perspiration on her brow, the scent of lemon or jasmine preceding her warm embrace and kiss, and her daily inquiry, 'How was your day, lover man?' But on this day, there was no warm embrace, only the icy frost of The Chill. The source was the kitchen, the heart of our home, so I went there to confront it.

Jeanne was at the stove, her back to me, her lithe body tense in its posture.

'Hello, Jeanne.' I glanced back as I said the words. The children, sensing disharmony, had disappeared to their rooms.

Jeanne turned, her eyes flashing. 'How could you, Teddy? I thought things were put to rest after the reception at Government House. But that woman, again? What kind of a hold does she have on you, Teddy, that you set aside your family – no, two families, the one you have now and the one you had with Icilda – for her?' A tear escaped through her anger, cutting a damp trail along her smooth cheek.

'Jeanne,' I said, moving to touch her arm. She shrugged away from me, turning up The Chill full blast. Now was plainly the time for explanation, not embrace. 'Cat Wells has no hold on me. She destroyed my life, Kevin and Tamia's lives. I will not, I am not, letting that happen again. I am not setting aside this family for her. I am not setting you aside for her.'

'Then why were you with her today?'

'It was police business, Jeanne. Having to do with the Letitia Lane murder investigation.' The words sounded unconvincing even as they escaped my lips.

Jeanne's very being flashed furious at my lame, even if true, explanation. 'What kind of police business is there off on the deserted track to Windlass Bight for a murder that took place at Government House on Tortola? Wasn't Windlass Bight where you told me that you and that woman used to go fuck?' Could a word ever be pronounced with more vituperation than when Jeanne said that word? I think not.

'It's not that way.' I faltered in my explanation. 'It's nothing. There's . . .'

'Oh, Teddy.' The tears flowed unabated now. 'I thought what we had could overcome that. Her. Now, what I've seen, what you say – I just don't know. I guess I don't know anything. I just . . .' Jeanne gathered herself, shoulders back, injured but dignified. For a moment, the barest moment, I was proud of her, proud of her strength, her poise, but then the other shoe dropped.

'Leave, Teddy.' Jeanne looked at me evenly. 'You need to leave.'

'Jeanne . . .'

'Leave.'

She turned away from me.

I went to our bedroom, the place where our hearts and bodies joined, now so sad and cold, and packed a bag.

The house was like most in the cookie-cutter collection of homes in The Settlement. A tin roof, rusted red brown; three bedrooms, divided by paper-thin partitions; exterior daub-and-wattle walls that had managed to bend and sway their way through dozens of tropical storms and hurricanes; a back porch looking out on to a tiny yard enclosed by a low limestone wall, the plot's only adornments a few cacti, a century plant, and a cement cistern that caught the infrequent rainfall that was the house's sole water supply. On an easy chair on the porch, my ninety-three-year-old Dada, Sidney Creque, dozed until he detected my presence through some kind of old-man extrasensory perception.

'Boy, what brings you here at the dinner hour, when I'd expect that woman of yours would just now be getting ready to fatten your skinny backside with pot fish and plantains? She is one fine woman, and one fine cook.'

'I thought I would stop by to see you and Madda for a bit,' I lied.

'What about that tasty supper that handsome woman is right now cooking for you in your house?' Dada was like a shark with a whale carcass when he got on some topics. He would just keep coming back and coming back.

'I thought maybe I'd have a bite to eat with you and Madda, if I'm not too late and you have some food to spare.'

'Always had 'nuff on the table raisin' the ten of you babies and I'm sure your Madda got 'nuff in the pot for you tonight.' Dada paused, his rheumy eyes giving me a squinting once over. 'You can stay the night too, boy, if you're inclined.'

Was my need for a crash pad that apparent? Foolishly offended that it was, I said, 'Why would I be inclined to stay over?'

'Call it an old man's intuition. Your Madda always says she has women's intuition. Why can't I have old man's intuition?' The corners of his mouth bent into a wry smile, a sign of his pleasure with himself for as long as I could remember. 'Besides, I see the end of your overnight bag peeking round the corner of the house where you dropped it before you woke me. So, now, boy, is there trouble in paradise?'

That old-man ESP again. 'There seems to be some trouble. Yes, Dada.'

'Do you want to talk about it?' He stared out into the yard as he said the words, seeming to look at the century plant or maybe the cistern. I sat on the porch floor beside him and stared out in the same direction, our lack of eye contact allowing me to pour out what had happened between Jeanne and me with a minimum of manly embarrassment.

When I was done, he said, 'Boy, you remember that cat your Madda had when you were about three or four years old?'

Baffled by the non sequitur, I said, 'Vaguely, yes.'

'I never did figure out why she took in that cat. What did she name it?'

'Puss.' I might as well play along.

'I never understood why she took that cat Puss in. She was just a feral cat, like the ones that run all over the island. It wasn't starving or sick. All those wild cats here have more than enough to eat, with the lizards and the crabs they can catch, and all the little birds migrating through, and fresh bait fish on the shore when the 'cudas and the jacks chase them up out of the water and they're flopping on the beach for the cats' picking. And your Madda didn't lack for companionship none, what with you and your nine sisters and brothers keeping her running hither and thither all day and me seeing to her other needs at night.' Dada gave a lurid wink here, a thing no child should ever have to endure when already trying to wipe from their imagination carnal relations between their ninety-year-old parents.

Dada came back to his rambling story. 'Anyway, she had this cat, Puss, for a year or two and decided it was lonesome for other feline companionship. So she got another cat, Tilly, that had been the house cat of old Evelyn Frett until Evelyn passed on. Do you remember?'

I hesitated, not sure I remembered all of this cat drama in the house of my youth. Not waiting for an answer, Dada kept on. 'Your Madda brought Tilly into the house and it was evident from the start that neither Puss nor Tilly felt the need for any companionship that actually involved another cat. As soon as they saw each other, the house was filled with spitting, hissing, posturing cat flesh. Then the two seemed to be everywhere in our cramped three rooms, and no one room, nor the entire house, was big enough for the two of them. But your Madda persisted, so those cats expanded their war. Not to your Madda, to me. Puss started to crap in my shoes. The good shoes that I wear to church every Sunday.'

I remembered those shoes, his only ones, fifty-some years old now, polished with layers of black polish. The first time the soles wore out, Dada took them to the only cobbler in Road Town, and watched him make the repairs. Thereafter, Dada resoled the shoes with shagreen when needed, the smooth sharkskin leather lasting almost as well as cowhide on the sands of Anegada.

'At first, Puss did her business in my shoes once a week, on Saturday night so it greeted me on Sunday morning right before church. When that didn't get her desired result, she stepped up the frequency, until the shoes were getting a daily dose of cat nasty. Your Madda scolded Puss and cleaned the shoes daily, trying gamely to wait out the feline war of attrition. Finally, though, she saw the handwriting on the wall. She found a new home for Tilly, and my shoes were never defiled by Puss again.'

'Nice story, Dada,' I said. 'What does it have to do with Jeanne and me?'

'You have a Cat problem, too, Teddy. You brought that woman Cat Wells to the island, didn't you?'

'But for the right reason, Dada. To help with my work. To help with Princess Portia. To keep an eye on things inside the villa, where I am not welcome. And she has been helpful.'

'It don't matter, boy. You brought her here and you won't have peace in your house until she's gone from this island. You're smart enough to see that without me telling you. Now, do you want something to eat? Your Madda is making peas and rice, and she got a little bit of fat pork to go with it. It's good for a man to have a little fat in his diet.'

'Sure, Dada,' I sighed. 'And I guess I'll be staying the night.'

Dada stared off into the limestone-cluttered yard. 'Yep, a little bit of pork fat's fine, but too much gives you the indigestion.'

THIRTY-NINE

The anole twitched and darted its way along the underside of the tin roof in the weak dawn light on a search for an insect breakfast. I watched as it hunted without success. It was odd to awaken in my childhood bedroom. Madda had replaced the ten rope beds that had held me and my siblings during our growing years with a single twin bed. She called the room the guest room now, and it seems luxurious, the bed with a real mattress and all the space around it. But it was less cheerful without the chatter and joshing of my nine siblings.

Madda and Dada hadn't expanded into the third room of their tiny house, choosing to live in their bedroom and the cramped-cozy kitchen as they had when I was growing up. I could hear their regular breathing through the wall, just as I had heard it when I still lived there, Madda's a regular sibilant suspire, Dada's a throaty, sonorous male rumble.

In the peace of the early morning, I finally had an opportunity to reflect on my problems, domestic and professional. Dada was, as always, right about the domestic side of my life. My problems there had no chance of going away until Cat was gone from Anegada. I assumed her absence would eventually allow me to engage in a dialogue with Jeanne that would be emotional but leavened with calm by Cat's permanent departure.

And the way to the solution of my domestic problem was the one thing that was crystal clear to me. Solve the professional issues and Cat was gone, off to her new life, landed on her feet after prison, reformed and traveling in the society of wealth to which it appeared she had always aspired.

So how could I get Cat on her way? She was on Anegada solely because of Lord Sutherland's unwillingness to be inter-viewed by me. If an interview could be obtained, and assuming it revealed nothing new or important, the Princess, the Viscount, and, collaterally, Cat could all go on their way. It was an easy solution, cured with a single conference of an hour or two. So why hadn't that already occurred? Princess Portia had been amenable and forthcoming. On the basis of our interview, I could all but eliminate her as a suspect.

Her consort was another matter. Why was he so intractable? Was it just in his nature, a product of the very wankerness that had earned him his tabloid nickname? Or was there something he did not wish to reveal when the police wanted a conversation about a crime? Much as I wanted him gone from Anegada, he was still a viable suspect, maybe my only suspect if the Deputy Commissioner was eliminated. But I had no inkling of a motive for him, or for anyone other than the DC and his paramour, Consuela Lettsome.

And what of the pit bull? Her approach was aggressive but unorthodox. Aggressive in the sense of cutting off all communication between police and her client, a time-honored approach in the United States, if less often used here in Great Britain. The unorthodox part was her apparent aversion to the law courts. She had filed nothing with the coroner nor any court in Road Town asking to have the material witness warrant against her client quashed or dissolved. Maybe she had not had time, but it seemed as if she could have brought some motion, ready to file, with her when she traveled here. She had given no indication of doing this to me, but maybe her intentions had been communicated through higher channels. I resolved to give Inspector Stoutt a call when his office hours began. Perhaps word of some court action had reached him before finding its way to remote Anegada.

And what if the pit bull didn't file anything in court but continued to stonewall my interview with Lord Sutherland? I suppose it could be a strategy but it would result in the continued detention of her client, a Caribbean version of a Mexican standoff, eye to unflinching eye on a sunny beach with reggae and the gentle surf as background music. I guessed that Jeremy Sutherland's tolerance for this strategy would be short-lived. He had brought in the pit bull for action, not inertia. She would be forced to do something soon, but if not in the law courts, then what? Stumped, I decided to consider alternatives to anything involving the Viscount or his lawyer.

Could I mine some further information from the few but more cooperative witnesses on Tortola? I could go back to Jubbie

Watson but I was convinced that everything that could be extracted from him already had been. The information he had given was vital but only to place Jeremy Sutherland in the garden doing some unusual, but not incriminating, things. He was not a witness to the actual murder and knew nothing that would allow me to definitively name the perpetrator. Could Jubbie himself be a suspect? I thought not. He had no motive and there was no other reason for him to be considered. He was just a waiter, shirking a bit of his duties, caught in the wrong place at almost the wrong time.

What about Consuela Lettsome? Should I consider her to be a suspect? She did jail-break, or rather, hospital-break my principal suspect. She had a motive, a desire to see her long-time lover shed of his wife, the door open to her finally having the DC all to herself. But nothing put her at or close to the scene of the crime. If there was a conspiracy to do away with Letitia Lane, she was at the top of the list as a co-conspirator with the Deputy Commissioner. But her willingness to confess to the plan to remove the DC from the jurisdiction was so contrite, and so genuine, that I doubted that she would have skipped confessing to a murder conspiracy, too, if one had existed.

Which brought me back to my prime suspect, the man standing over the victim with his service weapon in hand. The man conveniently unable to speak about what had occurred for days, and who still, at the last interview, remembered almost nothing that had happened on the night of the crime. True, Nurse Rowell's investigation of his drugged state supplied some explanation for this. Some explanation. But the DC is a robust specimen. It was difficult to believe that a dose of roofies could erase an entire evening as effectively as he claimed. Was there something he was holding back?

There was. There had to be. No man could go through all that he had on that night and have so little memory of it. That is what my training told me. That is what the easy way out told me. That was what the old Special Constable Teddy Creque told me, the obvious answer. Go with the circumstantial evidence. It was damning. It was obvious. It was supported by a possible motive – the DC's long affair and his pre-retirement dispute with his wife. A pugnacious King's Counsel from the Office of

Public Prosecutions could easily spin that information into a conviction.

But Special Constable Teddy Creque, he of sloppy instincts and taking the easy way out, was gone. The poor policeman I had been was replaced by Constable Teddy Creque, of similar name and title, but dissimilar instincts. And my good cop instincts, the intuition of an experienced police officer that the Special Constable version of Teddy Creque had aspired to, told me that I had received the truth from the Deputy Commissioner. The entire truth. And any further effort to gain information from him would be a wasted effort.

The fact was that Jeremy Sutherland was my man. I knew it in my gut. But I only had witnesses who could put him near, but not at, the scene at the time of the murder. I could not place the murder weapon in his hand. I could not demonstrate that he had drugged the DC. And, maybe most importantly, I could not attribute a motive to him. I felt I knew who had killed Letitia Lane but I had no idea why he had done so. Or how I could find out. What I was sure of was that if I did not locate the needed evidence on Lord Sutherland, my mentor would probably go down for the crime.

I, like the anole casting about for insects on the ceiling of my boyhood bedroom, was looking failure in the eye.

I purposely delayed my short walk from Madda and Dada's house to the police station to miss the morning procession of children headed for the Anegada School. I didn't want to face Kevin, Tamia and Jemmy on the street, to field their questions about where I had been overnight, and when I would be home again.

The administration building was empty and silent when I entered. Pamela Pickering appeared to be taking one of her frequent days off. All the better, though no coffee awaited as it always did when she was in. I made a pot, poured a hot, black, bitter cup, watched the clock hand click over to nine o'clock, and placed a call to Inspector Stoutt at headquarters.

'Constable Creque, you sister island cops start your day early,' Rollie answered.

'Not early, just on time. Just like you in the hustle and bustle of the big city.'

'Not much hustle and bustle here. There are no cruise ships in port today, so many of the officers are taking a day off. And things are very quiet in the office without the Deputy Commissioner here kicking butt and taking names.' Rollie sounded like he genuinely missed the DC's strict discipline, though he had often been on the receiving end of it. 'Speaking of the Deputy Commissioner, is there any news? And by that I mean good news.'

'If you mean did Lord Sutherland break his silence and implicate a three-time felon in Letitia Lane's murder, absolving the DC, the answer is no. In fact, the part about him breaking his silence isn't even true. I can't get him to agree to an interview and now he has got an American lawyer here advising him not to talk to me.'

'Those Americans do love their lawyers.' One of Rollie's patented but-what-can-I-do-about-it sighs traveled over the phone line beneath the Francis Drake Channel and north to Anegada, reaching my ears unaltered.

'They do. This one seems particularly unfriendly. Her name is Susan Racey. Have you heard anything about her at your end, Inspector?'

'Such as?' Rollie could be obtuse.

'Such as has she been in contact with anyone in the Governor's or the Premier's office? Or with Commissioner Miles? Has she filed anything in court seeking to quash the material witness hold for Lord Sutherland?'

'I've heard nothing on any of those questions. And I'm sure if any of those things would have happened, as the case supervisor I would have been contacted. Shoot, Teddy, if the Commissioner got wind of a motion to quash the hold, he probably would've called me with glee. But there's been nothing.'

'Odd. Why have a lawyer if she doesn't take any legal action on your behalf?'

'Maybe it's too early. Give her some time. I'm sure you won't be disappointed.'

'Maybe so. In any event, if you get wind of anything on that front, Inspector . . .'

'I will give you an immediate ring, Constable.' The line clicked off.

FORTY

Another dead end. And no idea where to go from there. I am the sole police presence on Anegada and the investigation of Letitia Lane's death did not mean that I ceased to be that sole presence. My regular duties included a daily patrol around the perimeter of the ten-mile-long island, checking the beaches for shipwrecks or, more likely, stranded and sunburned tourists. It had been days since I had run a patrol. Maybe, I reasoned, some time on patrol would help to jar me loose from my impasse on the murder investigation.

I started, as I always do, with a slow roll down the short unnamed main street of The Settlement. This morning found the town quiet, the most significant event being a wave from Minnie George and her neighbor, Ruth Lloyd, as I passed by. From The Settlement, I drove along the dusty limestone and sand track northeast toward the Flash of Beauty restaurant, dodging goats in the road, to peer down the shoreline toward Spanish Camp and the rare Caribbean wilderness of the East End. I was out with my binoculars when the citizen's band radio in my car crackled to life.

'Teddy, Teddy, come in, Teddy.' Only in Anegada does one summon the police by calling an officer by his first name over an open channel monitored by everyone on the island. I immediately recognized the voice of De White Rasta, calm but urgent. Urgent wasn't something I had heard from him very often. As in never, up to that moment.

I leaned in the window of the Land Rover for the mic. 'This is Teddy. Over.'

'We need to switch channels.' Anthony's voice, still sounding calm to anyone not familiar with him, had a brittle edge to it.

'Switching to the alternate channel, Anthony,' I said, and clicked the radio dial over to channel 22, the channel we two had agreed in the past to use for conversations that the entire population of the island had no need to hear.

The turn of the dial resulted in an instant rush of incoming words from Anthony. 'Teddy, you'd best get over here, to the Setting Point Villa, right away. Sir Roger is dead.'

'Dead? Are you sure?'

'He collapsed in his food at lunch. He is not moving. I'm certain he is no longer with us.'

Not wanting to deprive Sir Roger of whatever chance he might have, I said, 'Maybe we had better get Ivie Rounds from the clinic. I can pick her up on my way.' I was in the police car and making a U-turn in the deep sand as I spoke.

'You can bring Nurse Rounds, Teddy – probably should – but there is no doubt that Sir Roger is dead. I've seen my share of dead men during my tour of duty in Helmand Province. To paraphrase the Bard, the sudden hand of death has closed Sir Roger's eyes. We still need you and Nurse Rounds here as soon as possible.'

'OK, Anthony, no need to start quoting Shakespeare. I am on my way. Out.' I floored the accelerator on the Land Rover, spraying the scrub thorn and seagrape bushes beside the path with sand. Maxing out to an almost-unsafe speed of forty miles per hour, I kept my head low to avoid hitting it on the roof as the car shuddered and jumped along the washboard road surface. At the same time, I radioed the clinic in The Settlement and was lucky enough to find Ivie Rounds there, holding her weekly walk-in session. By the time I roared down the short stretch of macadam in town, Ivie was standing at the front of the clinic, her first-aid bag in hand. She entered the passenger side of the vehicle as soon as I screeched to a halt. I filled her in as best I could as we drove the six miles to the villa.

'He's an assistant to the Royal family?' she asked, seeking to confirm what I had just told her, daunted by the prospect.

'He's a man in desperate need of medical help,' I said. 'That's all.'

What I told Ivie Rounds about Sir Roger turned out to be quite untrue. When we arrived at the villa and were waved through the entrance door and to the kitchen by Cat Wells, it was immediately evident that Sir Roger Chamberlain was a man beyond all need of medical help. His body was seated at a small table in one corner of the kitchen, his back to the entrance door. The upper half of his torso was slumped across the table's surface, his head resting on its side in a plate of conch fritters. As Nurse Rounds and I rushed to him, I saw that his eyes were wide open and fixed. A grimace, of horror, or terror, or agony, was frozen on his face. His skin was already a ghastly shade of gray.

Nurse Rounds placed her fingers on Sir Roger's neck, searching for a pulse I knew she would not find. She kept her hand there for a few seconds, her eyes on Sir Roger's rigid gaze all the while, and then drew back, shaking her head. 'He's gone, Teddy,' she said.

'The poor man went quickly,' Anthony said from behind me. 'Though he suffered quite horribly before he went.'

'You were here, Anthony?'

'Yes. I ran into the kitchen when Belle Lloyd called out for help. He was face down in that plate of conch fritters when I came in, twisting and flopping like a fish on the beach, like he couldn't get his body to do what he wanted it to do.'

'Was it some kind of seizure?' I asked.

'No, old man, not really. He wasn't unconscious or semi-conscious, as with a seizure. He seemed fully aware. There was panic in his eyes. They were moving from side to side, the whites showing like he'd seen a duppy I turned his head to the side, so he wouldn't aspirate if he vomited. That was when I saw his eyes. I thought about getting him off the table and started to do that when he tried to speak. His voice was weak and . . . odd. It was not just that his words were feeble as a whisper. He was having trouble forming them and they sounded different, like his voice wasn't his at all.'

'Could you understand him? What was he trying to say?'

'I leaned in and he said "bugger me." And then he stopped flopping and was dead. Quickly dead, no movement, no pulse, eyes fixed. Like someone had turned out all the lights.'

Nurse Rounds located a tablecloth and was about to drape it over the body. Something told me that was the wrong thing to do. Maybe it was the suddenness of Sir Roger's death. Maybe it was the unusual agonies that he had suffered in the process of dying. Whatever the reason, I said, 'Don't cover him, Ivie. Don't touch anything. You either, Anthony.'

Nurse Rounds stepped back, still holding the tablecloth like a bullfighter holds a *muleta* when enticing a bull. Anthony looked at me quickly. 'What is it, Teddy?'

'I think this may be a crime scene,' I said.

FORTY-ONE

'I must say, Constable Creque, you are certainly making David's encore career – our encore career – more exciting than he ever envisioned. Much more so than I ever envisioned.' Mrs Shapiro was somehow able to sound positively icy on this otherwise balmy BVI afternoon.

'I am so sorry for the inconvenience . . .' I started to say.

'Don't be sorry, Constable. While I want our golden years to be spent relaxing by the pool with his hand in mine, it has become painfully evident that he would rather have his hand elbow deep in a cadaver, searching for a piece of evidence and a cause of death. I have learned to accept it and to try not to hound him too much. You will please do the same, Constable.'

'Yes, ma'am.'

'I'll get him now. Return him to me as soon as you can. After all, some is better than nothing at all.' I heard the telephone receiver dropped, none too gently, on some hard surface, followed by the click of Mrs Shapiro's heels on the tile floor moving away from the telephone.

Seconds later, Dr Shapiro's elderly but strong voice came on the line. 'Constable Creque, it seems that you continue your efforts at destabilizing the marriage Mrs Shapiro and I have endured for the last sixty-two years.'

'Doctor, I'm sorry,' I stammered.

'Don't worry, Constable. I meant that in a good way. When she gets angry, it lights a fire and, well, to be perfectly candid, the make-up sex is great. Just between us gents.'

That tidbit prompted silence from me as I tried to erase the image of entangled geriatric limbs and a glass filled with dueling dentures on the nightstand from my mind.

Dr Shapiro plunged ahead. 'But I can't get the make-up sex without being called away first. So, what do you have that requires my attention, Constable?'

'We've had a death on Anegada,' I said.

'For such a small spot, it seems a very dangerous place to inhabit these last few years.' Dr Shapiro was correct. On reflection, the last decade had seen a virtual epidemic of corpses on my once-idyllic island home.

'Yes,' I said. 'True.' I tried to focus on the murder but the tangled, wrinkled arms and legs were still forcing themselves to the forefront of my mind.

'Not very talkative today, are you, Constable?' Dr Shapiro chided. 'Come on, man, tell me what you have. Details, details.'

'Sir Roger Chamberlain, assistant to the Royal family, has died while eating his lunch here at the Setting Point Villa.'

'Assistant to the Royal family? What is he doing on your island? On holiday?'

'No, Doctor. He is here with Princess Portia and Lord Sutherland.'

'I thought when I issued the warrants for you that they would remain on Tortola, ensconced in Government House.'

'Complications arose.'

'Ah, I see. I'm not "need to know,"' Dr Shapiro said. 'Suits me just fine. But a death involving someone associated with the Royal family, even a functionary who is not a member, is always touchy. I can see why you want a post-mortem, even if it is natural causes.'

'That's just it, Doctor,' I said. 'I don't think it was natural causes.'

'Choking? Accident is hardly need for a particular concern.'

'It doesn't appear to be choking. Anthony Wedderburn witnessed the death. He didn't see any evidence of choking. Or anything that sounds like a heart attack or stroke. Sir Roger went face down in his food but he had body movements. Anthony said it was like he was struggling to control the movements of his arms and legs.'

'Possibly a seizure then,' Dr Shapiro mused. 'It's unusual to die from a seizure, absent drowning or obstruction of the airway. Or trauma occasioned by convulsive movement.'

'That's the thing, Doctor. I observe no evidence of a traumatic injury and Anthony didn't see him hit his head or otherwise injure himself. And as for an airway obstruction, Anthony heard him speak. It was only two words, but two words would seem to me to be enough to indicate there wasn't anything blocking his airway.'

The coroner was noncommittal. 'Arguably. What were the two words he said?'

'Bugger me.'

'That indicates a consciousness that one does not exhibit during a seizure. It also indicates an understanding of the dire nature of his situation, which is also not consistent with a seizure. OK, Constable. Ice the body down and ship it to Road Town. I will be able to attend to the post as soon as it arrives.'

'Well, Your Worship . . .'

'Not that "your worship" crap again, Constable. It sounds like you want something. Just speak your mind and save the worshipping for some other time.'

'I'd like you to come here, to Anegada, sir. I think you would benefit from a look at the scene.'

'Oh you would, eh, Constable? I'm not a police officer, you know.'

'I understand, sir. I just think it would help in pinning down the circumstances of Sir Roger's death.'

'Circumstances? Are you thinking that a crime has been committed?'

'I've declared the location a crime scene at this point. I will be calling the Scenes of Crime Unit in as soon as I get off the line with you.'

'The tabloids will have a field day. First a murder and then a suspicious death in proximity to the Princess and the Viscount in such a short time. Are you sure you are ready for this, Constable?'

'I must follow my . . . instincts, Doctor,' I said. 'That and where the evidence leads me. And if my instincts are correct, there's less chance that the tabloid press will pick up on it in remote Anegada than in Road Town.'

'Ah, yes, Road Town, metropolis of the western world. You do know that chickens wander unharmed in the streets here, don't you, Constable?'

'And feral cattle wander unharmed in the sand paths we call roads here in Anegada, Doctor.'

'I see your point, Constable. All right, I'll come out. I suppose you expect me to buy my own ferry ticket, too?'

'I will make sure you catch a ride out with Scenes of Crime. I'll have a police vehicle pick you up at your home. Would half an hour give you enough time?'

'Just have a tot of Mount Gay waiting for me when I arrive. And don't think you can make these coroner house calls a habit, Constable.'

'Yes, sir.' I probably deserved the admonition.

'Although it seems you already have.'

'Constable Creque, did you intend to call me on the line for Scenes of Crime?'

I will never get used to caller ID. Or to the sigh of disconsolation that issues from Inspector Stoutt when he hears the prospect of real work in the offing. He was fine answering just a day ago when the call from me went in on the administrative line, probably because it meant the odds were remote that he would be called out into the field in his role as Acting Deputy Commissioner. The call on the line for Scenes of Crime came with the opposite prospect and Rollie's entire being – his allergies, seasickness and corpulence – always rebelled at the prospect of work away from a desk.

'I did intend to call on the Scenes of Crime line, sir,' I said.

'Jeezum. Nothing with Princess Portia, I hope?' Rollie's dread of fieldwork was overtaken by the prospect of work involving the Royals, and the attendant scrutiny from the Commissioner.

'Neither Princess Portia nor the Viscount are injured, or involved,' I said. Inspector Stoutt's exhalation on receiving that welcome news could only have been matched by a humpback whale surfacing in the Anegada Passage after a deep dive. 'But a member of the Royal party, Sir Roger Chamberlain, is dead.'

This news was received with the sound of Rollie reinflating before his next exhalation. 'What? How?'

'It appears to have been some kind of medical episode while he was eating his lunch.'

Now Rollie's sigh was one of relief. 'Tragic. But at least no crime occurred.'

'Well . . .' I began.

'Well, what? Oh, no, Teddy. Don't tell me a man dropping off into his Caesar salad—'

'Actually, sir, it was conch fritters.'

'Into his conch fritters spells crime to you. The man probably had a heart attack or a stroke. Ship the poor unfortunate back to Road Town for a routine autopsy. And do it as quietly as you can. We don't need any more negative press around the Royals than we've already created. Than *you* have already created.'

The last line hit like a blow. I have always considered Inspector Stoutt a friend and a solid, if sometimes reluctant, ally. My resolve hardened. 'I have already declared a crime scene.'

'What? With nothing to demonstrate that a crime can even be suspected?'

'A man is dead.'

'Yes, Constable. A man is dead. They come to the Virgin Islands to die all the time. They snorkel too far from shore and get lost at sea. They get drunk on rum and think they are cliff divers. They stroke out after trying to eat every lobster on Jost van Dyke. They have heart attacks. They drown. They get burned at beach barbecues. They travel from far and wide to our shores and a few of them die here, but every death isn't a crime.'

'I already have the coroner on his way to Anegada.'

'Jeezum, jeezum, jeezum.' For a minute, Inspector Stoutt was only capable of his favorite church-mild expletive. 'Why?'

Unsure if Rollie was asking for an explanation or merely firing a rhetorical question out into the universe, I decided on the former and said, 'Because my instincts tell me a crime has occurred.'

If I had given an answer like that to Deputy Commissioner Lane, the almost certain result would be to have my own head delivered into my hands, followed by the assurance of an even stronger reprimand to occur later. But Inspector Stoutt allowed for one last 'Jeezum!' followed by a final audible deflation and a resigned, 'Fine. I will be out on the *St Ursula* as soon as possible. Anything else?'

'Dr Shapiro needs a ride to Anegada. Can you have him picked up at his house and bring him with you on *St Ursula*?'

'Fine,' Rollie snapped. The phone went dead.

I retrieved my crime-scene tape from the police car and went to work.

FORTY-TWO

I had just placed a zig-zag of yellow plastic tape declaring 'crime scene' across the doorless servant's side entrance to the kitchen of the Setting Point Villa when the main door to the dining room swung open.

'Oh, how horrid, how horrid. Poor Sir Roger,' Princess Portia said, fortunately hesitating to come in the entrance I had yet to tape. Her face went as pale as it could go beneath the healthy tan the Princess had acquired on her short stay in Anegada. 'I'm sorry. I just had to see for myself.'

Not sure of the protocol when confronting a member of the Royal family about to enter an area which is being isolated as a crime scene, I bowed deeply from the waist, said, 'Your Royal Highness,' and, completing the gesture, stepped forward to block the Princess's progress into the room. Unused to such conduct by commoners, the Princess took a step back. She bumped into Cat Wells, who had come rushing upon hearing the Princess's words. It was at that moment that the sight of Sir Roger bobbing in his conch fritters registered. Princess Portia fainted away, a dignified quintessentially Royal swoon, landing delicately in Cat's outstretched arms as airily as a zebra longwing settling on a pygmy orchid.

'Help me with her, Teddy,' Cat said, as I gawked, hesitating to touch the Royal person. I finally mustered the courage to take her by the knees. Cat and I carried her to a couch in the living room.

'I will call for the nurse,' I said.

'Don't worry, Teddy, this happens all the time. The Princess is prone to faint.'

'Still, I'll get Nurse Rounds.' I did and a whiff of smelling salts from her bag revived Princess Portia.

'Please excuse me, Constable,' the Princess, flushed, said. 'Poor Sir Roger.'

'I must ask, ma'am, that you stay away from the kitchen for now,' I said. 'I have declared it a crime scene.'

'A crime scene? Dear God! Do you mean Sir Roger was killed?' The paleness returned and I thought the Princess might pass out again.

'Just a standard measure in the instance of unexpected death, ma'am,' I lied. 'Nothing to be concerned about.'

Princess Portia lay back and closed her eyes, calmed by my prevarication.

'Were you in the kitchen when it happened?' I asked Cat.

'No. I was on the patio outside. With Her Royal Highness.'

'I was there,' said a voice over my shoulder. It was Belle Lloyd. 'Just me and Sir Roger alone, when he first began to have his troubles. And then I called for help and that's when De Rasta came in. That poor man went fast, God rest his soul.'

'Are you OK to come back to the kitchen with me, Belle? I need to ask you a few questions about what happened.'

'I guess so, Teddy.'

'Will you stay with Princess Portia?' I said to Cat and Nurse Rounds. They nodded in agreement.

When Belle and I were alone in the kitchen, I wound the crime-scene tape across the remaining open door. Belle sat on a stool beside the stove, not coincidentally the point in the room farthest from Sir Roger's remains. I took a second stool and seated myself with Belle after closing off the door.

'Do you want coffee, Teddy? I got a pot on.'

'No thanks, Belle.'

'Do you mind if I have a cup? I could use it to calm my nerves. Truth is, I could use a couple fingers of rum. I never had a customer die on me before. If you could call him a customer. I guess you could.'

'So what happened, Belle?'

'I was getting lunch ready. I was making conch fritters. Princess Portia never ate them until I give them to her on the first day she was here. Now she wants them every day for lunch and dinner. I had a batch about ready to fry when Sir Roger comes in and says he wonders if he could have his lunch early, that he's got a telephone call back to England scheduled during the noon hour. "Sure," I say and told him to sit down at the table in the kitchen and I'll make him a salad, and I got a pot of fungi on the stove to go with the conch fritters. He said he didn't want to eat too heavy, that he would just have some of the fritters and an iced tea. I wasn't worried that I wouldn't have enough for the Princess, 'cause I had enough for another batch for her and anybody else that wanted them for lunch. Except that no one but the Princess and Sir Roger would eat my conch. The Viscount, he turned up his nose and said he wouldn't touch no snail meat. He only wants a steak all the time. And now that Lawyer Racey, she don't seem to want to eat nothing but lettuce leaves and coffee. With ice in it. Whoever heard of ice in coffee?' Belle huffed.

'You were saying about Sir Roger,' I said.

'Yeah, right, Teddy. I finished frying up the fritters and put them in front of Sir Roger. He dug right in like there was no tomorrow. I guess there was none for him. He horsed a couple of fritters down fast and then he made this noise, not like being strangled but real loud, like he couldn't make his voice work right. Then he flopped face down in his plate of fritters, almost like he slammed his face into it. His arms and legs was moving, scrabbling against the table and floor like he was trying to get up but he couldn't get any purchase.'

'Like he was having a seizure, Belle?'

'Not like any seizure I ever saw, Teddy, and my cousin, Gerald Pemberton, is epileptic. I saw him have a seizure a couple times and it wasn't nothing like what Sir Roger was doing.'

'In what way?'

'When my cousin Gerald would have a seizure, he would twitch and shudder but he wasn't really moving anywhere. Sir Roger was moving *a lot* but not involuntary like. He was trying hard to move, and succeeding, but he was just not able to control it. And the other thing, when my cousin Gerald had a seizure his eyes got this faraway look, like he was staring all the way out to a single point on the horizon. And he couldn't see you or anything else but that point he locked on to. But Sir Roger wasn't like that. His eyes were moving all around like one of those dolls with the googly eyes that move whenever you move the doll. He couldn't control his eyes but you could tell he was *trying* to control them, that he was trying his hardest to look at you. And the other thing that wasn't like Gerald was the pain. When Gerald had a seizure you could tell, you could just tell, that he wasn't having any pain. And afterward, if you talked to him, he would tell you that he didn't hurt or feel any pain during the seizure. But with Sir Roger it was just the opposite. I could tell that whatever was happening to him hurt real bad, that he was in a lot of pain. I could tell that he knew what was happening, that he felt almost trapped in his body and that he was panicked about it.'

'Did you try to help him?'

'I went for help but I didn't touch him. I was taught with cousin Gerald that you didn't touch anyone with a seizure unless they were having trouble breathing or they were swallowing their tongue. And I knew whatever was happening to Sir Roger wasn't keeping him from breathing. It wasn't much like the seizures I'd seen with Gerald, but that was the closest thing I knew. So I didn't touch him.'

'You left Sir Roger?'

'Yep. But just for a few seconds. I poked my head out the kitchen door and called out. De Rasta come running. By the time De Rasta and I got back, Sir Roger was in a bad way, a real bad way. De Rasta got close, turned Sir Roger's head to keep it out of the food on his plate and I heard Sir Roger say something to De Rasta, struggling to force the words out. I didn't hear what it was. I had to come over here and sit down. I was shaking.'

'And it was just you and Sir Roger in the kitchen up to the time Anthony came in after you called for him?'

'Yes. No, wait. Lord Sutherland and that lady lawyer came in the kitchen, right when I was plating the fritters. I had just pulled them out of the fryer and was going to put some lettuce on the plate as garnish when the two of them came in together. They were talking, something about suing. Suing you, Teddy. Talking like I couldn't hear them. They were always acting like I was invisible, unless they were ordering me to do something. They walked in the door, ignoring me until Attorney Racey says to me, "I need an iced coffee." No "Please" or "Thank you", "Do you have time" or "Sorry to interrupt." Just "I need an iced coffee." And the Viscount just stared at me after she said it, both of them did, like, "Well, are you going to get the coffee as ordered, servant?" If I had been in my own place I would've told them both to get out, but I wasn't and I knew how important it was to have the Princess's people treated nice, so I didn't say a thing. I had just put a pot of coffee on for myself, so all I had to do was go to the freezer for some ice and pour the coffee over it. It didn't take but a minute, and then they were gone, and good riddance to that pushy man and his pucker-faced lawyer.'

'They did not speak to Sir Roger?'

'Not that I heard. They didn't move from where they asked me to get the coffee, that I saw. Sir Roger was sitting in the corner so quiet, monkeying with his phone that I'm not sure they even saw him there. Why?'

'Nothing, Belle. I'm just trying to gather all the facts.'

And the fact was that if there was a crime here, my three prime suspects were Belle, Attorney Racey, and the Viscount of Newent. But was there a crime?

FORTY-THREE

The Scenes of Crime Unit of the Royal Virgin Islands Police Force, in the form of a perspiration-soaked Inspector Rollie Stoutt, and the Office of His Majesty's Coroner, in the form of the feisty David Shapiro, MD, arrived just as I finished taking Belle Lloyd's statement. Rollie looked the worse for the boat ride down the length of the Sir Francis Drake Channel in the face of an increasing swell, a condition sure to be cured by an hour on the firm sands of Anegada. Dr Shapiro looked the worse for the lack of a supply of Mount Gay Eclipse Barbados rum in the galley of the RVIPF police boat *St Ursula*, a condition he set about curing as soon as he caught the sight of me inside the spider's web of crime-scene tape segregating the Setting Point Villa's kitchen from the rest of the residence.

'It was a long, dry ride out here, Constable, and I could do with a dram.' Dr Shapiro dispensed with all niceties in favor of his urgent need. 'Is the cellaret in there with you or do they have the good stuff elsewhere? And, by the way, when you pour one for me you had better do the same for Inspector Stoutt. He had a tough passage, didn't you, Inspector?'

Rollie responded with a groan, and mopped sweat from his forehead with a white handkerchief in a gesture that also might have been taken as indicating surrender. He was all business, though. 'Where is Sir Roger?'

I pointed to the corner where Sir Roger was still splayed in his lunch. Rollie clicked open his camera case, pulled out his Nikon, and followed me to Sir Roger, watching his and my feet along the way to make sure we didn't step on any evidence. Dr Shapiro toddled on behind us, his pace slower than ours but blazingly brisk for a ninety-year-old.

'What a time to go,' Rollie said. 'He didn't even get to finish his lunch.'

Dr Shapiro edged up behind us. 'It looks as if his lunch

may have finished him, Inspector. Constable Creque, were there witnesses?'

'Yes, Doctor. Two, who I have spoken to briefly.'

'And did they see him choking on his food? Not that I'm looking for the easy way out on this but it's often the case with a death in the presence of food.'

'They described his behavior and it didn't sound like choking to me. No one mentioned that he was coughing or clutching his throat. And he made noises, loud noises. Not something I've ever heard of a choking man doing.'

'Well, if it wasn't choking, our old friend myocardial infarction comes to mind. But let's have a look in his airway first.' Dr Shapiro pulled a pair of blue nitrile gloves from his coat pocket and snapped them on with an alacrity born from seven decades of practice. Or maybe eight or nine decades; he was one of those physicians who seemed like he had popped out of the womb with a stethoscope in hand, a tiny doctor in diapers.

'Do you mind if I take a few photographs first?' Rollie asked. He held a mini-dictation machine in one hand, his Nikon camera in the other.

'Knock yourself out, Inspector. I don't think our victim has a ferry to catch, and neither do I.'

Rollie started shooting, the camera's flash illuminating the kitchen like heat lightning. He dictated a description of what each photo depicted into the recorder. At the end of fifteen minutes, he had photographed every perspective of the body and its immediate surroundings.

When Rollie was done shooting, Dr Shapiro stepped in. 'Let's see if this poor unfortunate went the way a little less than one-half of one percent of the population goes, suffocated by their own nutrition.' He carefully tilted Sir Roger's head back without lifting it from the table. With the body's jaw open wide, he shined a pen light into the mouth and probed methodically inside with his gloved fingers. After a few seconds, he grunted and pushed deeper and more vigorously. The rough handling of the corpse gave me pause until I reasoned that Dr Shapiro knew what he was about and Sir Roger was in no position to mind.

Dr Shapiro shook his shining bald pate. 'Nothing in the upper third of the airway, and that's where objects usually lodge in most choking victims. The post-mortem will tell the full story. There may be something deeper in the airway but that would be unusual. I think we should look for another cause of death. Besides making noises, how else did the victim act?'

I described Sir Roger's last moments as related to me by Anthony and Belle Lloyd.

'The severe pain Sir Roger experienced squares with what many have when they suffer an MI.' Dr Shapiro paused, deep in thought. 'But the loss of body control . . .' The coroner's aspect shifted from thoughtfulness to urgency. 'Did you touch Sir Roger or his food, Constable?'

'I . . . I may have,' I stammered, trying to recreate my actions from the first instant when I walked into the kitchen. 'No. No, I didn't. But Nurse Rounds did. She checked Sir Roger for a pulse. And Anthony Wedderburn did. He turned Sir Roger's head to make sure he wasn't face down in his food. Why?'

'Where are they? Where are they, NOW!'

'Anthony, I'm not sure. Nurse Rounds is in with Princess Portia, in the living room.'

With that, Dr Shapiro fairly sprinted out of the kitchen toward the living room, calling over his shoulder, 'Don't let anyone touch anything in the kitchen. Anything.'

'You heard him, Rollie,' I said, the apparent urgency of the situation causing me to fail to use my superior's title in addressing him. I dashed out after Dr Shapiro.

In the living room, we found Nurse Rounds seated beside Princess Portia. Anthony Wedderburn was standing to her left.

'Nurse Rounds and Mr Wedderburn, don't touch anything.' Dr Shapiro was winded from his short sprint, and paused. 'Did either of you touch the Princess? Or anybody else?'

'Why?' Anthony said.

'Dammit, man, did you touch Princess Portia?' Dr Shapiro's shouted question shocked the room into motionlessness.

'No,' Anthony said, sheepish in the face of the doctor's shouting.

'I did,' Ivie Rounds said.

'Where?' Dr Shapiro was close to frantic now.

'On the arm. And on her neck.'

Dr Shapiro turned to Princess Portia. 'Your Royal Highness, you must shower. Immediately. Go directly to the bath, drop your clothing on the floor and leave it there. Touch it as little as possible. Do not touch your mouth or face to wash them until you have thoroughly washed your neck, arms and wherever else you can remember Nurse Rounds touching you.' Dr Shapiro delivered these instructions with such rapid-fire exigency that Princess Portia didn't question them. Her face folding into itself with fear and concern, she stood and left quickly for the bath. Cat followed, keeping a few steps between herself and the Princess.

'Now, you, Nurse, and Mr Wedderburn, come with me to the kitchen.' Dr Shapiro was in full drill-sergeant mode now, barking orders left and right.

'But it is a crime scene,' I said.

The doctor did not mince words. 'Do you want these people to die?'

'No, sir.'

De Rasta and Nurse Rounds followed Dr Shapiro into the kitchen, to a sink far removed from the table where Sir Roger and his last meal remained a tragic tableau.

'Now both of you, wash up. Nurse, do it like you were scrubbing for surgery. Mr Wedderburn, do exactly as Nurse Rounds does.' Dr Shapiro, instructions concluded, sagged on to a stool, looking his advanced age for the first time since I had known him.

'Dr Shapiro, what is going on?' I asked.

'If I am correct, Constable – and I hope to God I am not correct – Sir Roger has been poisoned. With a particularly deadly poison.'

FORTY-FOUR

'Poison? What kind? How?' Inspector Stoutt asked. He had abandoned the crime-scene corner and huddled with Dr Shapiro and me, within earshot of Nurse Rounds and De White Rasta. I noticed that after the mention of poison, their scrubbing-up had become more vigorous. Much more vigorous.

'I believe what we are looking at is poisoning by botulinum toxin, Inspector Stoutt,' the doctor said.

'Botulism? Food poisoning?' Rollie's time with Scenes of Crime had imparted just enough scientific knowledge for him to be dangerous. 'If it is just food poisoning, shouldn't Sir Roger still be with us, popping Imodium and staying close to the gents'?'

'You would be correct, Inspector, if Sir Roger had been subjected to the minute amounts of poison generated by the presence of the bacterium *Clostridium botulinum* sometimes found in poorly preserved food. Or to the small doses used to remove those unsightly wrinkles when injected just below the surface of the skin. Botox, of course. But the dose in this situation was something much more significant and much more lethal.'

'How much more?' Anthony asked from the sink, where he was finishing drying his hands.

'On the order of hundreds of times over the dose that would give a normal human the belly rumbles and the trots.'

'How would he get a dose that large?' Rollie asked.

I had already guessed the answer. 'Anthony, go guard the bath where the Princess is showering. Don't let anyone near her. Not anyone, do you understand?'

Anthony underwent a mystifying but undeniable transformation from uber-laid-back administrative assistant to former Royal Marine without any overt change in his demeanor, barked 'Aye, aye' and dissolved from the room.

'What is going on here?' Rollie looked from Dr Shapiro to me and back.

'In answer to your question, Inspector, an intentional poisoning,' Dr Shapiro said. 'The dose of botulinum toxin that would cause death in the manner described for Sir Roger's passing would be about two hundred nanograms.'

'Nanograms?'

'One nanogram is one billionth of a gram. Two hundred nanograms would be many times the dose delivered by an extreme case of food-borne illness. The dose seems small and it is. Keep in mind, however, that forty grams of botulinum toxin, about the weight of a small lime, would be enough to kill every human being on earth.'

'Jeezum. Jeezum!'

'And a dose of two hundred nanograms means what?' I asked.

'It means that the source of the poison is not from *Clostridium botulinum* found in bad food. The bacterium in spoiled food does not produce a dose that large. That means the poison had to find its way into Sir Roger's system by an unnatural means.' Dr Shapiro's tone was matter-of-fact, belying the momentous import of his words.

'A poisoner here, at the Setting Point Villa.' Inspector Stoutt's words were not a question.

'We already have a perimeter of officers guarding the premises, so no one can leave without our knowing,' I said.

'Correction,' Rollie said. 'No one *is* leaving. Period.'

'But we can't hold anyone here. We have no basis to hold any particular individual, Inspector.' I said. 'Other than Lord Sutherland and Princess Portia, under the warrant issued by Dr Shapiro.'

'The others don't need to know that they can leave. They will only find out if they try to go. I am notifying the sergeant in charge of the perimeter contingent now.' Rollie was out the door as fast as I have ever seen him move his chubby backside. His departure left me in the kitchen with Dr Shapiro and the corpse of the poisoned Sir Roger. On the other side of the kitchen door was a houseful of suspects in the knight's murder, and an heir to the throne of the United Kingdom. These facts swirled around in my head for a panicked minute.

Then Dr Shapiro spoke. 'Quite a shit storm you find yourself in, eh, Constable Creque?'

The old doctor's plainspoken observation almost made me laugh. Almost. What it did do was break the wave of panic enveloping me. I had a job to do. People's lives might depend on how well I did it. The very Crown might depend on it. On me. Shake it off, Teddy. There is a murder investigation to conduct.

'How would you deliver a dose of toxin when the poison is so lethal?' I asked Dr Shapiro.

'The small amount needed means that the delivery medium could be almost anything. A single drop from a syringe. A microdot the size of a grain of salt. If I were doing it, I would place it in the food, rather than trying to inject it into the victim or have him directly ingest the dose. The food might provide the cover that it was ordinary food poisoning. It might fool a sloppy medical examiner.'

Good thing my medical examiner was a whip-smart crusty old codger. 'Can the food be tested?'

'I wouldn't want to get any nearer to it than we already have been without a full biohazard set-up. I would want a level-A encapsulation suit with a self-contained breathing apparatus. The same precautions are needed for the remains, by the way. Sir Roger isn't going anywhere any time soon.'

'What about the delivery or storage system for the poison?'

'What about it?'

'What would it look like?'

'Small. Easily concealed. Probably metallic rather than plastic, to prevent damage and accidental release. Any container would likely be stainless steel.'

'And could it just be tossed away after use? Into the sea, or into the interior of the island? Or buried?'

'It could be disposed of in that manner but that risks someone finding it, and being exposed. That makes further questions possible, even years later. If I was doing this, I would take the storage and delivery mechanism with me when I left, and hand it over to whoever had provided the poison to me in the first place.'

'So it's here, somewhere, you think?'

'Constable, I am a man of science and I don't engage in rank speculation. But if I were a police officer investigating a murder, I would certainly try to locate the murder weapon.'

'I can search this villa for something like you described in plain view but I will need a warrant for anything beyond that. And a warrant takes time.'

'Leave that to me, old chum.' The voice of De White Rasta came from behind me.

'You are supposed to be with the Princess, Anthony.'

'Inspector Stoutt and two armed officers are outside her bedroom door, and another is posted below her window outside.'

'I suppose that's better than just you,' I said. 'Now, how are you going to find the murder weapon?'

'An old Royal Marines trick, Teddy. Leave it to me.'

FORTY-FIVE

'If this is some kind of stunt to interrogate my client, I'll have your badge and own whatever crappy little hovel you call home after I sue your ass.' Attorney Racey's threat was delivered in a half-snarl, half-whine that was so irritating in and of itself as to distract me from the import of the actual threat. 'Just who do you think you are, ordering us to assemble in the living room at two o'clock? This isn't some cheesy murder-mystery television show on the BBC. But maybe yokel cops like you get your training from watching TV. It sure seems like it.'

'Where is Her Royal Highness?' Lord Sutherland made a show of concern for Princess Portia which had been completely absent when I made my way through the villa to gather the participants for the meeting. I had found him and Attorney Racey closeted in the library, whispering in conspiratorial tones. 'I demand to see her immediately.'

'She is being isolated for her safety.'

'What?' The Wanker went red-faced. 'All because Sir Roger choked on his lunch? That is preposterous.'

'Sir Roger didn't choke on his lunch,' Dr Shapiro said.

'What do you mean?' Cat Wells, the sixth participant in our cozy confab, chimed in. 'Anthony said that he had choked.'

'From initial appearances that seems to be the likely reason Sir Roger died.' Dr Shapiro dropped the bomb shell. 'Actually, the cause of his death appears to be poisoning. Botulinum toxin poisoning.'

I studied the faces around the room. Cat Wells' lovely green eyes were red-rimmed. She had been crying. Belle Lloyd covered her mouth with her hand but her eyes were upset and concerned. Susan Racey was the same as the first time I had met her – reptilian, with seething anger at me, or the situation, or the entire world, just below the surface and ready to burst forth at any second. Jeremy Sutherland was untroubled and indifferent, so indifferent I expected him to complain that I would bother him about Sir Roger's death, when he was too important to be bothered about another man's demise. I realized that of the four suspects I had in the room, the latter two were the ones my good cop instinct told me should be my focus.

But it was neither Attorney Racey nor Lord Sutherland who spoke up first. Belle Lloyd reasoned over the thousands of orders of conch fritters she had safely and expertly prepared in two decades at the Cow Wreck Beach Bar & Grill and said, 'Botulism? You mean like food poisoning? Ain't no way Sir Roger got food poisoning from my conch fritters. I got my conch from Kendrick Smith. He dove for them out at the East End this morning. I used fresh oil. No way those fritters weren't good. And I keep a clean kitchen. No one who ever et my food got sick from it.'

Listening to the cook say what she said reinforced it further, and when Belle finished, she glared at me. I remembered that look from the last time I had considered her as a suspect. And I decided then that Belle was not the perpetrator. Besides, she was without a discernible motive.

None of the three who remained had a discernible motive to kill Sir Roger, either, I realized. Had someone else made their way into the villa? What was I missing?

Dr Shapiro stirred the pot. 'I'm not saying that Sir Roger suffered food poisoning, Ms Lloyd. Based on his symptoms, the amount of botulinum toxin which entered his system far exceeded the amount which would be delivered because of food contamination.'

'You mean somebody purposefully poisoned him?' Cat's question was spoken in a near whisper.

Attorney Racey began to rise from her chair. 'Come on, Jeremy. We don't have to listen to this drivel. We are done here.'

Lord Sutherland bestirred himself but wasn't on his feet yet when Dr Shapiro, addressing Attorney Racey, said, 'Sit, young lady. We are not playing around and you know we are not.'

The pit bull fell back into her seat. The only reason that I could fathom was that, contrary to my earlier speculation that she had not been born to human parents and had been raised by wolves, somewhere in Attorney Racey's distant past was a firm, grandfatherly figure who had been the only one to rein in her otherwise antisocial contrarianism. She shot eye daggers at me from her seat; avoidance of Dr Shapiro's genial gaze was her only defense against him.

Her eyes were not the only ones on me. Everyone in the room had turned expectantly toward me. My mind churned away on the motive issue. Who here would want to kill Sir Roger? Then I realized that might not be the correct question. The real question might be: 'Who here would want to kill someone here?' Once I had determined that the broader question was the key, I decided to let my thoughts play out in front of the four potential killers and watch their reactions.

I went back to Cat's question. 'That's correct, Cat. Someone poisoned Sir Roger. But it may have been an accident.'

'How can a poisoning be an accident?' Cat asked.

'I am thinking that the poisoning accidentally killed Sir Roger instead of the intended victim.'

The room fell quiet until Attorney Racey, in typical lawyer fashion, felt compelled to fill the silence. 'That's preposterous.'

'I first thought that, too,' I said. 'Until I considered the matter of motive. Why would anyone want Sir Roger dead, and want it strongly enough to go to the trouble of bringing in a very deadly poison to carry out the job? Sir Roger was a petty bureaucrat. A pain in the butt. A stickler for protocol, a manipulator, an irritant. Does one plot to kill someone because they irritate them?'

'No, of course not,' Cat said. 'If that were the case, there would be a dozen murders a day in the British Virgin Islands. Twice as many in Puerto Rico. A thousand times as many on the mainland.'

'Exactly,' I said. 'And carrying the thought further, who among the four of you here would have been so irritated, so vexed by Sir Roger's petty officiousness as to want to kill him? You, Cat?'

Cat shook her head, denying.

'No, of course not. Sir Roger had proven himself untrustworthy, even underhanded, to you, misleading you. But hardly a killing offense. Especially when you have already experienced the sting of a prison term. It would hardly be worth a disruption of your posh new lifestyle and the risk of a return behind bars to get rid of a pesky fly like Sir Roger. You and Edmund Steinmetz could simply fly away in his helicopter or sail away on his yacht, and leave Sir Roger behind.'

'That makes sense to me.' Dr Shapiro was relishing his role as my sidekick in this little ruse.

'Belle is equally lacking in motive,' I continued. 'Sir Roger leaves in a day or a week, and the problem is gone, if he was a problem to her. Or she could just quit if he's so obnoxious, and be back at the Cow Wreck Beach Bar & Grill in ten minutes, staring out at one of the most beautiful beaches in the Caribbean.'

'Damn right, Teddy.' Belle's glare was replaced by a look of vindication.

'Which leaves Attorney Racey and Lord Sutherland. And they have absolutely no motive to do in Sir Roger. Good God, he was actually helping them, assiduously stonewalling my investigation into Letitia Lane's murder.'

'Here, you fucking copper, you . . .' the Wanker began.

Attorney Racey placed a hand on her client's arm. 'Jeremy, I'll do the talking.' Turning to me: 'We resent the implication. Your investigation, and I use that term loosely for the farce that you are engaged in, is the real problem here. You do not know what you are doing. You are an incompetent, Constable Creque, and you cannot foist your incompetence on to Lord Sutherland or me.'

'Well, foisting or not, I couldn't discern any motive for you, Ms Racey, or your client to harm Sir Roger.'

'Damn right,' Lord Sutherland said, picking up the phrase that Belle Lloyd had coined so eloquently moments before.

'So I decided to look at opportunity instead,' I went on. 'Who had been in a position to place the fatal dram of botulinum toxin in Sir Roger's lunch? No one in the police guard. And Princess Portia?'

'Now wait a minute here, man.' Jeremy Sutherland's bluster lacked the edge of a husband truly offended on behalf of his spouse, I noted.

'No, the Princess was nowhere near,' I said. 'Nor was Ms Wells, who never entered the kitchen during the meal preparation. But two other persons did. Lord Sutherland and Ms Racey came in to get coffee. And, of course, Belle Lloyd had an opportunity to place the poison in the food from the beginning to the end of the process.'

'Teddy Creque.' Belle's glare reappeared.

I held up an open hand to Belle, asking her patience. She settled back in her chair.

'Yes, it has to be her.' Attorney Racey almost smiled as she spoke, the customary twist of her lips looking for a fleeting time as if they had tasted honey rather than the usual vinegar that perpetually played upon their surface.

'But, as I have said, Belle lacks a motive. To kill anybody.'

Attorney Racey's focus on Belle was laser-like. 'You are discounting her as a suspect just because she is an islander.'

'I assure you, Ms Racey, that justice on Anegada is blind. The fact that I have known Belle Lloyd for my entire life, and that she is an upstanding citizen, does not color my judgment of the evidence in this case in any way.'

Attorney Racey continued to hammer away at her favorite suspect. 'You had better look deeper than that, Constable. She could be a professional killer.'

'That seems unlikely. Just as you and Lord Sutherland seem unlikely as suspects. So, with no obvious motive for any of you and an equal opportunity to commit the crime for all of you, I had to look at the means to commit the crime. Which of the three of you had the poison? It has been too soon for whoever did the poisoning to get rid of whatever container held the toxin and whatever mechanism was used to deliver it. So it seemed to me that a search of certain rooms here at the villa would turn up the container or the mechanism and reveal the person or persons who had committed the murder.'

That is when Anthony Wedderburn, Viscount of Thetford, or, depending upon your viewpoint, De White Rasta, arrived right on cue.

FORTY-SIX

Anthony stood in the entry to the living room, a cherubic smile on his face and a merry twinkle in his eye. One might have thought that he was entering a much-anticipated party rather than an assembly of murder suspects. 'Got it,' he said, lifting an opaque plastic bag bearing a red EVIDENCE label in nitrile-gloved hands for all to see. His entrance had the desired effect.

'You don't have a warrant.' As I had counted on, Attorney Racey could not contain her pit bull self.

'He is not a police officer,' I said.

'You stupid hayseed, he's acting as an agent of the police, even if he isn't actually a police officer.' She relished putting the hayseed in his place.

'Possibly that is the way it is in the United States, but our laws on search and seizure are different in the Virgin Islands.' I gave Ms Racey my warmest and most taunting smile.

The pit bull became a mad dog, her pasty-pale complexion incandescent with anger, her thin lips stretched taut. 'No. The fruit of the poisonous tree doctrine governs. The evidence in that bag is useless and so is anything else you found in my room.'

'Your room, Ms Racey?' I said. 'Why would you be concerned about Anthony finding something in your room? Unless you had the means to commit the murder of Sir Roger hidden there. Did you?'

The pit bull dodged my question. 'You know what you have in that bag is worthless, Constable. And you know that anything your boy found in my room is tainted, too. Don't blow smoke up my skirt. I've taken apart way tougher cops than you on the witness stand after an illegal search.'

'Search?' I said in my best baffled bumpkin voice.

The crestfallen expression on the pit bull's face said it all.

'Anthony, you didn't search Attorney Racey's room without a warrant, did you?' I asked.

De Rasta's imp smile broadened. 'Oh, no, Constable Creque. I would never do that. You taught me that we should never do a search without a proper warrant. The only thing I did was to get this empty evidence bag from your police vehicle, in case we came upon the murder weapon in plain view here in the villa. I have not come upon anything of that nature yet.' Anthony turned the evidence bag inside out to show that it was empty. 'Sorry, old man.'

'You lying bastard.' Attorney Racey fairly spat as she said it.

'I told no lies,' I said.

'You deceived me, then.' She turned to Anthony. 'And you did too, you smarmy English twit.'

'Guilty except for the twit part, Ms Racey. As the Bard said, "False face must hide what the false heart doth know,"' Anthony said. 'However, my guilt for the deception seems to be minor in comparison to the guilt of others in the room.'

As planned, Inspector Stoutt and an armed officer now entered the room. 'I have stationed an officer at the door to Ms Racey's room,' Rollie said.

'Thank you, Inspector,' I said. 'With the admissions we have, we should be able to secure a warrant for a search of her room from a judge in Road Town by this afternoon. In the meantime, I think we have enough to hold Ms Racey for the murder of Sir Roger. Officer, please handcuff her.'

Attorney Racey stood and the handcuffs were applied. She was uncharacteristically quiet and seemed lost in thought during the process. Finally, she said, 'I wasn't trying to kill him, you know.'

'I know,' I said. 'You were trying to kill Princess Portia.'

FORTY-SEVEN

My words threw the room into an uproar. 'What? An attempt on the life of the Princess?' Inspector Stoutt said, then to the armed officer, 'Double the guard on the Princess's room immediately.' He took Attorney Racey by the arm and held her.

'How do you know that, Teddy?' Cat asked.

'As I said, she had no motive to harm Sir Roger. Nor Princess Portia, that I could discern. But recall that Belle was originally preparing the meal for the Princess. And that the Princess had developed an affinity for conch fritters during her stay here. When Ms Racey entered the kitchen and saw the fritters cooking, she thought that Princess Portia would be the one eating them. And she would have been if Sir Roger had not appeared hungry and in a hurry and Belle had not accommodated him.'

'This is an outrage!' Lord Sutherland's explosion made up for in sound what I suspect it lacked in sincerity. 'If we hadn't been ridiculously held here, my wife would not have been placed in danger of her life. And who knows what other plots are afoot? Inspector Stoutt, I demand an apology and, for her and my safety, that we be released from this foolish house arrest and allowed to go home to England immediately.'

Rollie was in the process of mumbling his regrets when I looked from the raging Lord Sutherland back to Attorney Racey. Behind her small black eyes the wheels were turning. My good cop instinct told me to take the chance.

'Are you going to let that happen?' I asked her.

She answered my question with a fair question of her own. 'Will there be an appropriate accommodation?'

Inspector Stoutt looked from Attorney Racey to me, and back, baffled.

'Yes,' I said. 'I will do everything I can do. There is no death penalty in the United Kingdom. Everyone convicted of murder receives a full life sentence, with a minimum tariff to serve. In a carefully planned murder, the sentence may be a full life tariff. But police and the Office of Public Prosecutions can recommend a lesser tariff. No gun was involved here, so that can be a part of a recommendation for a lesser tariff. As can be cooperation where there is a conspiracy to commit murder.'

'Fifteen years.' Attorney Racey's voice was steely and even.

'Twenty-five years for such a crime, even with full cooperation,' I said.

Now, not just Rollie's but Lord Sutherland's eyes pinballed back and forth between his attorney and me. 'What the hell?' he blurted.

'Twenty,' Ms Racey said.

'Done,' I said. 'Inspector Stoutt, do you have an additional pair of handcuffs? In my haste to get to Sir Roger I seem to have left mine in the police vehicle.'

Inspector Stoutt, still holding Attorney Racey by one arm, drew a set of handcuffs from a sheath at the small of his back and gave them to me.

'Jeremy Sutherland, I am placing you under arrest for the murder of Sir Roger Chamberlain and for the attempted murder of Her Royal Highness Princess Portia,' I said. 'Please stand, turn your back to me and place your hands behind your back.'

'I'll have your badge, filth.' At least Lord Sutherland had learned the local pejorative for the police since marrying his way into the Royal family, though I expect he didn't learn it from them. Now he said to Rollie, 'I'll have both your badges and your pensions.'

Inspector Stoutt's free hand, the one not holding Attorney Racey, waved in agitation, as if it had a life of its own. 'Teddy, are you sure . . .?'

'I have a plea and cooperation deal with Attorney Racey, don't I, Counsel?'

Attorney Racey settled her vulturine black eyes on Lord Sutherland. 'Yes.'

'No, you can't.' Now it was Sutherland's turn to be agitated. 'There's attorney–client privilege. You can't say what we spoke about.'

'There is an exception to the privilege where it involves a conspiracy to commit a crime, numb nuts,' she said. 'Besides, breaking client confidentiality only means that I could be disbarred and I'm not really worried about saving my license at this point. I'm worried about saving my ass. So I'm handing over yours.'

And then, Attorney Racey bestowed upon her former client a most beatific smile.

FORTY-EIGHT

'The hell you are,' Lord Sutherland bellowed. During the course of events, he had risen from where he sat in a wing chair next to Cat. Now, rather than turning his back and allowing himself to be handcuffed, he dragged Cat to her feet, placing her between himself and me. She struggled briefly as he held her with one arm but he was a big man and powerfully built. Her efforts to free herself ended when he produced a Glock G42 semi-auto pistol and held it against her neck. There was terror in her eyes as she looked toward me.

'Give up. You'll never get away, Sutherland,' I said, removing reference to the title he had earned through deception and that I now considered he had forfeited by trying to kill Princess Portia. 'Put the gun down. This is an island. You have nowhere to go.'

'That's where you're wrong, cop,' Sutherland said. 'Ms Wells and I are about to go flying, away from you and this island where you think you have me trapped. You see, I've learned in life that everyone with half a brain has a contingency plan. Unlike my esteemed former counsel and freelance hitwoman, who apparently has no contingency plan, and knuckled under at the first hint of trouble. Sorry, baby, no room in the helicopter for you. Enjoy prison, you traitorous bitch. As for Ms Wells and me, we're off to Punta Cana. Her helicopter has more than enough range to reach there and, God bless them, the good people of the Dominican Republic don't have an extradition treaty with the United Kingdom. I've got some cash stashed there in an offshore account, nowhere near as much as I would have inherited if Ms Racey had successfully performed the job I hired her to do, but enough to live a quiet life well. Now, step back. And you, Officer –' Sutherland waved his head in the direction of the armed policeman who had just handcuffed the pit bull – 'remove your sidearm from its holster. Slowly now.'

The officer looked to Inspector Stoutt, who nodded an OK to him. He did as Sutherland said.

'Good. No fast moves. That's right. Now step to the patio door, open it, and throw the weapon as far away as you can.'

The officer had a good arm. His gun splashed yards out into the clear water of the Caribbean.

There was another gun in the room, beneath the jacket Inspector Stoutt wore as a plain-clothes officer. I knew he wouldn't draw it in this situation unless Sutherland began firing. I wondered how Sutherland had gotten the baby Glock into the Virgin Islands. I guessed that His Majesty's Immigration Department had been pretty lax in the search of the Royals' luggage when he and Princess Portia had flown in. If there had been a search at all. Not that that mattered now.

'Everyone over by the sofa,' Sutherland said, directing us away from the door to the patio. He edged out, holding Cat in front of him. She fixed her green eyes on mine, as she had done so often when we were lovers, but the message in them was different now. She was going to try something. Unfortunately, she could not convey what it was with eyes alone.

The helicopter was a mere hundred feet from the patio and soon the whine of the engine turbine started up. 'Give me your gun, Inspector,' I said. 'Stay here. Protect the Princess. I'm going after them.'

Rollie, though my superior officer, gave his tacit approval to my plan by handing me his weapon, if you could call it that. It was a ridiculously pint-sized derringer, a North American Arms .22 caliber mini.

'What is this?' I said, holding the dinky revolver. Flat in my hand, it barely covered my palm.

'I don't like to carry a lot of weight.' Rollie was sheepish. 'Full-sized pistols drag my belt down and my pants sag in the back.'

'Best call Road Town,' I said, and was out the door just in time to see the Jet Ranger lift off from its perch at the edge of the narrow beach. Sutherland sat holding his gun on Cat, and flashed me a two-finger goodbye wave as the helicopter gained altitude and swung in a wide turn to the north-west. It was no more than a few hundred feet in the air above Flamingo Pond when the turbine engine coughed once or twice and went silent. There wasn't much time but Cat's combat experience from Desert Storm allowed her to bring the unpowered bird down, moving at sixty or so miles per hour across the pond's pinked waters as it quickly descended. At the last second, she flared the helicopter upward to slow its airspeed and then plummeted the final ten feet to a hard landing. The aircraft's skids crumpled in the inches-deep waters of the pond but the main cabin was undamaged.

Now that it was down and most assuredly not flying back up, I had to reach the wrecked helicopter as quickly as possible. It had come down almost in the middle of the pond, a half-mile from the shore in any direction. Sizing up the situation, I ran to the Land Rover and gunned it back down the road toward The Settlement. At a point where the road passed nearest the pond, I cut the wheel in a sharp left turn on to a sand path toward the water. The path was short, no more than a few car lengths, before it debouched directly into the pond.

The ponds of Anegada – Flamingo, Bumber Well, Bones Bight, Budrock, and Red Pond – are unlike any you will encounter anywhere else in the world. They are a warm pink in color, due to minerals in their waters. Together, they cover over one-third of the desert interior of the island. They are the home to many birds, including our famous flamingos. The water in them is extremely saline, the habitat of various brine shrimp species, and very shallow, usually only a few inches or, at most, a foot deep. At the bottom of all of the ponds is a thick gumbo of decomposing vegetation, which grabs and sucks at the feet of pedestrians or the tires of vehicles that happen to wander into the roseate waters.

It was this latter feature of Flamingo Pond which posed a problem for me now. With a hard bottom, I could have driven the Land Rover to the crash site, and once there, used the vehicle for cover. But with the bottom as it was, I was sure to get stuck long before reaching Sutherland and Cat. The alternative was to park and walk, slowed to a snail's pace by the sucking mud and exposed the whole way across the featureless pond. I opted to drive and, figuring speed was my friend, floored the accelerator of the Land Rover as I entered the water. For a hundred yards it looked like I had made the right choice. The big car almost skated along the surface of the water, elevated by speed and held above the muck bottom by a combination of surface tension and hope. Then I was stuck, the wheels quickly burying themselves to the axles.

FORTY-NINE

I threw open the door to the Land Rover and stepped out. My feet went six inches into the ooze of the pond bottom, which sucked back against my sandals with each step I took. Ahead, Cat and Sutherland emerged from the wrecked helicopter. I hoped against hope that the crash had dislodged the baby Glock from Sutherland's hands and that Cat would come out with the gun. My hopes were soon dashed. Cat walked a few feet ahead of Sutherland, as he waved directions with the gun. They moved sluggishly away from me, toward a dry sandy point. If they reached it, Sutherland would try to find another means of escape, maybe steal a boat in The Settlement or make his way to Auguste George airport and hijack a small plane.

I fell, rose covered in gunk, and redoubled my efforts. Sutherland spotted me but did not risk a shot. He would wait until I slogged closer. So the chase, if you could call it that, went on at a ridiculously glacial pace, cop, hostage and perpetrator all stepping forward and sinking in, then pulling out their trailing foot and starting the process over again. After ten minutes, the initial adrenaline rush wore off for all of us. It was blisteringly hot, the sun reflecting off the mirror surface of the water, and humid. Cat fell, recovered, and fell again. Sutherland dragged her up, pulling her with him. She was doing her best to slow their pace. Pulling her along sapped Sutherland's stamina and momentum. I was gaining. There was a chance to catch them before they reached the edge of the pond and the dry land there.

After twenty minutes, Sutherland stopped, hands on knees, nearly spent. Cat slogged a step or two away from him.

'Hold up there, or I'll shoot you.' Sutherland's threat to Cat was made in a conversational tone but the unruffled waters carried it to me as if he was standing beside me. 'We'll wait for him here.'

I stopped, trying to recover some strength for the final push. Sutherland caught up the two steps to Cat and pulled her close in front of him, pistol again pressed against her elegant neck. He was waiting for a final confrontation. He still needed Cat. Her skills as a pilot might facilitate his escape. I, on the other hand, was a problem, a problem to be disposed of. He could see that there were no other police on the way. They had all remained at the villa to protect Princess Portia. If he could get rid of me, he could run unimpeded. He was patient as I struggled to cross the three hundred feet that separated us.

I stopped a hundred feet from where Sutherland and Cat stood, hoping he would be uncomfortable taking a shot at that range. I know I was.

'I'll give you a last chance, copper,' Sutherland called. 'Walk away to the north. It will take you a while to get out of the pond and by then we will be gone. Cat will come out all right. She will fly me to where I need to go and won't receive a scratch. And you'll be a fucking hero, saving the precious Princess from her nasty wanker of a husband. Go on now!'

'You know I can't, Sutherland. You are responsible for the death of a man in a murder for hire. And you tried to kill Princess Portia.'

'Damn you. Go!' Sutherland fired a shot in my direction for emphasis, a far miss.

'And I still need to talk to you about what you saw on the night Letitia Lane was killed.' I'm not sure why I said that. Maybe it was dogged insistence on completing the investigation that had started me down this road. Maybe it was just to stall for time, to think, to extend events that I was certain were going to have a gruesome ending.

'Oh, Jesus Christ, not that again. What is it with that case?'

'A good man, my mentor, is the accused. You were out in the garden. He was drugged. I know that you got a couple of glasses of champagne.'

'How do you know that?'

'Jubbie. The waiter.'

'Huh. Aren't those people supposed to blend into the background? Instead, they always seem to blab away.' Sutherland was incensed that a mere waiter would give information against him.

'I need to complete my investigation,' I said. 'I need your statement. What do you know?'

'Really? I am somewhat busy now.' Sutherland laughed.

'I'm not going anywhere.'

Even at a hundred feet I saw Sutherland's eye roll. 'OK, you know what, I'll tell you. I'll have to kill you, as the silly saying goes, but, OK, if you want to die that badly. That big stupid slab of a cop didn't kill his wife. I did. Happy?'

A flock of flamingos lifted off from the far shore behind Sutherland and Cat, assembled into a long pink 'V' formation and flew east. I wondered if it was the last beautiful thing I would ever see.

'Why?' I asked.

'Because the unfortunate broad was wearing a dress that showed up as white in the moonlight that night. You remember the moon that night?'

'Yes, vaguely.'

'Well her dress looked white when I saw it. Portia was wearing a white gown that night too. I thought I was shooting Portia.'

'You planned to kill Princess Portia that night?'

'I need cash. She is stingy with it. I'm in debt up to my neck on my real-estate holdings and the Russian mob is the creditor. They can be unforgiving – very unforgiving – when the loan comes due and they aren't paid. I couldn't get the prissy little bitch to even discuss it.' He mimicked Princess Portia's aristocratic accent. '"I won't have my family's money used to pay an illegal debt. I simply won't hear of it." So I had to get the money the old-fashioned way. I had to inherit it. And to do that, Portia had to die. So I pitched a fit, had her Royalty and Specialist Protection security contingent left behind in England for our visit to the BVI, and planned to have an armed local police officer accidentally shoot her on the night of the reception. It all went to plan. I roofied the cop – he couldn't refuse a glass of champagne with Lord Sutherland when I insisted. When he went out, I got his service weapon and waited. The lady in the white dress appeared and I shot her, wiped the gun, and pressed it into the cop's hand. I figured it would look like an accident. Of course, all hell broke loose when the shot was heard. What surprised me was that that big ugly brute of a cop was able to stand up and walk over to the woman on the ground. I'd given him a dose large enough to put down a Clydesdale.

No matter, though, the deed was done and I thought he would get the blame. I started to run away and then decided to hide in the bushes for a time until things settled a bit. Then I figured the best way to throw suspicion off myself was to "happen upon" the scene and be indignant. You remember that part, don't you? I didn't really look at the body on the ground then, darkness and all. It was quite a surprise when I got back to Government House and found Portia there, still quite alive. No matter, I thought. There would be other opportunities. Best to get back to England and work on another plan. Then you bollixed things up by not letting us out of the country. But when a friend of mine found Racey, a real professional hitwoman, for me, it became a second opportunity to cleanly inherit Portia's money. And you bollixed it up again. So you must die. Come closer.' He beckoned with his pistol.

I had tucked Rollie's toy pistol into the waistband at the small of my back. Now I drew it.

'You call that thing a gun?' Sutherland jeered but hunkered more closely behind Cat. 'Come close and die.'

I slipped and clawed my way forward, hunched down to make a smaller target. Sutherland snapped off a shot at seventy-five feet, missing me by inches. Then he held his fire, waiting for me to get close enough so he wouldn't miss the next time, counting on me not to fire as long as he was shielded by Cat.

At fifty feet, Sutherland decided I was in range and swung the Glock away from Cat's neck. She slammed her heel into his instep and twisted away, throwing herself into the inches-deep water to his right. Sutherland paid her no attention, quickly firing twice at me. I was pushed back into a sitting position, and felt a sear of pain in my left arm. Seeing that I remained upright, Sutherland fired again. I emptied Inspector Stoutt's five-shot toy at him as fast as I could. As soon as I began firing, Sutherland did the same with his Glock, an Old West shoot-out in the mud of Anegada's arid interior, flamingos wheeling overhead, the crash of waves on the barrier reef of the North Shore audible between the clapping gunshots.

Then the world went silent. I found myself standing, Cat beside me, pressing a bloody kerchief into my arm to staunch the bleeding. She was crying, tears and gasping sobs released by the horror of the day's events. I wrapped my good arm around her.

Jeremy Sutherland lay dead at my feet, his life emptied from a barely visible wound in his neck, the rose-pink water of Flamingo Pond turned deep scarlet by the blood.

FIFTY

'Constable Creque, you look as if you have been dragged through the proverbial knot hole in the banyan tree,' Boss Claudie greeted me as a phalanx of the former drug kingpin's cousins and nephews parted to allow us to shake hands.

'And you, sir, look spruce as ever,' I said.

'Clothes make the man, on a superficial level.' Claudie ran a hand along the lapel of his Ermenegildo Zegna sports jacket to emphasize the point. 'But it is a mind willing to explore the deep questions of life that make the true man.'

'Philosophy today?'

'And every day since you delivered my two house guests,' Claudie said. 'Today it is Kant, Hume, and Hammurabi on the existence of right and wrong. I must say your friend Howard Lane is keen to explore the concepts and quick in his analysis. And young Mr Watson, while a touch immature in his logical processes, is a lively thinker as well. I shall miss them both when they depart.'

'That is why I am here. They will both be departing today,' I said.

'In custody?' Claudie frowned. 'Or free as the albatross that rides the wind? The latter I hope.'

'Just so.'

'Good. Come in. I will show you to them.' He led me through the dark interior of his tasteful but modest home on to a rear patio with a sweeping view of Road Town and its harbor. There Deputy Commissioner Lane and Jubbie Watson sat drinking coffee and playing French with two of the nephews, the pips fairly jumping off the bones as each domino was slammed to the table. Seeing the approach of a policeman, the nephews melted away.

Jubbie was to the point after shaking hands. 'Constable, am I at last free to go?'

'Yes, Jubbie, you are free to go. And thank you. The information you provided helped free an innocent man and may have saved the Crown,' I said.

Jubbie puffed up with pride and fairly dashed out the door, exclaiming to the various nephews and cousins along the way, 'You hear dat, mon? I-mon save de Crown! De Crown! Dat Ms Myrthlyn Nibbs will gib mi my waitin' job back now!'

'You are a mess, Constable. Your uniform is a disgrace.' The DC couldn't help his spit-and-polish self. His attitude changed to concern when he saw the bandages on my left arm. 'You are injured, Constable. You need to seek medical attention immediately.'

'I have already had it, sir. And the wound is not that bad, a bullet, through and through. I will recover with no impairment.'

'Is the wound the result of events leading to Mr Watson's freedom?'

'Yes,' I said. 'And your freedom, too.' I explained the happenings of the last several days in detail to the Deputy Commissioner, an oral report to my commanding officer. He received it with his customary scowl, his face not betraying the personal effect the information must have had on him. When I stopped, he said, 'So Ms Wells was not injured?'

'She was not, sir. Badly shaken but uninjured.' My mind returned to Cat's trembling hands and tears as we walked back to the Setting Point Villa. 'She is as much responsible for solving this matter and apprehending the perpetrator as I was, sir. When she started the helicopter after being taken hostage by Jeremy Sutherland, she switched the fuel feed to an almost empty tank. She had expected to crash into the sea somewhere between Anegada and Hispaniola and was pleasantly surprised when the tank ran dry shortly after take off.'

I didn't tell the DC the rest of what had passed between us. That she had said she knew when she survived the crash she might live but that she was not sure that I might risk my life to save her. I'd told her then that we were even, all accounts between us reckoned and settled. We had both almost died and each had been saved by the other. She had cursed Anegada, claiming the island was unlucky for her. When we parted at the RVIPF Marine Station after the St Ursula had returned Princess Portia, Cat,

Anthony and me to Tortola, I knew she would never return to Anegada. We would never see each other again. Just as well for her. Just as well for me.

'So Letitia's murder was an accident? A case of mistaken identity? All because her dress appeared to be the same color as the Princess's in the moonlight?' The DC's professional scowl was gone now. He had the fragile mien of what he was, a man recently widowed.

'Yes, sir,' I said. 'It is so arbitrary, so unnecessary.'

'So unnecessary.' The DC's look was far away. 'And she would be alive today but for my being a police officer.'

'It's not your fault, sir.'

'Isn't it, Constable?' The DC shook his head. 'I'm tired, so tired.' He looked directly into my eyes. 'You have been through this. How can I get through it, Teddy?'

DC Lane was right, I had been through this. I'd had a marriage of partnership more than love, of convenience without passion. And, as with Letitia Lane, in the end my Icilda had paid the ultimate price, leaving her spouse to pick up the pieces. Letitia Lane was blameless, my Icilda less so. But both left behind a man filled with doubt, a man wallowing in probably justified self-blame. I had made it though the hard days and the long nights, and come out on the other side. DC Lane would, too, I believed. I gave him the only advice I knew to give.

'It takes time. You have to give it time.'

EPILOGUE

I stood with teeth chattering, feeling as if I was freezing despite the long pants and buttoned-to-the-neck tunic of my formal police uniform. Lord Anthony Wedderburn, Viscount of Thetford, stood on my left, comfortable in the same kilt, sash and sporran that he had worn at the reception for Princess Portia at Government House so many weeks before. On my right, Jeanne Trengrouse was resplendent in a magenta suit, with a matching calot nestled in the wild tumble of her hair. Dada was right; all that had been needed to mend the rift between us was the departure of Cat Wells from Anegada.

Dada and Madda were there, too, along with Kevin, Tamia and Jemmy, all the people I love, all wide-eyed with fascination. Our small group was rounded out by the presence of Royal Virgin Islands Police Force Commissioner Sir Fleming Miles, whose Saville Row tailored uniform put my regulation-issue garb to shame. It mattered not a whit to me.

We all waited in the biting wind behind a velvet rope, in a kind of bullpen. We had arrived early. Early enough to stand through spitting rain showers and fleeting glints of weak sunshine for half an hour before a man in a uniform of dark blue, with a red belt and a cascade of gold braid falling from his shoulder, came to greet us. By then, others had gathered with us behind the velvet rope, dressed in all manner of finery. The man in the blue uniform said that he was from the Lord Chamberlain's office and, after providing a short explanation of the details of the ceremony, shepherded us into the ballroom of Buckingham Palace.

If it was meant to inspire awe, the ballroom, with mile-high ceilings and enough red velvet to outfit a thousand Vatican cardinals, certainly delivered. The place was abuzz with several hundred guests and ten honorees. A platform or dais, elevated two steps above floor level, dominated one end of the room. A stool stood at the foot of the dais.

As the first honoree, I was seated in the front row. I was more frightened than a sprat facing a school of barracudas.

A man called the cushion brought out a decoration, a Maltese cross, on a purple velvet pillow and the ceremony began. A fanfare, and two Gurkha soldiers in dark uniforms and carrying long staffs, marched in. Then came King Charles in a naval uniform, relaxed and smiling. My name was called. I rose, stepped forward to the stool, and knelt. The King was handed a sword. He gave me a reassuring smile and wordlessly touched the sword to both my shoulders, making certain to use the same side of the blade on each. He made a motion for me to rise and the cushion stepped forward with his purple pillow. The King placed the decoration on its ribbon around my neck and said, 'Teddy Braithwaite Creque, for personal service to the Crown, I name you Knight Commander of the Royal Victorian Order. Thank you, Sir Teddy, for your exceptional efforts in safeguarding Her Royal Highness Princess Portia and the entire Royal family.'

The King then shook my hand and whispered out of earshot to all but me, 'Good job, Teddy. I never did like that wanker.'

'Thank you, Your Majesty,' I managed to stammer.

There must have been more to the ceremony but I remember nothing further of it. As if Queen Ya-Ya had directed one of her spells at me, the next thing I knew I was at a reception in an anteroom, a glass of punch in my hand, surrounded by my family, and receiving congratulations all around.

Suddenly the group surrounding me parted to make way for a veiled woman dressed from head to toe in black. She stopped before me and lifted her veil. Princess Portia. I had not seen her at the investiture, nor, indeed, since I had ridden back with her to Tortola on the *St Ursula*. I attempted to bow but she pulled me up, silently hugged me, and was gone.

'Not bad, Teddy, to have a friend in the family,' De White Rasta said. 'A true friend in *the* family.'

Commissioner Miles had hovered at the edge of our small group, chatting up Dada and Madda. Now he saw his moment and pulled me aside.

'Constable . . . Sir Teddy, well done,' he said. 'On behalf of the entire Royal Virgin Islands Police Force, congratulations on your accolade. It is well deserved.' Sir Fleming hesitated as if unsure about something.

I filled the silence. 'Thank you, sir.'

'Sir Teddy, I learned a bit of news just before coming here to see you receive your KCVO. News that affects all of us in the RVIPF but may matter especially to you.' Sir Fleming, I noticed, was now speaking to me not like I was a subordinate but like we were chums, members of the same exclusive club. I supposed now we were. 'Deputy Commissioner Lane has elected to retire. Even though he was completely cleared of wrongdoing. I had a chance to speak to him briefly about it. He mentioned something about waiting for a very important person in his life to resolve some issues with which she was dealing, and how he wanted to be there for her. But he said, more than that, he needed time. That was it, he said he just needed time. Unusual but I can understand after what he has gone through, poor man.'

I understood, too. Consuela Lettsome would not be without a caller on visiting days at His Majesty's Prison. And I was sure Deputy Commissioner Lane would be waiting for her on the day she completed her sentence and was released.

'I will miss him,' I said, and meant it.

'The RVIPF will miss him, too. His departure will leave a huge void in our small force.' Sir Fleming paused. 'His natural successor, according to rank, time of service and administrative experience, would be Inspector Stoutt of the Scenes of Crime Unit. I thought a great deal about that on the flight over and it did not satisfy. Pulling Inspector Stoutt away would leave the RVIPF without his considerable Scenes of Crime experience and, to be frank, he has little to no experience in general policing. I tried to think if the force had other suitable candidates for the position with more policing experience. One stood out, a man with a stellar investigative record in the field, good instincts for the job and even a Queen's Police Medal to his name. A quality officer. As the Yanks say, a good cop. And now a knight. You. I am offering you the job.'

'Sir. I don't know what to say.'

'Of course, there might be those who will question elevating a constable several ranks at once to Deputy Commissioner, but your record in high-profile cases should silence any detractors.

And, keep in mind the considerable increase in compensation. Not to mention that you would be based in Road Town. You would be able to leave that backwater island and bring your family to a real town, with opportunities for all of them. So what you should say, Sir Teddy, is that you accept the position.'

I thought about leaving Anegada. About taking Jeanne, and Kevin, Tamia and Jemmy from the island we all love. About Madda and Dada, old and alone across the Sir Francis Drake Channel. 'I'm deeply honored, Commissioner. It is a very tempting offer but I am satisfied where I am. I hope you understand.'

Sir Fleming, I was sure, didn't understand but he was unfazed. 'It's a great disappointment but I understand. The pull of home and such. Well, good job, old man. Congratulations on your KCVO. Again, earned and well deserved.' Spotting another knight of his acquaintance, Sir Fleming called after him and dashed away.

Jeanne came to my side as soon as Sir Fleming departed. 'What was that all about, Teddy?'

'Nothing much. Just some knight talk.'

'Ah. So do I have to call you Sir Teddy now?'

'It wouldn't hurt.'

'Even in the bedroom?' She gave me her bedroom eyes. My mind immediately flew to whether Madda and Dada might be willing to take the children to Harrods for the afternoon while Jeanne and I tested the resilience of the massive four-poster bed in our room at Claridge's, where we were staying at Crown expense.

'Especially there,' I said.

De White Rasta sidled up.

'He expects me to call him "Sir Teddy" now, Anthony,' Jeanne announced, taking faux offense to my faux arrogance.

'Really?' De Rasta said. 'The cheek of the gentry.'

'But, Anthony, I'm willing to call her "lady,"' I said.

'Sorry, Teddy, but the woman of a knight is only called "lady" if she is his wife.' Anthony said it just as we had planned it.

'I know,' I said. 'And I am willing to call her "Lady Jeanne," if she will have me.'

'Lady Jeanne Creque,' Jeanne said, the mischief that I loved shining in her blue eyes. 'I like the sound of that, Sir Teddy.'

And she threw her arms around my neck and kissed me.

ACKNOWLEDGEMENTS

My gratitude to my wonderful editor, Rachel Slatter, for her sagacity and kind nature. Every communication received from you leaves me with a smile.

Thanks as well to Tina Pietron for her diligent work in bringing this book to completion; to Claire Ritchie for her copyediting prowess; to Martin Brown for his steady hand steering publicity and marketing; and to everyone else on the team at Severn House for making this book possible.

And my most special appreciation to my wife and gentle first reader, Irene, for her insights, support and unconditional love.